The Ultimate Betrayal

Annette Mori

Affinity
eBook Press
NZ
2016

The Ultimate Betrayal
Annette Mori

The Ultimate Betrayal
© 2016 by Annette Mori

Affinity E-Book Press NZ LTD
Canterbury, New Zealand

1st Edition

ISBN: 978-0-908351-83-1

This is a work of fiction. Names, character, places, and incidents are the product of the author's imagination or are used fictiously and any resemblance to actual persons living or dead, businesses, companies, events, or locales is entirely coincidental

Editor: Nat Burns
Proof Editor: Alexis Smith
Cover Design: Irish Dragon Designs

Acknowledgments

A huge thank you to JM Dragon who helped tighten the first draft with her insightful feedback on how to improve the manuscript. Of course, I once again have to acknowledge Erin O'Reilly who helped me with the re-writes based on JM's advice. Often a writer is so close to the work that a needed friend can help them see the light. Erin gives of her time freely, without the expectation of anything in return. I am honored to call her a friend and loved having a chance to meet her in person at GCLS.

I would also like to express my gratitude to Affinity Press and the wonderful trio (JM Dragon, Erin O'Reilly and Nancy Kaufman) who continue to support this new and somewhat unconventional writer. I am eternally grateful for the opportunities they give me to let my stories see the light of day.

On my journey, I elicited advice from my older sister, Val, who gave me valuable feedback that helped shape the final version of the story. She continues to be an incredible encouragement to me. My other beta readers include, Sharlie and favorite fan, Gail. Gail especially gave me feedback about my need to spruce up my sex scenes and with this novel, she noted that I've come a long way. My other family members who were also very supportive, include my nephew, Aaron and his wife, Chelsea, and my little sister, Kim. I always enjoy working with the beta editor and Kay Carney helped to improve my story.

Thanks to Nat Burns for her magic again as the final editor to tighten the story even further. Inevitably, there are those pesky final errors that slip through and I am thankful that the final proof editor, Alexis Smith, caught those before the book went to print.

Nancy Kaufman is a rock star with her covers. Nancy is also a promoter extraordinaire.

A huge thanks to all the other readers and fellow writers who have sent personal e-mails, written reviews, and posted nice things on Facebook (you know who you are). The Affinity authors are an especially supportive group and often share posts or send words of encouragement. Finally, my wife, Jody, continues her support even when it interferes with our weekend time.

Dedication

To all the fans, especially Gail, who continue to support my books. To my wife who I love dearly for her patience when I get in a groove and ignore her during "our" weekend time.

Table of Contents

Also by Annette Mori

Locked Inside

Out of This World

Asset Management

The Incredibly True Adventure of Two Elves in Love
(Affinity 2014 Christmas Collection)

Love Forever, Live Forever

The True Story of Valentine's Day

Vampire Pussy…Cat
Nicky's Christmas Miracle X3
(It's in Her Kiss Affinity's Charity Anthology)

Chapter One

Summer 2013

Lara Beck smiled as she watched Rachel Mathis walk along the rose petal strewn path leading to the intricate gardens where they'd decided to get married.

A flowing white dress clung to Rachel's athletic body and there was no argument that Rachel made a stunning bride. Her hair fell in soft waves across her shoulders and shimmered in the sunshine as the highlights reflected the rays of the sun.

As Lara took Rachel's hands in her own, she looked into sapphire eyes that reflected nothing but love. Lara felt like the luckiest woman in the world. Rachel had been difficult to ensnare, but she'd won her heart.

The only other time Lara had felt the same way toward a woman was eight years ago when she'd watched her first love walk down the aisle in New York's St. Patrick's Cathedral. Her emotions had been so intense then that she'd almost convinced herself she would be able to remain faithful. Lara couldn't help thinking about her first marriage, today of all days.

Lara shook her head to bring herself back to the present and the beautiful woman in front of her, who was ready to say her vows. They both had written their own words and Lara was excited to hear what Rachel would say.

"Lara, I never thought someone would capture my heart until I met you. Your relentless pursuit and never-ending passion takes my breath away every time we come together. I cannot imagine ever growing tired of you. I'm afraid our combustible desire for one another will burn so brightly that it will leave nothing behind but blissful ashes, but I'm willing to take the chance at a love that I suspect I'll never find again. Thank you for never giving up your pursuit. I love you. Now let's do this," Rachel said.

Lara laughed and started reciting her own vows. "The moment I met you, I knew I had to make you mine. You were worth every bit of energy I put into wooing you. I don't think I've ever met a woman who sparked my interest quite like you. When we come together it is like poetry in motion—fiery poetry. I couldn't resist circling your orbit because the gravitational pull was just too great. I love you, too, and will always celebrate the day I met you at that cheesy fundraiser."

"Hey, I planned that event. There was nothing cheesy about it," Rachel argued.

Lara chuckled. "Just teasing, hon. Can we get to the I do's now, please?"

†

On the eve of her second marriage, Lara pondered what love, sex, and marriage meant to her. Of course, those thoughts didn't make it into her vows.

Lara didn't think there was anything wrong with using sex to further her business interests. In her opinion, too many people had hang-ups about sex. She'd been told that she was a lot like a man in her perspective, but to her, love and sex were not the same thing. She could have sex with someone and not love them. She was a healthy, sexually active woman who could appreciate that sometimes sex was just a means to an end or a physical release without the added complication of love. Of course, it was a bonus if you loved the person you were having sex with. She would concede to that point.

If there was one thing she despised, it was a double standard. It was 2015 and men no longer cornered the market on sex, power, and control.

Marriage, in her estimation, tended to suck the excitement out of sex, which is why men and women took mistresses. It was practically a requirement for ambitious, successful executives. Lara reasoned that, to maintain a healthy marriage, it might be necessary to venture outside the boundaries of matrimony and that had nothing to do with whether or not she loved her wife.

Deep down Lara adored her wife but humans were not designed to be monogamous. She'd listened to an anthropology professor lecture that only seventeen percent of human cultures were monogamous. That lecture stuck with her and helped justify her behavior.

She believed that if she had the stamina and the resources to keep multiple lovers satisfied, what would it hurt? Perhaps some might judge her and believe she had impulse control issues. *Fuck them.* She had the world at her feet and nothing would stop her from taking every bite out of life.

Chapter Two

Summer 2005

Sophia Torre squinted into the bright sunshine as she looked up at the familiar brick building. The City University of New York campus felt like home. She'd spent four glorious years here before attending Rutgers University for her doctorate. She was grateful to be back in New York but anxious about her interview with Dr. Francine Forester. She didn't have anything against New Jersey, but it wasn't New York.

Dr. Forester was her favorite professor when she'd attended CUNY, earning her undergraduate degree from the innovative LGBT studies program. She'd wanted to absorb every bit of information from the course and had managed to get a choice internship with the warm-hearted professor. Dr.

Forester was instrumental in Sophia's decision to pursue her doctorate. Now, Sophia was back, after the professor had tracked her down to ask her to consider a position in that same life changing program.

Joy, her best friend, was delighted to have Sophia back in New York. During their conversation last week, she'd told Sophia that New York was where she belonged.

Sophia retrieved her cell phone from her purse when she heard the muffled ring.

"Hello," Sophia answered.

"Hey, gorgeous. I just wanted to call and wish you luck. Not that you will need it. Call me as soon as the interview is finished and we can celebrate—just like old times. You, me, a bar full of hot women to choose from, and an intimate party back at my place afterwards. You've become a huge disappointment since starting grad school. Who knew Jersey would be so bad for you. They must have beautiful women in New Jersey, so what's the deal?" Joy asked.

"Don't start with me. Graduate school was not a walk in the park and I wanted to do well so I could return to New York. No celebration plans until I know whether I've got the job or not."

"Oh ple-eze, she called you. Remember? You are going to rake in the little baby dykes. Their program will grow to epic proportions with a hot professor like you. That Dr. Forester is a shrewd one. She knows that you will draw in more students," Joy insisted.

"Gotta go. I promise to call after the interview. Don't buy the champagne just yet. Okay?"

"Righteo, but I got a good feeling and it's about time you came back. I missed hanging out with my best bud. Talk to you soon. Love ya."

"Love you too, goofball."

Sophia closed her cell phone, took a deep breath, and walked up the stairs to face what she hoped would be her future.

†

Sophia's high heels sounded unusually loud as she walked down the hall. The echo reverberated in the empty corridor. Students were always sparse during the summer term. She smiled as she trod familiar territory.

She knew her way around the building and like a homing pigeon she found herself in front of the door where she'd spent countless hours discussing everything from politics to religion, helping her favorite professor with whatever research project she was working on at the time. The small conference room was a short distance from Dr. Forester's office.

Sophia knocked on the door.

The five foot tall prof, with curly brown hair that always looked disheveled, opened the door, and pulled her into a warm hug. "Sophia, you look wonderful. I am so delighted you are interested in our position. I can't think of a better fit for our program."

Dr. Forester was a quirky middle-aged woman who seemed to love every part of her job but obviously reveled in the energy and enthusiasm of her students. Sophia knew that, as a gifted teacher, Dr. Forrester would never completely give up teaching for a job that required her to spend one hundred percent of her time on administrative tasks. Sophia admired that.

"Thank you for thinking of me, Dr. Forester."

"Stop with the Dr. Forester. Call me Francine. After all, we are going to be colleagues shortly."

Sophia chuckled. "I thought this was an interview."

Francine waved her arm in the air. "Merely a formality. Come in, come in. Can I get you some coffee or tea?"

"No, thanks." Sophia took a seat at the conference table.

Francine poured herself a cup of coffee and sat at the head of the table next to Sophia. "Let's get right to it. We'd like you to start teaching some of the one hundred level classes in the LGBT studies program, but intersperse some of them with the upper level courses. I know the youngsters can tire a person out, so we're not expecting you to take the entire entry-level curriculum. I don't suspect it will take you very long to achieve tenure. The pay is horrific as an associate professor, but the hours are divine and eventually you'll do okay when you become a full professor. We always have someone on sabbatical, so I can make sure you have a place to stay where you won't have to pay an outrageous amount of rent. That should help with expenses for the first few years until you become a full professor. Any questions?"

"Am I to understand that you are offering me an associate professor position?" Sophia asked.

"Well, yes, of course. I didn't track you down to have coffee. Although we will have to find some time to get together after all this is settled so we can catch up properly. I have a contract right here for you to sign."

"Um, okay." Sophia laughed. "Why the heck not? The program meant so much to me as an undergrad, I guess I can't really see myself teaching anywhere else but CUNY. Just how crummy is the salary?"

"I pushed a little and got you sixty thousand to start, even though there is a collective bargaining agreement I was supposed to adhere to. Human Resources hates dealing with me because I pointed out that the union contract has a clause allowing the university to pay above scale. They spouted some crap about fairness and equity, but I went above them to the president." Francine grinned and pushed the contract toward Sophia.

Sophia glanced at the piece of paper in front of her and turned to the final page, noting the line for her signature.

Francine handed her a pen and two minutes later, the deal was done.

"Welcome to CUNY. Oh, by the way, we have a couple of big fundraisers each year and it would be a crime not to take advantage of your good looks and charm. Can I count on you to attend both of them? There are a lot of prominent women who attend and a few of them have very deep pockets." Francine waved her arm in the air. "I know, don't lecture me on feminism and all that crap. Do you really believe that Gloria Steinem would have been as popular as she was if she looked more like me? Welcome to the politics of academia."

Chapter Three

Winter 2005

Sophia hated attending the stuffy fundraisers for her college, but she didn't want to let Francine down. The annual holiday black tie fundraiser that brought in money from affluent New Yorkers and alumni, was the first of many that she was expected to attend.

Sophia hung toward the back of the room, practically plastered to the wall, sipping her glass of Riesling, when she noticed a stunning honey blonde prowling confidently into the room. In Sophia's mind, prowl was the right word because the woman seemed to have a kind of animal magnetism about her. She reminded Sophia of a sleek lion or leopard. When the woman came closer, Sophia came face to face with brilliant green eyes. Sophia remembered seeing a friend's pictures of her African safari where a leopard peered back at her with the same color eyes as this woman.

The fundraiser no longer seemed boring to her as she locked eyes with the woman. A slow, sure, grin made its way across the woman's face as she came closer. Sophia felt like she was this woman's prey for the evening. Somehow, the thought of this woman hunting her was not at all unappealing.

Sophia knew what it felt like when another woman was cruising her, but this woman's appreciative look was more like a caress. The woman screamed class and sophistication. Sophia suspected that her self-imposed celibacy as a result of the intensity of graduate school and settling into her new job was about to end.

"You must be the new professor everyone is talking about," the huntress said.

"Excuse me?" Sophia raised her eyebrow.

"Criminally sexy Italian. That's what they are saying about you. The lesbian students in your program are going to love you." The woman stuck out her hand. "I'm Lara Beck. I run a boring financial services company," she stated.

Sophia chuckled. "Well, I must admit that's a pretty good line, using others to deliver a compliment. Yes. Sophia Torre. Nice to meet you." Sophia shook Lara's hand. "I am the new professor in the LGBTQ studies program. They only hired me because I was a right pain in the ass when I was a student in their program and they knew they'd never get rid of me unless they hired me to teach for them."

"Somehow I doubt that very much. I'll bet you're brilliant and it certainly doesn't hurt that you're attractive. Enrollment in the program will most likely increase now that you're a professor."

"I can already tell that I'm going to have to watch myself around you. You are quite the charmer," Sophia admitted.

"Any chance I can charm you into having drinks with me after this soiree is finished?"

"I'd love to—especially if it will get me out of staying until the bitter end."

"How about if I promise to make a very large donation in exchange for stealing you away earlier than the minimal, acceptable amount of time?" Lara asked.

"Oh, I think that would be a fair compromise. Let me just make my excuses to my boss and you can lead the way," Sophia answered.

†

A limousine pulled up in front of the circular drive and Sophia gracefully folded herself inside after her charming companion used a feather light touch on her back to guide her to the vehicle.

A bottle of wine was chilling in the compartment opposite the two women.

"Although this isn't exactly the drink I was referring to earlier, would you like a glass of wine?"

Sophia didn't want to drink too much alcohol and miss the opportunity to get to know this intriguing woman better, so she declined the drink.

"We have a couple of choices for where to go for drinks. We could either go to one of the loud, obnoxious, dance clubs, an unhealthy smoke infested jazz club, or my smoke free penthouse that would be quiet enough to actually have a conversation."

Sophia chuckled. "You are a crafty one. By describing the other two options in a very unappealing manner, I suspect you hope I will choose your penthouse."

"Beautiful and intelligent—that is a lethal combination for me. Sophia, I'm not one to play games. I find you positively delicious and I would like nothing more than to take you back to my place and make love to you all night long, but I won't push for anything more than you willingly wish to offer. If sharing drinks and conversation is all that evolves tonight, I'll just bide my time and keep asking you out until it's the right time for both of us."

"I'm not opposed to having drinks at your penthouse and then we'll see where it takes us," Sophia offered.

†

Sophia had never been in such an opulent apartment. She stood at the floor to ceiling windows that revealed a spectacular view of the city, the glimmering lights winking at her. She knew places like this existed in New York, she'd just never been invited to one before. It was a bit overwhelming to her and she took another large sip of the drink in her hand. She was surprised to see that there was nothing left but a few ice cubes.

Lara gently removed the glass from her hand and tucked a stray hair behind her ear. Sophia instinctively moved closer and their lips came together in a gentle union.

Sophia felt Lara's hand caressing her face and the next kiss slowly increased in intensity until she heard herself moan loudly. "Oh God, I swear I felt that all the way to my toes."

"Are you more relaxed now?"

Sophia thought that, while the kiss managed to break the ice a bit, she was anything but relaxed. She imagined this was a lot like when someone revved up a sports car engine. Her engine was definitely purring.

"If you're intending to relax me, it would be best not to kiss me like that again."

"What do you want, Sophia? I want to give you whatever your heart desires. Tell me and I'll make it happen," Lara whispered.

Sophia was definitely not a prude, but had never slept with anyone after just meeting them. She wasn't the kind of person to have one-night stands. Tonight she would venture into new territory. "You, I want you."

"You have me."

Lara took Sophia by the hand and led her into the bedroom.

Chapter Four

July 2011

Sophia walked slowly beside her father and smiled up at her love who was waiting at the altar. This was happening. This was really happening. After six years together, they were finally able to legally marry. They'd had a commitment ceremony a little more than five years ago, but there was something very different about this. Sure, there were all the legal advantages to marriage, but it was more than that. It was standing up before all your friends and family and sharing your love for that one person and having them celebrate with you the special commitment that a marriage signifies.

Dominick, Sophia's father, smiled at her, kissed her on the cheek and stepped back.

Her sister, Marie, was standing next to her, performing to perfection all the duties expected as her maid of honor.

Joy, Sophia's best friend, stood next to Marie. Sophia chuckled as she saw Joy checking out one of the women standing next to her future wife. Joy would never change and would never lack for female company.

Sophia looked into the eyes of the woman she'd fallen so desperately in love with on the night of that fundraiser and smiled at the love she saw reflected back.

That one night had led to many more which had sealed their relationship. It was a whirlwind romance, starting with that night of passion and quickly led to a commitment ceremony only six months later. Sophia had moved into the penthouse after only a month, despite, Joy's minor protestations that she should date a bit more before settling down. Sophia tossed away Joy's advice because she just knew she'd found her one and only.

"Shall we begin?" the officiant asked.

Sophia nodded.

Everything was a blur as they each recited their vows.

Sophia was so nervous, wanting to say just the right things. She tried to remember everything she'd written down. "You were like a freight train barreling down on me. From the first moment I laid eyes on you, I was lost. Some people say that love at first sight is not possible. That it's only a romantic notion strictly relegated to books and movies, but they're wrong because I'm convinced I fell in love with you the moment our eyes met. I can't imagine living my life with anyone but you. You had my heart then, you have my heart now, and you'll have my heart until the day I die."

"Until I met you, I never thought it was possible to settle down and love just one woman. You were the first to turn me into a believer in love. From the moment I saw you hiding in the corner, I knew in my heart that I would have to make you mine, no matter what it took. I will do everything in my power to make you happy for the rest of our lives."

It wouldn't be long now and they would finally get to the fun part – the enormous party that practically all of New York was invited to attend.

"Sophia, do you take…."

Chapter Five

Spring 2015

Lara grimaced as she looked out the tiny window of the Boeing 767 jet. Even the first class windows were small on the airplane. The constant drizzle created tiny beads of water on the glass.

"Big surprise. It's raining again," she muttered.

"Excuse me?" Chelsea Martin, the international head of Microtech, inquired.

"Nothing," Lara responded and smiled.

Lara was a master of deceit. She could fake just about anything and Chelsea might come in handy later. She would smile and continue showing Chelsea how interested she was in her prized greyhounds. Lara knew that the chance meeting with the famed executive might prove fortuitous. A little flirting here and there wouldn't hurt either. Chelsea Martin was one of the most powerful lesbian executives in the United States. Her wealth and connections could mean several additional large accounts. Lara thrived on money and power. It was like air to her—she needed it to sustain life.

"We should really plan on having lunch together. I'd love to hear more of your ideas for my financial portfolio. It would be such a pity to not get together now that I know your home base is right in my back yard." Chelsea's mouth bent up and her brilliant smile left Lara with a hint of promise.

If Lara really wanted to seal the deal and pave her way into this woman's fortune, all she had to do was accept this formidable executive's veiled invitation. She'd heard that Chelsea enjoyed entertaining other powerful women in business and Lara was well known in her own right. Lara didn't consider it cheating to have a brief intimate encounter with a potential business client. It was all part of the game and she was very good at this form of entertainment.

As the Chief Executive Officer of Fortified Financials, Lara had achieved a certain amount of fame and status, but her aspirations were always two steps higher. Being a millionaire wasn't enough anymore, she wanted billionaire status. Her ruthless approach to business would not let her stop at anything to achieve her ultimate goal. Integrity and morals had no place in a successful financial planning business.

"I'd be delighted to have lunch and give you a few pointers, but of course to receive the full benefit of my extensive knowledge, I'd have to sign you up as a new client. I am convinced you would not be disappointed with my performance." Lara smiled seductively at Chelsea.

Chelsea pulled out a business card as the voice on the speaker sounded.

Flight attendants, please prepare for landing.

"Here is my card. I'll expect a call on Monday. I look forward to connecting with you again. It's been a pleasure talking with you," Chelsea said as she nodded.

Lara frowned before taking the card and then quickly displayed her own brilliant smile. The nod from Chelsea felt like a dismissal or even worse, an order. Lara did not do well when another woman was in charge, but Chelsea's connections were necessary to propel her to the next level. She would continue to let Chelsea believe she held the reins.

"I will definitely call on Monday to arrange lunch. Shall I call your assistant, or would you prefer that I call you directly?" Lara asked.

Lara noted the look of surprise in Chelsea's eyes before they narrowed in scrutiny. "For now, why don't you go through my assistant?"

"Perfect."

As the plane came to a stop, the sound of unbuckling seat belts and shuffling bags filled the small cabin. Lara leaned back in her seat and decided to let all the passengers around her gather their belongings and deplane before attempting to pull her overnight bag from the bin above. She didn't want to take the chance that Chelsea would see her reunion with her wife, Rachel.

Rachel always greeted her at the airport with a passionate kiss. The greeting created an internal conflict with Lara. Although she thoroughly enjoyed the physical experience, her more reserved side did not enjoy what she considered was a flamboyant and unnecessary display of public affection.

Early in their relationship, Lara tried to temper her passionate wife. As a hot-blooded Italian woman, Rachel refused to moderate her passion with Lara. Most people who met Rachel would never guess she was Italian with her long blonde hair and piercing blue eyes, but Rachel's ancestors were from the Northern territories where blond, blue-eyed men and women were the norm.

In the end, Lara wanted the passion more than she needed the reserve. Rachel was a spectacular bedmate, so she allowed this one idiosyncrasy.

When the last passenger began his descent down the narrow aisle, Lara stood up, moved into the tight passageway, and stretched her long, lean body. She lifted her Louis Vuitton carry-on bag from the overhead bin and slung it on her shoulder. She smiled as she envisioned Rachel's generous lips devouring her mouth. She felt a trickle in her silk panties as the scene played out in her head. Lara had plans for Rachel and could barely wait to unwrap her. It would take at least a half an hour, depending on traffic, to reach their expansive home on Lake Washington. Maybe Rachel would agree to a quick release in the car as she drove.

†

Rachel was running late to pick up her wife. She shoved the mail littered on the kitchen table aside looking for her keys. Espresso, their black cat, up on the table again, blinked his green eyes at her and Rachel imagined he was saying, "Why so stressed, mom? Do you want me to help you?"

Espresso began batting the pieces of mail with his paws.

Rachel sighed. "This is not a game, Espresso. Get down. You know how mommy Lara hates when you jump up on the table."

Espresso yawned and plopped down on the table, resuming his lazy attack of the mail as he sprawled out on top of half of the envelopes.

Rachel petted his head before picking him up and placing him on the floor. Two seconds later, he jumped back on the table and reached up to place one of his paws on her shoulder. "Okay, you big baby, you can come with me, but we have to find mommy's keys first."

Rachel pulled Espresso close to her as he wrapped his other paw around her neck and licked her chin. When he poked his tongue in her mouth and licked sloppily, she placed her right hand over her mouth to serve as a barrier.

"No French kissing. How many times do I have to tell you that's reserved for mommy?"

Rachel picked up Espresso and shifted him to her left arm while continuing to move the mail around. "There you are, you naughty keys. I thought I told you that playing hide and seek right before I have to pick up Lara is strictly forbidden."

With Espresso still in her arms, Rachel rushed out the door and into the garage. Placing Espresso on the passenger seat, she settled into the buttery soft leather of her Tesla. Pushing a button on the large touchscreen, the garage door whirred open and she eased out of the three-car garage.

"Let's hope traffic is light today. You'd think it would be on a Sunday, but it's Seattle so you never know. Lara will be plenty pissed if I'm late again. I might have to make the trip back home a little more pleasurable to make up for my tardiness." Lara grinned at Espresso. "You need to jump in the back and settle in for a nap while I welcome mommy home properly."

"Meow," Espresso answered.

"I'll give you extra treats and let you climb on the counters when mommy Lara isn't there if you're a good boy while I help mommy relax."

"Meow."

"Good boy. I knew I could count on you."

†

Lara glanced at her watch. "Where the hell are you, Rachel? It's Sunday for Christ's sake. How hard can it be to get to the airport on time on a flippin' Sunday?" she grumbled in frustration.

Lara was not the kind of woman you kept waiting. This was yet another small irritation that she considered less than ideal regarding her wife. Rachel would be late for her own funeral, Lara often teased.

Lara pressed a button on her watch and rapidly recorded a message, "You're late again. Don't park. Meet you at arrivals."

The ping and haptic notification on her watch was instantaneous. Lara smiled as she saw the, *sorry*, with a smiley face in her tiny 38mm watch screen. Rachel might be chronically late and a bit too demonstrative for her at times, but she was also a hellcat in bed and one of the most beautiful women Lara had ever laid eyes on. She knew the instant they met at the Seattle Children's Hospital fundraiser that she would make this gorgeous creature hers. The fact that she was already involved was a detail that Lara found irrelevant to what she wanted—and what Lara wanted, she always got.

With her carryon bag slung over her shoulder, Lara briskly walked outside to wait for her errant wife. Tapping the toe of her black Gucci pumps, Lara waited impatiently for her wife to drive up. Without her nylons, the pumps rubbed uncomfortably on her sensitive heels and the sides of her feet. After she removed her silk underwear and the extra nylon barrier while visiting the restroom, she realized that Gucci did not design the expensive shoes to function as a bedroom slipper.

The drizzling rain, her late wife, the rubbing shoes, and her uncomfortable suit left Lara irritable and primed for an argument of epic proportions. This was not how she envisioned her homecoming. She shivered in the overhang that protected her from the Seattle rain. Even though it was a short distance to the car, she knew that a few raindrops would penetrate the light silk fabric on her shirt, adding to her irritation.

Ten minutes later, Rachel's sleek black Tesla screeched to a halt in the arrival lane closest to the overhang. Rachel jumped from the car and rushed up to Lara, pulling the bag from her shoulder and placing it on the ground while she wrapped her arms around Lara's neck. Her mouth found its target like a heat seeking missile and blanketed Lara is a searing kiss that sent tingles of arousal all the way to her toes.

Lara's irritation dissipated quickly as she settled into the kiss. Her arms wrapped around Rachel's tiny waist and their bodies melded together in a sensual dance. Lara wanted to toss Rachel on the sidewalk and rip off her clothes, but she would have to wait until later. The kiss was a promise of things to come.

"God, I missed you so much. I still don't understand why you can't just hire someone to run your New York office," Rachel purred.

Lara frowned. She enjoyed the fact that her wife missed her so much, but she did not like when Rachel questioned her in any way. She had more reasons than her tendency toward total control for keeping a New York office under her command. Lara couldn't let Rachel know about that other reason, so she needed to school her reaction to the challenge.

"Oh babe, you know how much I miss you too, but we've talked about this before and I explained how poorly things went when I left someone else in charge. You know I can't let that happen again," Lara said.

Rachel placed her hand on Lara's collarbone and slowly let her hand slide down across her breasts before picking up the overnight bag. As Rachel popped the trunk, Lara chuckled at her blatant seduction and the fact that she never cared who was watching when expressing affection for her wife. In fact, Lara suspected that a small part of Rachel's penchant for public displays of affection was due in part to the thrill of knowing she was creating a show for the passing voyeur. Some days this bothered Lara more than others. Today she craved her wife's fiery passion, so it didn't bother her as much. Rachel was insatiable in bed. They were still newlyweds, so the fires were still burning bright.

Lara caught the twinkle in Rachel's eye and she knew the ride home would be just what the doctor ordered. When she opened the door, she groaned. "Did you have to let the little bad boy come?"

"Meow."

"Now is that any way to treat your son? He's missed you almost as much as I have. Don't even try to sound mad. I know how much you love the little shit," Rachel teased.

Lara reached down to rub Espresso's head as she leaned in to kiss his wet nose. "Be good for mama and climb into the back seat while your sex starved mother enjoys the ride home," she whispered.

Espresso blinked, yawned, and stood his ground as he steadfastly refused to move from the passenger seat.

Rachel laughed as she picked up the cat and gently placed him in the back seat. "Time for a nap, little bad boy, your mama and me have unfinished business to attend to and we don't need your help or your rough little tongue getting in the way."

Rachel climbed into the passenger seat as Lara walked deliberately to the driver's side. After adjusting the mirrors, she glanced at her wife. "At least you could have grabbed his carrier. I swear if he tries to lick your hand while you're, you know…"

"Well, can you blame him? Your scent is intoxicating. I might lick my own hand after I delve into your luscious juices. Just push him away. Eventually, he gets the message."

Lara groaned as Espresso poked his head between the seats. She scratched his chin and then pushed him back. "Not today, Espresso. You just march your furry butt back and curl up to take a nap like a good boy."

Espresso's eyes turned to tiny emerald slits as he swished his tail back and forth before settling into one of the bucket seats in the rear of the car.

"See, he just needed a few little pets." Rachel raked her gaze across her wife's business attire. "Not that I don't love you in your sexy suits, but are you trying to make this challenging for me?"

Lara eased the car into traffic as they exited the airport arrival area. She grinned at Rachel. "Nylons and panties are in my purse. I wanted to feel the breeze between my legs."

Rachel moved her hand up Lara's silky leg and pushed the skirt up. "Mmm, commando, and someone is especially happy to see me. I should have noticed you weren't wearing pantyhose—how unobservant of me."

Rachel's hand kept circling dangerously close to Lara's clit and her frustration peaked as she blurted out an order. "Stop teasing me. I'm ready to burst."

"Mm hm. Patience is a virtue you know. Maybe I want to merely get you ready for when we get home."

Rachel's lazy smile was Lara's undoing. "I have no patience and I can't wait. We can do the slow tease later, right now I just need quick and precise."

"As soon as you get on the highway," Rachel purred.

Distracted, Lara nearly plowed into a car speeding to her left as she tried to merge onto I-5. She jerked the wheel to the right just in time. "Okay, maybe I can wait until I'm safely on the highway," Lara agreed.

The black Tesla jerked forward several times as Lara's foot pushed against the gas pedal and her head hit the backrest in ecstasy. The appetizer before the full meal was enough to stir her hunger.

Chapter Six

Sophia looked out the window of her luxury high-rise penthouse in the exclusive New York City building, Central Park West. The gray sky mirrored her mood. Her wife had left early that morning after two glorious weeks in which they'd felt like a normal couple.

She hadn't wanted to spend their short time together fighting about the pitiful amount of time they managed to share with one another. Sophia didn't care about the money. She desperately wanted her wife to give up the west coast office. Since she'd opened the office, Sophia felt like she'd begun to slip away from her.

Sophia did her best not to put pressure on her hard-working spouse and the old arguments remained strictly off the table during the precious two-week visit. She chuckled to herself as she realized that's exactly what it felt like—a two-week visit.

Sophia was grateful for the fact that the visit coincided with her spring break. She loved teaching and was fortunate enough to have a lot of free time during the university breaks. She couldn't imagine doing anything else, but she'd grown tired of city life.

Sophia's roots were in the sparsely populated cities in the rural Midwest. Good old boys, mom and apple pie, did not create an easy life while growing up as an out and proud lesbian. She thought she'd died and gone to heaven when she first learned of a university that taught gay and lesbian studies.

The shiny new bobble that was New York City had not worn off for many years and her return to the city seemed inevitable, but lately Sophia had begun to think about other things that she wanted from this life. She wanted to spend more than two weeks at a time with her wife and she wanted to have kids. It wasn't too late—yet.

She'd just turned thirty-five and she could feel her biological clock ticking loudly in her head at night. The ticking got especially loud when she found herself alone in the five thousand square foot luxury penthouse. What good was a boatload of money when you rarely were able to enjoy the fruits with the one you loved?

Fawn, her tan tabby, waddled closer and barely made it up on the arm of the plush moss green sofa resting perpendicular to the floor to ceiling windows that overlooked the twinkling lights of the city.

Sophia smiled down at her sole companion. "Who keeps feeding you treats? Pretty soon you won't be able to jump up on the bed and then what'll you do? Maybe while your other mommy is away again, I can keep you on a strict diet." Sophia stroked his soft fur and could feel him purr as she absently continued massaging his head.

Her sigh was loud enough that if anyone had been in the master bedroom, they might have heard the depression in that one quick expulsion of air. "Oh Fawn, remember when we first got together, we couldn't keep our hands, or any other part of our body, off one another. I don't want to feel like an old married couple. If I didn't know any better, I'd think she was cheating on me, but how in the world would she have time. Running two successful offices on opposite sides of the country doesn't leave time for much else besides working, eating, and sleeping. I need to get a life that doesn't revolve entirely around my wife's business schedule. Let's call Aunty Joy and see what she's up to tonight. I'm done moping around for now."

Sophia picked up her smart phone, swiped the large screen, and punched several buttons until she heard her best friend's voice. "Hey, Joy. Yeah, she left this morning. I'm bored, depressed, and something else I don't care to mention. Get two. I'll be able to devour one whole container myself. Yep, nothing like ice cream therapy to cure whatever ails you. Oh yeah, can you also pick up some double A batteries? Oh, shush, it's for the something else I didn't want to mention and no, you cannot watch."

Sophia chuckled as she ended the call. "Now, why couldn't I fall in love with Joy, who is a constant in my life and who I'm sure will never fall prey to the dreaded lesbian bed death."

As Sophia wondered why she hadn't heard from her wife yet, the ding on her phone signaled that a new text message had arrived.

Flight delayed. Just got in. Love u.

Love u 2. Call me tomorrow after u get some sleep.

OK

At least Sophia wouldn't worry about her wife making it safely back to her satellite office. Sophia wondered if her love felt as lonely and lost as she did every time she left. *Probably too busy to get lonely.*

Hearing the doorbell, Sophia scurried to the door to let her best friend and the two pints of Ben and Jerry's ice cream into the penthouse.

"About time you got here. Did you have to milk the cow?" Sophia asked.

"No, smartass, but I almost had to pay Johann in ice cream to let me come up this late at night. He told me chocolate chip cookie dough is his favorite and then he gave me his best puppy dog eyes. Too bad for him that I'm a big old dyke and those puppy dog eyes only work when they are attached to a buxom blonde."

"Ooh, is that the color of the week now?" Sophia prodded.

"Ha ha. I've always been a sucker for blondes," Joy offered.

"And brunettes and redheads and silver foxes, anything with two legs...."

"I'm ignoring that because I know you're distraught because your honey lips just left. How long will she be gone this time?" Joy asked.

"Honey lips? Ew, that's just wrong. She'll be gone for a whole month," Sophia lamented.

Joy whistled. "Whoa. She'll be gone for her fortieth birthday. I thought you were planning a big surprise party for her?"

"I was, but my plans just got shot to hell when she laid the big bomb on me today. She was terribly apologetic, but that doesn't make up for the fact that I won't get to spend the big day with her. Poor baby." Sophia plucked the pint of Ben and Jerry's chocolate chip cookie dough from Joy's hand and walked into the kitchen, retrieving two spoons.

Stainless steel appliances with a built in wine refrigerator adorned the kitchen. The imported Italian marble countertops sat on top of rich, cherry wood. Her wife insisted on the best of everything, but Sophia would gladly trade it all in for a normal marriage where people got to sleep together every night.

"Why don't you just go to her? I'll bet she would love the surprise. The university loves you, I'm sure they could get someone to cover your classes for a few days," Joy offered.

Sophia waved Joy into the living room and plopped down on the sofa next to Fawn, while Joy settled into the leather recliner. Sophia started laughing when Joy removed the top to the ice cream and didn't know where to put it after snuggling into the comfortable chair. She popped up from the sofa and grabbed the top, placing it next to the cap on the coffee table that she'd already removed from her pint. A plastic bag settled haphazardly next to the chair where Joy had tossed it. Sophia suspected it contained her batteries. She was thankful that Joy hadn't remembered to tease her about them.

"You know, Joy, that isn't a half bad idea," Sophia said, getting excited. "I think I'll do it. I can surprise her at her office. God knows why she decided to set up an office in loggersville. I suppose all those Microtech millionaires might be reason enough, but geez it rains there all the time."

"I heard the Seattleites are wild in the sack. All that free love, granola shit makes them completely unconventional. I wouldn't mind taking a trip out west to check it out. I feel an illness coming on and I'm sure in two weeks it will be a full-fledged contagion that I must absolutely resist exposing others to. Take me with you, please," Joy begged.

"Absolutely. We can play tourist while my lovely wife works her ass off. I don't know why she's never let me visit.

There are a few places that I'd love to see. They have Orca whales in the sound right outside some cluster of islands not too far from Seattle. I want to see the whales," Sophia enthused.

"We can go see the whales only if you promise I won't have to put on some smelly jumpsuit that five hundred sweaty people previously wore. I saw this special TV show once about those whale watching tours and what those people wore was simply disgusting—not to mention totally unflattering to the figure. I want a luxury boat for our whale watching adventure. Oh, and you need to take me to a gay bar so I can meet the local talent," Joy insisted.

"Deal. Thanks for coming here, Joy, and cheering me up. I don't know what's happening with our marriage, but I get the feeling that she's slipping away from me. We made it through the scary sevens, but after ten years, we should be more settled. Something is off. I can't put my finger on it, but I feel like I'm missing something really important. Maybe I'm being paranoid, but as my granny always said, *just cause you're paranoid, don't mean they ain't out to get you, honey.*"

"She did not say that. You're making that shit up," Joy said.

"I am not. My granny was bat shit crazy, but a wise woman just the same."

"Is she the one that drank a glass or two of red wine every night?" Joy asked.

"Yep. That's the one. My other grandma was the hussy with six different husbands."

"Okay, now you're pulling my leg."

"No, I'm not. I swear. She was a real looker in her time, but she got bored easily and the men she married never seemed to keep her satisfied for too long. She married her last husband in the nursing home, but that only lasted six months before he caught her in bed with the guy down the hall. Granny had an active libido all the way into her eighties. Grampa number six caught her with her legs spread eagle and old man Harold's head nestled right in the middle. He couldn't get it up anymore, but granny swore his tongue was golden."

Joy burst out laughing. "Damn, girl. No wonder you're a lesbian, our equipment functions well into old age and it sounds like to keep up with you and your ancestors, that's what it takes to keep you happy in your golden years."

Sophia looked at her best friend. "Joy, are you really serious? Will you go with me to Seattle? I might need someone to pal around with while I'm in a practically foreign land."

"You know you can always count on me. Besides, I'd love to drool over your wife again. She is a fine looking specimen, even though she is so not my type."

Sophia got a dreamy look on her face. "She is something, isn't she? I hit the jackpot when I met her. She's beautiful, charming, intelligent, rich, and mine, all mine. Now if we could just reside in the same city three hundred and sixty five days a year—life would be perfect."

"You've been living apart like this for at least two years. Why are you, all of a sudden, desperate for your best friend's ice cream therapy?" Joy asked.

"I want to have a family," Sophia blurted out.

"So, Miss Perfect doesn't share your long-term plans, huh?"

"Well, I thought she did, but lately she keeps dodging the subject and whenever I try to have a serious discussion about it, we go down the bad road. I see her so little as it is—I've just stopped mentioning it," Sophia admitted.

"Oh hon, you two have to get that settled and soon. Being on the same page about having kids is one of those make or break marriage subjects. Didn't you two discuss that when you got married?" Joy asked.

"We did, but that was before her business took off and she became so successful," Sophia explained.

"Have you ever thought of marriage counseling?"

"Are you kidding? You've met my wife. She has serious control issues. No way in hell would she agree to that." Sophia stuck her spoon in the ice cream container, dug out a large chunk, and wrapped her mouth around the spoon, letting the creamy sweet treat melt on her tongue. "Mmm, that is orgasmic. Something I've been missing lately."

Joy picked up the plastic bag sitting next to her chair, pulled out the package of batteries, tossed them to Sophia and began singing. "Sisters are doin' it for themselves."

Sophia chuckled. "Yep, you got that right. I always thought that being a lesbian would ensure that I'd never have to revert to *doin' it* for myself."

"Oh, honey, sometimes it's fun to incorporate that into the total love mix. Nothing wrong with a little toy action now and again."

Sophia scooped out some ice cream and held her spoon up while Joy dug out her own treasure as they clicked their spoons together. "Amen to that."

Chapter Seven

Two seconds after the Tesla came to a complete stop in the garage, Rachel unbuckled her seat belt, jumped out of the car, and grabbed Espresso.

Lara oozed out of the driver's side and followed her wife's path to the door.

After tossing Espresso in the door, Rachel clutched Lara's silk shirt, dragging her into the house. Pushing her against the wall, Rachel crushed her mouth against Lara's. She didn't waste any time tugging on the zipper of Lara's skirt, unzipping her in seconds and pushing the skirt to the floor.

Espresso ran to his favorite daybed and settled in, watching his two moms perform their favorite coming home ritual.

"If I don't taste you right this instant, I'm sure I'll die of starvation," Rachel exclaimed.

Lara stepped out of her skirt, tossed her purse on the floor, and gently pushed Rachel's head between her legs. "We can't have that, now, can we?"

Rachel urged Lara's legs apart and covered her sex with her mouth—licking and sucking while she penetrated her with her middle and index fingers.

Lara threw her head back and moaned. "Ooh. So good. So fucking good. Remind me to insure that tongue of yours." When her orgasm finally crested, the pulsations and quivers that ran up and down her body created an out of body experience.

Rachel pulled her fingers from inside Lara and slowly licked each one clean. "Mmm, finger lickin' good. Better than Kentucky Fried Chicken, and I loves me some fried chicken," Rachel exclaimed in a poor imitation of a southern lady.

Lara chuckled. "That is a horrible southern accent, darling." Lara clasped Rachel's hand and began leading her to the bedroom. "I seem to be the only one partially dressed here. You and me. Naked. Now. I've brought home a few presents, but we seem to have left them in the trunk in our haste to finish what you started in the car."

"Ooh, presents. I like the sound of that, but I'd rather leave the bag until later. I left the silk ties on the bed. I'm in the mood for some extended playtime and excruciating delay of pleasure. Tie me up and tease away, my talented lover. I won't even try to escape," Rachel exclaimed.

"Now where's the fun in that? I'll have you squirming and begging in no time," Lara taunted.

†

Lara peeked at the neon green light flashing ominously in the dark. Damn it was midnight already. Rachel had been insatiable for two hours as they brought one another to the height of pleasure multiple times. Rachel was lightly snoring now as Lara slipped from their bed to send her text.

Creeping quietly into the mudroom where she left both her purse and her phone, Lara muttered, "Shit, she's probably biting off her toenails now with worry." Digging into her purse, Lara retrieved her phone and walked quietly into the living room. She jabbed at the phone in irritation, forming the quick text. Fortunately, it was late and she wouldn't expect a phone call. Only a text, letting her know she'd arrived safely.

Lara smiled as she thought of her soft brown eyes and the way they watered when she'd left her standing in the doorway. She was a vision of loveliness—a classic Italian beauty from the southern regions of Italy. Lara could never give her up. She was Lara's first true love.

Lara felt a ping of guilt that she quickly stuffed down deep into her black soul. Her justifications for the decisions made in her life were always completely logical. No one was really getting hurt. She cared deeply for both of them. Didn't she make sure they both had everything they could ever want or need? She spared no expense to ensure that she took good care of both of them.

The little voice in Lara's head kept shouting at her that she wasn't being fair. She'd only made love to her once during the visit. She would have to rectify that the next time they were together. Their lovemaking was so different from what she had with Rachel. No less satisfying—just different. Rachel was adventurous and creative. Her other lover was sensuous and passionate. She needed both in her life—what she liked to refer to as her sexual yin and yang.

"Lara? Where are you?" Rachel's sleepy voice called out.

Lara rushed back to the master bedroom and a rush of arousal hit her as she looked at Rachel's tousled blonde hair and crystal blue eyes. Rachel was a natural beauty. Without any effort, she turned both male and female heads the minute she entered a room. She had a kind of casual sexiness about her and could make a pair of jeans come to life on her body.

"You look positively delicious, but we both need to get some rest if I'm going to survive the office tomorrow," Lara tossed out.

"Can't you just call in sick or go in late, for once?" Rachel asked.

"No. I have a full day and I need to follow up on a possible lead. I met Chelsea Martin on the flight back to Seattle. I can't wait to get my hands on her billions. I believe she is in need of some expert financial planning. She gave me her card to call and arrange a lunch meeting. I'm not going to let the grass grow on this one. She'll be my largest client to date."

"That's great honey. I'm sure that your good looks and charm won't hurt one bit. I heard she's a shameless flirt. Not too shabby looking for an old lady either." Rachel laughed.

"Hey. You better not consider forty old because my fortieth is just around the corner you know and I would hate to think you believe I'm over the hill or something," Lara joked.

"Not a chance, especially the way you acted tonight. God, Lara, you tired me out and I'm ten years your junior. I better start taking vitamins if I hope to keep up with you in our golden years."

"No worries. I'll just trade you in for a younger model when you grow old and gray." Lara chuckled.

"Fine, then I'll take every last cent of those millions you've amassed and get my own hot Latin lover." Rachel grinned.

Lara set her phone on the nightstand and climbed into bed with her wife. She was thankful that Rachel was still a little groggy from sleep and hadn't asked any questions about why she had her phone with her. Lara thought that in many ways Rachel was young and naïve. She knew that Rachel would never suspect anything. It was one of the things she loved most—her trusting nature. Lara remembered

Rachel telling her once that it was always better to *assume good intentions.*

With Rachel curled up in her arms, Lara fell into a deep, satisfying sleep.

†

Rachel absently stroked Lara's stomach. She could feel Lara's slow even breathing as she entered dreamland. Rachel was now wide-awake after noticing that her wife was not in bed after calling out to her.

Rachel watched Lara saunter back into their bedroom with the moonlight spotlighting her beautiful naked form. Rachel thought Lara was one of the most exquisite women she'd ever met and the first time she'd laid eyes on her, she knew she had to have her. Their sexual chemistry was explosive. Lara was one of the few women who could keep up with her heightened need for physical intimacy. It didn't escape Rachel's keen observation skills when Lara set her cell phone on the nightstand.

Rachel wondered who Lara was texting or e-mailing in the middle of the night. She didn't hear her speaking to anyone on the phone, so she assumed that when she came back into the bedroom and laid the phone on the dresser, that she was checking e-mails or texting someone. That damn phone was tethered to her hand. Sometimes Rachel got irritated with Lara's laser-like focus on business which stressed their relationship. It was her only irritation with their marriage.

Finally, Rachel would have Lara all to herself for a full month. She was delighted that the Seattle office required her attention for that amount of time. It would be the longest timespan that Lara remained in Seattle before returning to New York since their honeymoon two years ago. Rachel intended on making the most of this time and was quite pleased with her plans for Lara's fortieth birthday party. It would be a night to remember.

Rachel had been extra careful not to let the cat out of the bag. She hoped that Lara would appreciate the surprise party she'd planned.

Rachel settled into Lara's protective embrace and nodded off to sleep with a contented smile on her face. Dreaming of the fancy black tie affair she had planned, she sighed and did not move until the annoying alarm startled her awake at six-thirty.

†

The song, *It's A Beautiful Day*, blared from the speaker of the tablet setting on the nightstand closest to Lara.

"Jesus, Lara, do you have to program that to blare, *It's A Beautiful Day*, so fucking loud that my grandmother can hear it from her grave," Rachel grumbled.

Annette Mori

Lara kissed Rachel on the lips and sat up, stretching her arms above her head. "Well, good morning to you, too, little Miss Sunshine."

"Now that I'm awake, I might as well send you off with a little motivation to return quickly." Rachel pulled her lover back to bed and quickly flipped her on her back while straddling her body.

Rachel's libido was wide-awake now as the hairs on her pussy mingled with Lara's. If she wiggled a little more into position, she might be able to rub her clit against Lara's. She was sure it wouldn't take long to experience a synchronized orgasm.

Lara chuckled. "Unfortunately, I don't have time. I have to be in the office by seven thirty this morning. Besides, don't you need to get up and get going?"

"Nope, I told my staff that I would be fucking you long into the night and wouldn't be in until later this morning. They completely understood," Rachel joked.

"You did not, you big liar."

"Well, I might not have used those exact words, but they did know you were coming in last night and assumed I would be in later," Rachel clarified.

"Must be nice to be the boss and have an understanding CEO."

"Um, you are the CEO of your company, so you get to make all the rules. That means you can go in late today," Rachel pleaded.

"Sorry, hon, no can do. I set up a meeting with my staff for seven thirty. I have a lot to go through before I approach Chelsea. I might even be able to set up the lunch for today and I need to be prepared," Lara answered.

Rachel shifted and was able to rub her aroused bud against Lara's. "Two minutes. I can feel your wetness beneath me."

"Oh, God," Lara moaned. "You are a temptress. You win." Lara wrapped her flexible legs around Rachel and positioned herself in such a way that her center of arousal was easy for Rachel to stimulate.

As they rocked and rubbed against one another, Rachel cried out. "So good, yeah, that's it. Come with me, Lara."

The two women cried out together in ecstasy as their combined orgasm hit simultaneously sending shivers of pleasure throughout their bodies.

Rachel collapsed on top of Lara and captured her lips in a sensuous kiss.

Lara rolled Rachel and pecked her forehead, "Uh, uh, uh, do not start anything. I really do have to get ready now." Lara jumped from the bed.

Rachel groaned as Lara's ass swayed seductively while she entered the master bath. "Now who's the temptress," Rachel called out before Lara shut the door.

Chapter Eight

Lara climbed into her silver Porsche with a satisfied smile on her face. Life was good. Even the morning traffic could not shake her from her good mood.

As she eased into her parking space in the garage under her suite of offices in downtown Seattle, she began to mentally prepare for the day.

A brief meeting with her vice presidents would bring her up to speed on the pending accounts. She expected to hear that, in her absence, the sales force had successfully secured those accounts. Failure was not an option if you worked at Fortified Financials. She had personally set those accounts in motion and all her staff had to do was close the deal. If any one of them went sideways, someone would lose their job. This was business and business took no prisoners.

The click of her heels on the marble floor tiles announced her arrival at the office.

"Good morning, Ms. Beck. Welcome back. The VPs are all in the conference room waiting for your arrival. I arranged for a light breakfast."

Lara had handpicked the receptionist and her efficiency had pleasantly surprised her. Not only was Chandra efficient, but she was very easy on the eyes. She was the perfect front person to represent Fortified Financials. Lara made sure that her salary was at least ten percent above any possible competitor. Although she was a tough businesswoman, Lara justly rewarded competence.

"Good morning, Chandra. Thank you for making those arrangements. I swear you are a mind reader." Lara winked at Chandra.

Chandra blushed. "My pleasure, Ms. Beck."

"You know, Chandra, you can call me Lara now. I think you've worked here long enough for us to be on a first name basis. Don't you?"

Lara knew that the young woman had a crush on her and she thought it was charming, but she wasn't about to dip her pen in the company ink well. However, a little flirting here and there would ensure that this competent young woman would remain loyal to her.

"Okay... um... yeah. I can do that," Chandra stuttered.

Lara strode confidently into the conference room and narrowed her eyes at the only man on her senior leadership team. She'd heard rumors that he was planning to branch out and start his own financial planning firm. She planned on rooting out this traitor and crushing him like a bug. *Too bad*, he was a brilliant strategist and a visionary, but she would not allow for any competition—especially from a former employee.

"Jason, would you mind getting me a cup of coffee, please?" Lara directed her predatory smile at him.

Yolanda, the VP of marketing, raised her eyebrow and coughed to cover up a chuckle.

Lara suspected that Yolanda knew what was coming. She'd worked the longest with Yolanda and, if she were so inclined to place her trust in anyone, it would be Yolanda.

Jason frowned, but got up and walked to the table where Chandra had laid out the breakfast and coffee. "Cream and sugar?"

"Yes, please." Lara smiled sweetly.

You little pissant, you know exactly how I take my coffee.

Yolanda looked at the other three women in the room and they all smiled in return. Lara suspected the rest of her team might also know what was coming. Lara was usually not so overt with her power plays.

Lara sat at the head of the table and accepted the coffee from Jason. "Thank you, Jason, now please sit so that we can get the meeting started. I'd like a report on the pending accounts first."

Selena, the VP of sales, began her report. "Everything is a go. I met with Mr. Tanner on Friday and all we had to do was finalize the contracts and obtain the authorizing signatures."

"Did you have to adjust the fee structure in any way to close the deal for any of them?" Lara asked.

Selena grinned. "Nope. In fact, I took a chance and increased our commission by one percent on the most lucrative contract. I got a gut feeling about that one and it paid off."

Lara nodded and smiled at Selena. She was glad she had hired this aggressive woman. Her instincts on business deals were always right on the mark. Lara wasn't worried about her loyalty. The previous company that Selena worked for did not appreciate her bold approach and as a result, the conservative firm had wasted her talents.

Selena confessed to Lara one evening, when they were celebrating an enormous account closure, that she was eternally grateful Lara had given her a chance. She told her that she would follow her to the ends of hell, if needed.

"Excellent job, Selena." Lara touched her index finger to her forehead. "I see a big bonus in your future. Yes, that's what the crystal ball in my head says." Lara turned her attention to the unassuming woman on her right. "Is everything ready for National Retirement Planning Week?"

"Yes, my staff has everything set. We have an event planned for every day. The employees really appreciate the recognition for good work. They love seeing you and the rest of this team let down our hair and have a good time at the bar-b-que. Some of them swear you do a better job grilling than their husbands."

"Thanks, Robin. I know it's not only your team, but that you have personally put a great deal of work into the week-long celebration and I appreciate it," Lara said.

Lara flipped open the binder with the quarterly financial report. "Jason, these numbers seem a little incomplete. Can you please share with me why the financial projections do not include the new accounts that Selena and her team did such a wonderful job securing?"

"We just closed those deals this past week. My team did not have enough time to prepare the numbers for this meeting," Jason said defensively.

"Selena, you provided the preliminary contracts to Jason, correct?" Lara asked.

"Yes. I e-mailed them to him two weeks ago and then sent a follow-up e-mail on Monday stating that I should have final signature copies by Wednesday. They signed them on Tuesday evening and the final contracts were on his desk at five o'clock that evening," Selena responded.

"I see." Lara turned her penetrating gaze to Jason. "Well?"

"It takes a bit of time to prepare those projections," Jason replied.

"Really? I thought you had models that allow you to plug in the appropriate numbers. How hard can it be to prepare a statement once you have the information—which it appears you received in plenty of time to arrange for a full report?" Lara's quietly controlled voice hung heavily in the air.

Twenty seconds passed before Lara interrupted the awkward silence. "Jason? I'm waiting for a viable explanation."

"Um, I guess I don't have any excuse to provide to you. The report will be on your desk by noon today." Jason lowered his gaze and stared at the papers in front of him.

"Don't bother. I went to your senior accountant and she was delighted to prepare a thorough report for me. I suspected you wouldn't have time while exploring rental options in the city for your new company. She was excited about her promotion to chief financial officer. Good luck with the development of the new company, because you're going to need it. Now, get the hell out of my sight. You will not be receiving a severance."

"Fuck you, Lara. One of these days you will get your just desserts and I hope I get to see it when it happens. I don't need you. Chelsea Martin is due to become my first client and that should be enough to get my firm started," Jason shouted.

A predatory grin spread across Lara's face as she turned around, picked up the receiver, and pressed a button on the conference room phone. "Yes, this is Lara, can you please send up security to escort Mr. Delgado out. His services are no longer needed at this company. Oh, yes, I almost forgot. Can you please send Ms. Rice into the conference room? She just became our new CFO. Thank you, Chandra."

Jason collected the papers in front of him and stood up. His face was bright red and Lara thought he might have a stroke in front of her.

"Leave the papers, Jason, they are the property of Fortified Financials. I would hate to call in the police and have you arrested for theft," Lara said.

"You are a bitch, Lara."

Lara shrugged.

Two very large men in security uniforms entered the conference room and Lara pointed to Jason. "Please make sure Mr. Delgado safely exits our premises and that the only items he leaves with are his personal belongings. Make sure he does not possess any thumb drives or any other items that belong to Fortified Financials. Frisk him if you need to."

After the men left and a stunning redhead entered the conference room, Lara resumed the meeting. "I'm sure you've all met Carrie Rice. Please welcome her to our team. I anticipate good things from Carrie and I believe she will fit right in." Lara pointed to the seat that Jason had recently vacated. "Now, where were we?"

†

Lara sighed as she sat down in her leather chair. The solid cherry desk placed a barrier between her and any prospective employee or client, which was why she rarely conducted business in her office. Firing Jason wasn't exactly pleasant, but it was a satisfying end to her one big mistake. She never should have hired the little weasel.

Lara plucked the business card Chelsea had given her from her purse and turned it in her hand, grinning at the prized possession. Punching the numbers on the card into the phone on her desk, she waited for Chelsea to answer.

"Good morning. Yes. May I please speak to Ms. Martin? She is expecting my call. Good morning, Ms. Martin, this is Lara Beck. We met on the flight back from New York yesterday. Why, thank you for remembering me and please call me Lara, as well. Yes, I was hoping you were free for lunch today or tomorrow—my treat of course. I can make arrangements at the Canlis for twelve or twelve thirty, whichever time fits your schedule. I hope that wasn't too presumptuous of me. Excellent. Shall I meet you there or would you like me to pick you up at your office around eleven forty five? Perfect, then I will see you tomorrow. I'll clear my calendar for the rest of the day so that I can provide you with my undivided attention. Yes, I look forward to seeing you again as well."

Lara hung up the phone and wondered if Chelsea would require her more personalized service or if the reputation of her company would be enough to seal the deal. There was no way she would let that little Benedict Arnold steal her potential client. Lara would do whatever was required to make sure Chelsea Martin was a new client by the end of the day. That would teach that little bastard never to screw with Lara Beck. He was way out of his league if he thought he would ever put one over on her.

Unfortunately, she might have to let Rachel know that she would be late again tomorrow night but Rachel would understand. She always did.

Lara pulled her cell phone from her purse and called Rachel's direct line at Seattle Children's Hospital. "Hey, babe. You sound out of breath. Still recovering from this morning?" Lara teased. "Same old, same old. I finally canned Jason today. The little bastard was trying to start his own company on the sly. Look, I know I just got home, but I might have to work late tomorrow night. I need to make sure everything is copasetic after my big move today. Jason unfortunately did have his own loyal minions. No, I don't anticipate huge issues, but I may need to smooth a few ruffled feathers and ensure his staff that no one else is on the chopping block. Yes, I hired Carrie to take his place."

Lara laughed. "Is that jealousy I detect in your voice? Ooh, so you like my choice. Just don't make your ogling noticeable. She may or may not swing both ways, but I don't want to compromise our working relationship. She's a bright and shining star that will only shine more brightly as she's given additional responsibility. I wish I'd have met her before hiring Jason. Since I'll have to attend to most everything tomorrow, I can make tonight an early night and I'll be home as soon as I can. I love you, too."

Lara pushed the button on her phone to end the call and leaned back in her chair. She hadn't exactly lied. Jason did have his loyal followers and she would need to keep her eyes open for any dissent in the ranks, but she could easily do that in the next couple of weeks. Chelsea Martin would be her main focus tomorrow.

Chapter Nine

Sophia's shoes clip clopped on the sidewalk in front of the dean's office. She wanted to catch her boss before she left for her first class.

During the years, Sophia had developed a close relationship with Francine and hoped that her last minute request for time off would not put a kink in their friendship.

Sophia really needed this time with her wife and she wasn't opposed to begging Francine to get it. She suspected it would never come to that, but she was prepared to do just about anything to get away and spend it with her wife on her fortieth birthday.

Sophia walked up to the heavy wooden door and knocked. When she heard Francine tell her to come in, she walked confidently into the cluttered office.

Stacks of papers covered every inch of the old oak desk. Francine had piled up books and file folders on the floor in a random pattern. Sophia shook her head as she attempted to navigate the narrow path to her boss who sat behind a massive desk. The desk dwarfed her short body and she looked like a kid playing a grown up game.

"Sophia. What brings you to my neck of the woods?" Francine said.

"Hey, boss. I have a huge favor to ask and I know it will put you in a bind, but I really need this," Sophia blurted out.

"Sit, sit," Francine directed.

Sophia looked around at the stacks of books and papers on every chair in the office. She picked up a pile of books on the chair with the least amount of debris and sat down. "You know, Francine, one of these days, someone is going to report you to the reality show, *Hoarders*. I'll bet one of those industrious students learning about Toyota Lean would just love to come in here and Five S your office."

"Five S?" Francine lifted her eyebrow.

"Yeah, one of the lean tools. Sort, set in order, shine, standardize, and sustain. Basically it's a fancy way of saying you need to clean and organize your space," Sophia explained.

Francine waved her hand in the air. "I know exactly where every single piece of paper is in my office. They better not touch a single one or I won't know where to find anything. You've heard the expression, if a cluttered desk is the sign of a cluttered mind, than what is an empty desk the sign of?" Francine laughed at her own joke. "Forget the clean freaks, now tell me what this ginormous favor is."

"I need to take off at least a couple of weeks, maybe three if I can get it, to spend time with my wife in Seattle and help her celebrate her fortieth birthday," Sophia pronounced.

Francine leaned back in her chair and narrowed her gaze at Sophia. "Okay, but what else is going on in that pretty head of yours?"

A single tear trickled down Sophia's cheek. "You're far too observant for your own good, Francine. I think my marriage is in trouble and I'm at a loss as to what I can do. I need to go to Seattle and see what the big draw is for her. She's starting to spend more time in Seattle than in New York and that worries me. I'd move in a heartbeat if I thought that would fix the problem. Don't get me wrong, I love teaching at CUNY, but I love my wife more and if I had to make the sacrifice, I would."

"Don't worry, Sophia, I'll get one of the adjuncts to cover for you. Look, I don't want to lose you, but I'll support you, no matter what. We're not just colleagues, Sophia. I'd like to think we're friends and your happiness is important to me. You go take that three weeks and fix things with your wife." Francine lifted her small body up and walked around the desk. Sophia easily accepted the hug from her boss and friend.

"Thanks, Francine. I don't know what I did right in this life, but I have the best boss in the world."

"Go on, start making those plans. That is if you can find a way out of my cluttered office," Francine teased.

"I promise to play interference whenever one of your do-gooder students starts talking about helping you organize your office."

"Have a safe trip and we'll talk when you return. Bring me a bottle of wine back. I hear Washington State has some very fine wines," Francine requested.

"You got it. Thanks again, Francine."

Sophia walked to the door and smiled. Everything was going to be just fine. Once she got to Seattle and was able to spend time with her wife, she knew they would work everything out and fix the chasm that had suddenly appeared in their relationship. She whistled to herself, feeling hopeful about the future.

†

When Sophia returned to her penthouse condominium, she launched into efficiency mode to pack quickly and catch the next possible flight out to Seattle. Of course, she would call her best friend, Joy, to make sure the arrangements worked into her schedule as well.

Fawn rubbed his fat body against her legs and let her know it was petting time. "Meow."

"Oh damn, I almost forgot about you, Fawn. We'll have to call Aunty Grace to come over and kitty sit. You love Aunty Grace. She's the person who sneaks you all those fattening treats when your mommy and I take our long weekends away."

"Meow."

"I know, you big baby, but this is something I have to do. Your mommy and I need some quality time together and if the mountain won't come to me, I'll go to the mountain."

Sophia pulled her phone from her back pocket and pressed the button on her favorites list to dial Joy's number. "Hey, bestie. Yes, I got the time off, no problem. Francine is the best. Now tell me you can leave tomorrow and you'll make my day. No, I haven't gotten the tickets yet, but I'm sure we have enough miles to get us the next flight out tomorrow—first class, of course. It pays to be married to a big shot financier. They practically drool all over me to make sure that the arrangements are to my satisfaction. I think she scares the shit out of them. Yeah, why don't you come here tonight and we can leave together tomorrow. I'll take care of all the arrangements. Don't forget that sexy black dress of yours. I'm sure there are single women in Seattle yet to be bedazzled by your beauty."

Sophia hurried to her walk in closet and pondered what she would bring to Seattle. She had no idea what the weather would be like in early May. Seattle was unpredictable, she'd heard. One day it could be in the seventies and the next day it might be cold and rainy. She hoped there would be a few nice days so that she could enjoy playing tourist.

She'd have to contact her wife's assistant or the receptionist. She couldn't remember which one her wife spoke so highly of. She knew this person could help her make arrangements for the surprise party she wanted to plan, but she couldn't quite remember her name. It was something unusual, that much she knew. She thought it started with a C. Oh well, she'd cross that bridge when she made her way to the downtown satellite office.

She pulled out her own sexy dress, a shimmering coral gown, and a variety of casual shirts to go with her jeans. As she selected the various outfits off the hangers and folded them neatly in the suitcase, she began to get more excited about her upcoming adventure.

The spontaneity bug was something that rarely bit her—it was completely out of character for her to make last minute arrangements to fly across the country. She was normally sensible and considerate of the wants and wishes of everyone around her. Rarely did she venture out and do something impulsively designed to meet her needs and ignore anyone else's. She needed to be with her wife. That was evident to her.

After packing her suitcase, Sophia retrieved her phone and dialed the number for her wife's travel agent. "Hey Claire, it's Sophia. No, I need travel arrangements for me. Yeah, don't act so shocked. Oh, and I'll need you to find a seat for my best friend, Joy. Yeah, she's tagging along to keep me company while the big shot wife is doing her thing in Seattle. Yeah, I'd like to fly out as soon as possible. Any time tomorrow will work for us. Oh, that is perfect, Claire, an early flight will work just fine for us even if I have to drag Joy out of bed at five in the morning. Cassidy. Yes, she has a passport. No, it's my treat. No, don't tell her, I want this to be a surprise. Yeah, oh, and can you arrange for a limo to take us to her office? Perfect. Thanks Claire, you're a doll."

Sophia ticked off the list of tasks to accomplish before the limo came to the condo to pick her and Joy up and take them to the airport in the morning. Although it would be a long flight and an even longer day, she would be in Seattle by early afternoon with the time difference. She couldn't help her ear to ear grin at the thought that she would be able to have an early dinner with her wife—as long as she was able to drag her wife away from her office.

In the beginning, Sophia was often able to entice her wife away from work. Sophia thought back to the first night she met the love of her life. It was certainly lust at first sight. Before meeting her, she didn't believe in love at first sight, but there was something about her that attracted her from the very first moment she captured her eyes. It changed her somewhat cynical view of love. Love and lust didn't seem to be too different from one another—they were at least in the same family.

Sophia felt confident that she would be able to ignite the fires again and regain the passion of their first year together. This would be her new mission for the next three weeks. She didn't see herself in the role of one half of an old, boring, married couple. That was unacceptable. She'd have her wife begging for her before the end of her three week vacation, just like old times. Complacency had crept into their relationship and that would stop the minute she stepped into her wife's fancy office. She might decide to take her on top of her lavish desk. Although she'd never been to her wife's Seattle office, there was no doubt in her mind that the office was extravagant.

Sophia was in high spirits when she opened the door to her best friend. They celebrated by sharing a bottle of wine and giggling like schoolgirls about their upcoming trip. They made plans to hit all the tourist attractions. Sophia explained that she planned to reserve the nights for hot steamy sex with her wife. She hoped Joy didn't mind being on her own in the evenings.

Chapter Ten

Rachel yawned and stretched her naked body as she glanced at the alarm clock on the nightstand next to her side of the bed. Espresso pounced on her stomach as soon as she moved.

"Thank you for letting me sleep in, Espresso. What a good boy you are today, letting mommy recover from her sexercise last night," Rachel cooed.

She stroked Espresso's sleek black fur as he turned his head to lick her hand.

"I guess I better get up and head to the hospital." Rachel popped up from the bed and smiled as she noticed the strap on that Lara had tossed on the dresser after using it so expertly. She was pleasantly sore in all the right places. She brought her fingers to her nose and inhaled. "Mmm, ode de Lara. What a delicious smell your mother leaves on me. I wonder if I can take a shower without removing this smell?" She looked at Espresso, who was kneading the covers. "Yeah, I guess not, that probably wouldn't work, would it, Espresso?"

Rachel picked up the sex toy and brought it with her to the master bathroom. Espresso jumped on the vanity and began purring. She turned on the sink faucets, testing the water until she achieved the perfect temperature to wash the dildo. After pumping the soap dispenser, she rubbed the soapy mixture on the toy and rinsed it off with the warm water. "That should do it. I'd better put this away before I give Mrs. Hanford a heart attack. I guess that's the price we pay for having a housekeeper. I always have to de-sex the place before she comes in to clean."

Espresso blinked at her before rubbing his body against her arm.

"You couldn't care less about my need to put away our toys, huh? As long as I make sure you receive your daily adoration, you're good." Rachel put Espresso's paws around her shoulders and allowed him to hug and lick her face while she massaged his shoulders and stroked his silky fur. "Okay, little bad boy, it's time for mommy to kick in gear and get ready."

Rachel patted the dildo dry and walked to her closet to store the item in a special box hidden in the back of the large walk in dressing area. She grabbed a pair of pin striped navy pants and a light blue shirt and tossed them on the bed. After rummaging through her dresser, she found a navy thong, matching bra, and silk knee high dress socks. She tossed the items on top of her pants and shirt.

"Now for a quick shower and hi ho, hi ho, it's off to work I go," she muttered.

Before Rachel finished getting dressed, she snapped a selfie while she was still completely naked planning to send the photo to Lara after lunch with a text message attached.

Just a little preview as an incentive to come home as soon as you can :)

Her marriage was getting better and better. It seemed like in the past six months, Lara spent more time in Seattle than her home office in New York. Rachel didn't know why there was a shift, but she felt grateful for the additional time with her wife. Maybe she would go to the adult store and see what new items there were to try out. Rachel giggled in anticipation of round two of their marathon lovemaking. She would make every moment of this four week stint memorable.

†

Lara approached the maître d', who was standing in the foyer of the Canlis. "Hello, George, I have a reservation for two at twelve thirty. I assume you have my table ready. The other person in my party should be arriving shortly. Can you please escort her back upon her arrival?"

"Of course, Ms. Beck. Please follow me. We have your table ready. Shall I send someone to help you select a bottle of wine today?"

"That would be lovely, George." Lara followed George to a secluded table in the back of the restaurant and he set a menu in front of her and on the place setting opposite Lara.

"I recommend the fresh caught Copper River Salmon special. It literally melts in your mouth," George suggested.

"Thank you, George, I think I'll take your advice on that. It sounds wonderful. Copper River Salmon is such a treat and only available a short time each year, so it would be a crime not to take advantage of the offering."

George bowed and walked back in the direction of the foyer.

Lara was planning her seduction of Chelsea when the attractive older woman approached the table as the server pulled out the chair for her. Chelsea wasn't much older than Lara, especially now that Lara was turning forty in a few short weeks. Lara wanted to look as good as Chelsea did at forty-five.

Lara looked up, smiled, and stood to greet her prospective client. Boldly taking Chelsea's hands in her own, she kissed her cheek in greeting. "Chelsea, I am delighted you could join me for lunch on such short notice. I've been looking forward to this since you made the suggestion."

"As have I. It was so fortuitous meeting you on the plane. I was planning to contact you before we met the other day. One of your staff members approached me a few weeks back and I've wanted to connect with you on that. I'm afraid I may have led the poor boy to believe he had my business, but I really wanted to discuss my options with you personally. I insist on your personal touch to seal the deal."

Lara smiled and leaned back in her chair. "Ah, you must mean Jason. I'm afraid Jason is no longer with Fortified Financials. I hope that will not affect our ability to serve your interests."

Chelsea waved her hand in the air. "Not at all." She leaned in. "I don't usually speak ill of those not present, but he seemed to be a bit of a tool."

Lara laughed. "That's one way of putting it." Lara saw her opportunity as Chelsea's arm rested on top of the table. Touching Chelsea's hand, she leaned in and whispered, "I would be delighted to provide you with individualized personal service to ensure every one of your needs are met. I guarantee you won't be disappointed with the outcome. I believe my reputation speaks for itself."

"Indeed, it does, Lara, indeed it does. Of course, I appreciate the personal attention and choose my business entanglements carefully. If you have the contracts with you today, I would be happy to sign them. I trust you have all afternoon to explain the finer details of those contracts once I've signed them. I do like to thoroughly understand every business deal I've committed to," Chelsea said.

"Of course, Chelsea, I want you to be completely satisfied with your decision. I've arranged for a hotel room that will allow us complete privacy without disruption from the hustle and bustle that tends to occur when I conduct business at the office. Hotel 1000 is only three miles away. It's very discreet and has an excellent reputation. Did you drive here today?" Lara asked.

"No, I had my driver drop me off," Chelsea answered.

"Perfect, we can drive together and I'll drop you off anywhere you need me to after I've gone over the finer details of the contract with you."

"I look forward to the thorough explanation. Now let's order a nice meal so that we can have plenty of energy to conduct our business later on. I'm famished. How about you?" Chelsea asked.

"Ravenous, but I'm sure that will be remedied shortly. George recommends the Copper River Salmon special and I've never been disappointed with any of his recommendations," Lara advised.

"Well, then, I believe I'll order the fish."

"Would you like me to select a wine to pair with the meal?" Lara asked.

"Yes, please. I like a woman who takes control."

"Very well then. How about the Resonance Pinot Noir from Oregon? It is a delicious single vineyard wine that pairs well with salmon. Perhaps we can order dessert when we get to the hotel—something that will pair well with our business collaboration," Lara offered.

"That's a lovely idea. I'm a bit partial to champagne and strawberries dipped in chocolate." Chelsea leaned back in her seat and Lara thought she saw a very satisfied smile grace her classic good looks.

"I like how we are on the same page with everything." Lara lifted her gaze and with a slight motion of her head, the waiter appeared at the table.

Chapter Eleven

Sophia fidgeted in her first class seat while absently scrolling through Facebook posts.

Joy lifted her head and stared at her best friend. "Geez, I can feel you squirming in your seat while I'm trying to sleep. I thought we were both going to catch up on sleep while flying in luxury. You haven't even closed your eyes yet. Aren't you exhausted, hung over, whatever, after our slumber party last evening?"

Sophia smiled at her best friend. "I'm sorry, Joy. I'm just too excited to sleep. I feel like it's Christmas Eve and Santa is about to bring me my Christmas wish."

"Well, I'll tell you my Christmas wish is to get some shut eye before I descend on the lovely ladies who reside in the Emerald City. I need my beauty sleep, unlike some of us that are naturally beautiful twenty four seven, no matter what amount of alcohol they consume," Joy grumbled.

Sophia smacked her arm. "Don't sell yourself short. The women will flock to you the minute your high heels hit the tarmac."

"Ouch. Yeah, I do all right, don't I?" Joy answered.

"Yes, you do and you know it. The humility gene certainly by-passed your zygote."

"Ooh, I love it when you talk all trashy and sciency with me."

"What the hell are you talking about? There is nothing trashy about zygote," Sophia declared.

"I know it's a geek term, but coming from your beautiful mouth, it sounds sexy."

"You're incorrigible. Now, go back to sleep and I'll try to keep my movements to a minimum," Sophia proposed.

"Thank you. You are a true friend and a goddess." Joy grabbed her pillow, fluffed it up, and settled her head against the window where she'd placed the cushion.

Sophia sighed as she looked at her watch, noting that they would not arrive in Seattle for at least another two hours. She began to fret that her wife would not appreciate her spontaneity, but quickly shoved those negative thoughts aside. She leaned back her chair, closed her eyes, and tried to meditate. She hoped the meditation might lead to sleep, considering that she was tired. Getting only a couple of hours of sleep was something she used to have no problem with when she was in her twenties, but now at thirty-five she needed at least six hours of sleep to properly function. She had big plans for her wife and could not afford to fall asleep on her in the middle of a steamy night of sex. Finally, with her eyes closed and her concentration on relaxation and taking deep breaths, Sophia nodded off, dreaming of the romantic reunion she'd conjured up in her head.

†

The modern building with reflective glass shimmered in a patch of rare Seattle sunshine. Joy and Sophia stepped out of the limousine and looked up at the contemporary architecture.

"Wow, that's some building. Your wifey sure picked a nice spot for her office," Joy announced.

Standing in front of the brass elevators that were encased in marble tile, Sophia began to get nervous. Would Lara be happy to see her? Or would she think that Sophia was crowding her? When the doors opened, Joy followed Sophia inside. Sophia pressed the button for the twelfth floor after noting the suite numbers for her wife's financial services company.

The doors opened to a bright airy space where a young woman sat at a desk. A headphone, complete with an unobtrusive mike, adorned her head. Her expressive hazel eyes tracked Joy and Sophia's progress.

"Good afternoon. Is Lara Beck available?" Sophia inquired.

"No, I'm sorry. Ms. Beck left earlier for a lunch meeting."

Sophia was surprised at how disappointed she felt to have missed her wife. Sympathetic hazel eyes met hers.

"I'm sorry. Did you have an appointment with Ms. Beck?" the young woman asked.

"No. I thought I would surprise her. I can just wait in her office for her to return. I don't imagine she will be much longer." Sophia glanced at her watch and noted the time. It was nearly three o'clock and surely her wife would be back shortly.

"I'm afraid that won't be possible. Ms. Beck—," the young woman started to say.

"You little twit, don't you know who this is?" Joy growled.

Sophia placed her hand on Joy's arm as the young woman turned confused eyes in Joy's direction. "It's okay, Joy. Let's go play tourist and then we can wait at her penthouse."

"Would you like me to give Ms. Beck a message?"

"No, that won't be necessary, uh, I'm sorry I don't know your name. I know it's an unusual name, but I've forgotten it," Sophia admitted.

"Chandra Hernandez. I'm sorry I don't know who you are, but you must be a good friend of Ms. Beck's."

"Oh, for fuck's sake, don't you recognize Sophia. Her picture must be plastered on Lara's fancy desk," Joy barked out.

"Stop bullying Lara's receptionist." Sophia smacked Joy's arm again. "Don't leave her a message. I want this to be a surprise." Sophia winked at Chandra.

"Okay. If you are planning to go to the penthouse, you may want to wait a bit. What I was going to tell you earlier is that Ms. Beck was planning to continue her business meeting at the penthouse. She left explicit instructions that she was not to be disturbed," Chandra responded, with hesitation.

"Hmm. She must have a really hot prospect on the line." Sophia turned to Joy. "Well, you wanted to see all the sights. Let's do the town and we can surprise her later this evening. I should tell the limo driver to drop our bags off at Hotel 1000. They can hold them in the lobby until we return from gallivanting around the city. I'll call him later to come pick us up after we've had a chance to see the city."

Joy smacked her hands together. "Oh, goody. Let the party begin. Chandra, can you lead Sophia and me to the nearest lesbian hot spot? Or, would you rather escort us personally? I've forgiven you for not knowing who Sophia is and you are rather cute."

Chandra turned bright red. "Umm...."

Sophia tugged on Joy's arm and pulled her far enough away from Chandra so she wouldn't overhear the conversation. "Come on, Joy, leave the poor girl alone. Her day is not through. She can't just abandon her job to play tourist guide."

"Well, why the hell not? Doesn't the fact that you're sleeping with the boss give us certain privileges to seek assistance from her employees."

Joy took a few steps back toward Chandra's desk. "I really need to find those hot lesbians you promised me and I think I've found the first one. Right, you darling creature. You know, as an older woman, I could teach you a thing or two." Joy winked at Chandra.

Sophia pushed Joy toward the elevators, turned her head to face Chandra, and called out, "Sorry. She's really not this bad most of the time. We've been cooped up in a plane for more than six hours."

She needed to connect later with Chandra so she could enlist her assistance with Lara's surprise party to celebrate her fortieth birthday. Perhaps she could get Joy to work with her—that ought to please her best friend.

†

Sophia exited the massive office building and headed to the limousine that was double-parked in front. The driver jumped out ready to open the doors for the two women. She waved her hand to indicate they weren't getting back inside.

"My friend and I plan on walking around a bit. Would you mind dropping off our bags at Hotel 1000 where my wife's penthouse is located? I'll call when we're done, but I suspect it won't be until after five and probably closer to six," Sophia directed.

"It would be my pleasure," the driver answered. He pulled a card from his pocket and handed it to Sophia. "Just call this number and tell me where you've landed and I'll come get you and bring you to the hotel."

Sophia pulled out a hundred dollar bill and handed it to the driver.

"Thank you, ma'am."

"How come Lara doesn't own a house or a condo here in Seattle?" Joy asked.

Sophia shrugged. "I'm not sure. At first, when she opened the Seattle office, she would only be away for a few days at a time and I guess she thought the hotel would be easier. Maybe she's considering buying real estate here now that she spends more of her time in Seattle than in New York. She hasn't really talked much about her plans."

"So, how are we going to get into her penthouse suite without a key?"

Sophia pulled a key card from her pocket. "She forgot the extra card in her jacket that she asked me to take to the cleaners."

"Why, you little minx. You stole her card," Joy exclaimed.

"It's hardly stealing when I'm married to the victim—community property and all that." Sophia laughed.

"I guess it makes it easy for you to surprise her."

"Yep. That's the plan. No offense, but when we get to the hotel, I'm getting you a separate room. I have big plans for my wife tonight."

"No offense taken, but it would have been fun to watch," Joy teased.

"Funny. Your jokes get more ribald as you age."

"Who's joking?" Joy grinned.

"God, we really need to locate that bar so you can find your evening entertainment."

"Now you're talking," Joy said.

Chapter Twelve

Chelsea Martin rolled out of the luxurious king bed and began putting her clothes back on. "Lara, I can honestly say it's been a pleasure doing business with you, but unfortunately I've got to run. I hope you don't mind."

"No, not at all. I understand what a busy woman you are," Lara responded.

"As lovely as this afternoon was, and I must say it was one of the better business meetings I've had, I believe you've clearly explained all the finer points of the contract in enough detail that I won't require any additional clarification. Perhaps we can do lunch on occasion, but it certainly won't be necessary to spend any more time on the deal. I hope you understand." Chelsea narrowed her eyes waiting for a reaction from Lara.

"I understand perfectly. Fortified Financials appreciates the trust you have in our corporation. I guarantee that I will hold everything in the strictest confidence. You don't need to be concerned about anything. Your privacy and personal information is of paramount importance to us."

Lara remained in the bed with the sheet covering her from the waist down, but leaving her creamy white breasts exposed. With her hair tousled and half-naked body exposed, she was a tempting sight.

Chelsea shook her head. "You are absolutely lovely, my dear, but rules are rules. It's time for me to take my leave before I return to bed and make a decision I am sure to regret later." She leaned down and gently kissed Lara on the lips. "Goodbye, my dear."

Lara stretched her arms above her head. "The limo is waiting outside the hotel, ready to take you wherever you need to go. I trust you can find your way out?"

"Yes. Thank you." Chelsea ambled to the door and quietly exited the penthouse.

Lara tossed the sheet to the side and walked to the dresser to retrieve her cell phone. She'd heard a buzz earlier in the day, but it had come at a most inopportune time, so she had forced herself to ignore the message. When she swiped the screen and retrieved the message with the naked picture, she laughed out loud. "Ah, Rachel, you will be the death of me yet."

Lara searched for any other messages and finding no other texts, she frowned. It was unusual for her not to hear from Sophia. She decided she needed to call her wife and see if anything was wrong. After dialing the number and the call going straight to voicemail, Lara became irritated. It would be eight o'clock in New York. Sophia rarely went out and she never let a day go by without calling to chat for a few minutes, especially on the first day after Lara returned to Seattle.

Lara began pacing her penthouse. A storm was brewing—Lara could feel it in her bones. Instinct was what made Lara such a successful businesswoman and she sensed something big was about to occur in her well-organized life. The prospect of change was not welcoming.

Lara went toward the bathroom. She wanted to be home by eight and would have just enough time to shower and remove all evidence of her very personal business meeting. Lara smiled to herself. Chelsea had certainly been a surprise in bed. The woman was insatiable. If Chelsea had not made it perfectly clear that this would be a one-time opportunity, Lara might have considered taking Chelsea as a lover. What the hell was she thinking? She already had one too many women in her life.

Lara entered the bathroom and walked into her shower. She would try to call her wife again before leaving for home. She let the water run over her sore muscles. Pleasing Chelsea had been a workout. Lara groaned and she thought about needing to satisfy Rachel tonight. Burning the candle at both ends was starting to take its toll on her body. By the look of Rachel's text message, she was sure there would be an expectation that, she had to admit, would be hard to resist.

†

When Joy and Sophia reached the front door of Hotel 1000, a doorman graciously opened the door for them. "Welcome to Hotel 1000, ladies. We hope you have an enjoyable stay. All of us are here to serve you."

Joy smirked. "Too bad you're the wrong sex."

"Behave," Sophia chastised.

Sophia walked up to the check in desk with Joy close on her heels. "Hello, I'd like to see about getting a room for my friend here. If you have something available that is close to the penthouse, that would be perfect. I believe the limo driver dropped off our bags. My bags need to go to the penthouse and my friend's need to go to whatever room can be arranged."

"I'm sorry ma'am, but the penthouse is permanently rented and not available, but we have another room that I think should meet your expectations."

"Yes, I know the penthouse is rented—to my wife. I'm surprising her today," Sophia clarified.

The desk attendant raised her eyebrow, "You are Ms. Beck's wife?"

Sophia pulled out her key card and laid it on the desk. "Yes, I am. Is there a problem here?"

Sophia was beginning to get irritated. It seemed as though Lara's life in Seattle was completely separate from New York. Hadn't Lara talked to anyone here in her west coast satellite about her wife? Sophia knew that Lara wasn't closeted, so why the big secret? Sophia talked freely about her wife to everyone in her sphere of acquaintances.

"No, not at all. I apologize. Ms. Beck is a valued customer of Hotel 1000." The desk attendant clicked the keys on the computer. "We have a lovely suite two doors down from the penthouse. Shall I charge the other room to Ms. Beck's account?"

"Yes, thank you," Sophia answered.

"How long will you be staying in Seattle?"

"We'll be here three weeks." Sophia touched Joy on the arm. "Let me follow you to your room and get you settled before I pounce on my wife. I'm kind of nervous. This is really out of character for me to be so impulsive. What if she's too pre-occupied with business to appreciate the gesture?"

"Not a chance in the world." Joy stepped back and her eyes traveled up and down Sophia's body. "Even after a full day of traveling, you look delicious."

"On second thought, can I just have the carry-on bag? I'll take that one up with me and you can deliver the rest of the bags when we order room service. I'd prefer not being disturbed for what I hope will be a fervent re-union."

The attendant nodded and handed Joy a key card. "Is there anything else we can do to make your stay at Hotel 1000 more comfortable?"

"No, thank you. I apologize if I was rude earlier, it's just that Seattle hasn't been as welcoming as I thought it would be," Sophia confessed. "Now if I was visiting New York, well, then that would be expected." She chuckled.

"Oh ma'am, I'm very sorry. It's just that normally Ms. Beck makes all of her arrangements in advance. Let me retrieve your carry-on bag. Would you like assistance from the porter?"

"No, I think I can handle one small bag on my own, but the porter can carry my friend's bags," Sophia answered.

†

Lara had just secured the last button on her shirt and was heading to the door with her jacket in her hand, when she heard the beep at the door. She cocked her head, confused that the maid service would be entering her room at this time of the day. She'd never had to put the Do Not Disturb sign on her door previously. The hotel staff were well aware of the arrangements she made when entertaining business clients.

When the door opened and she stood face to face with Sophia, Lara was not able to school her expression. Shock, fear, and a tiny bit of irritation showed on her beautiful face. "Sophia, what in the hell are you doing here in Seattle?"

Sophia stumbled back and her eyes teared up.

Lara immediately recognized her mistake, took Sophia's bag and set it down, and then pulled Sophia into her arms. "Sshh. Oh, babe, I am so sorry, you just startled me. Is something wrong? Of course I'm delighted to see you."

"Are you?" Sophia asked.

"Am I what?"

"Delighted to see me? I wanted to surprise you, but I suppose this wasn't the best decision I've ever made." Sophia's tears slipped from her eyes.

"I know I've been distracted these past couple of years with the start-up of the Seattle office and I promise, once the office is running smoothly, we'll get away just the two of us for a long overdue vacation. Of course, I am very happy to have you visit, but I just lost my CFO and things are particularly crazy in the office. There are nights that I don't even get home. I just stay at the office because it's easier. I was just on my way back to the office tonight," Lara explained.

The tears continued to fall and Lara gently wiped them away. Lara looked into Sophia's sad brown eyes and she knew that she would have to think fast to salvage this untenable situation.

Sophia took a big breath. "Lara, I'm not asking for your undivided attention for the next three weeks, but can I have that for tonight at least? Joy and I will find ways to entertain ourselves here in Seattle for the next three weeks and hopefully, you'll be able to make some time for me. I do have one more request. I'd like to have a special day with you on your birthday."

Shit, shit, shit. How can I possibly be in two places at once? Rachel thinks I don't know about her surprise party, but not much happens in this town that I don't know about. I'll have to think of something later.

Lara looked away while the internal monologue ran through her brain. She turned back to find Sophia's expectant eyes scrutinizing her.

Lara grabbed Sophia's hands and led her to the couch. She stroked her face and tenderly kissed her lips. "Oh, my sweet darling, I promise we'll reconnect tonight. I just have to make a few calls and then we can order some dinner and I'll show you how much I love you, all night long."

Sophia smiled for the first time since she'd entered the room. "Go ahead and make those calls and I'll order us dinner. I'm sure you have the menu memorized, so what would you like?"

Lara waved her hand in the air. "You choose. I like almost everything on their menu, except of course beef or pork. You know I don't eat red meat."

Sophia arched her eyebrow. "Wow, you're letting me order for you. This night might prove interesting. Perhaps I'll be able to turn the tables and exercise a bit of control later. That might spice things up a bit."

Lara laughed. "Now, don't get too carried away. Ordering dinner is one thing—taking control in the bedroom is something else entirely."

As Lara walked into the bedroom, she heard Sophia pick up the phone—presumably murmuring their dinner order. She quickly retrieved her phone to make a quick call to Rachel.

"Hello, sexy. I'm afraid I have some bad news. Since I met with Chelsea Martin today, I need to do a ton of work to secure her business. It will probably take the better part of the evening, so I'll just stay in town tonight. I know. I'm disappointed too, especially after receiving your naughty text. Oh yes, I'll be thinking of you too. I'll call you tomorrow when I get a breather. Sweet dreams to you, too."

Lara placed the phone on the nightstand and pinched the bridge of her nose. Life just got uncharacteristically complicated for her. She needed a clear head to help her juggle the two main women in her life—both of them in the same city. This was never supposed to happen. She had a brief thought that perhaps she should just come clean and see where the cards fell, but she shook her head, discarding that moment of insanity. She was Lara Beck and this was just another problem that she needed to solve. She would think of something.

After her day and a half of practically nonstop, rowdy sex, she was looking forward to making love to her sweet and gentle wife. Sophia was a skilled lover and after ten years, she knew just where to touch Lara to send her reeling. She missed her wife and needed to re-connect with her. Maybe this visit wouldn't be so bad after all. The balance between Rachel and Sophia might just be what the doctor ordered. She'd let her lust for the new shiny object—Rachel—take her away from her first love.

Lara walked back into the sitting area and marveled at Sophia's beauty. Sophia stood in front of the large window overlooking the city as the sunset created an exquisite backdrop. Sophia's chestnut hair fell in waves across her shoulders. Her tailored clothes fit snuggly against her curves. Although Sophia visited the gym regularly, her body retained the softness of a woman, while keeping her trim and fit.

Lara noted that Sophia didn't look a day more than twenty-six and would most likely retain her youthful appearance well into middle age. Her grandmother still had a fair amount of dark hair mixed with gray at the age of eighty-four. Before Sophia's mother died, her hairdresser had marveled at the fact that she could never find one gray hair.

Lara stepped behind Sophia and caressed her shoulders. She moved her thick, wavy hair to the side to give her unencumbered access to Sophia's neck. Kissing her neck, Lara turned her around and sought out Sophia's generous, inviting lips. The kiss grew more intense as Lara explored every inch of her mouth, pushing her tongue inside and stroking her in an ancient dance of passion. Sophia opened to her like a flower in the springtime soaking up the energy of the sun.

When Lara broke apart and looked at her wife, Sophia took the opportunity to warn her. "Don't start anything just yet. I expect a knock on the door within the next ten minutes. What do you do to those poor hotel workers? I swear the guy on the other end was falling all over himself to apologize because it would take ten minutes. I could almost hear him wetting his pants on the other end of the phone. Please tell me you don't terrorize the staff," Sophia joked.

Lara laughed. "I do not terrorize the staff. I just like things done a certain way and you know that patience was never a strong quality of mine. Speaking of patience, you're really going to make me wait to ravage your body?"

"Yes, I am. It will be so much sweeter if I let the anticipation build."

Lara groaned. "It's been so long, I don't know if I can wait. I've been terribly neglectful lately and I intend to rectify that tonight. I'm sorry that I've let business distract me from what's truly important in my life. I promise that when I am with you from now on, you will have my undivided attention—especially since I probably won't be able to spend every night with you while you're here visiting. I'll make sure that when we are together, you won't be left hanging."

"Oh, darling, that is music to my ears. Shall we sit and you can tell me who your hot prospect was this afternoon?" Sophia headed to the sofa to sit and took Lara's hand when she joined her on the couch.

"Hot prospect?"

"Yes. Your assistant or receptionist, Chandra, mentioned that you had a business meeting all afternoon. I assumed that it must be a hot prospect if you needed to spend all afternoon with your client," Sophia replied.

Lara calmed her breathing and forced herself to ask the question that she hoped would not reveal a certain answer. "Did you call or meet Chandra in person?"

Sophia quirked her head. "We went directly to your office after we landed. Chandra is very protective of your schedule. She would only tell me that you were not available. It was an odd exchange. Joy was her normal abrasive self and raked the poor girl over the coals. She has some archaic notion that I should be given special privilege to information since I'm your wife. I shut her down before she could do any permanent damage. I'm sorry. I don't think it would be a good idea to visit your office anymore. I don't want to scare your employees away."

Rachel often showed up around lunchtime on the off chance that Lara was available. Sometimes they were even able to eat lunch. Lara smiled as she thought about some of her more adventuresome lunches with Rachel. The ice in her veins allowed the practiced response to Sophia "Yes, it would probably be a good idea to avoid the office, especially when you have your attack dog with you."

A light knock on the door interrupted their conversation and for that, Lara was thankful. She jumped up to answer the door.

A young man in a crisp uniform carried the tray into the room. "Where would you like me to put this, Ms. Beck?"

Lara pointed to the table in the small kitchen area. "You can set it there."

Sophia frowned. "Oh, damn, I guess I forgot to ask you to bring up my bags." She waved her hand. "No worries, you can bring them up tomorrow morning. I'll call when I'm ready."

"I'm sorry, ma'am, just let us know when you want those bags."

When he handed Lara the bill, she glanced at the amount, scribbled her signature, and added a generous tip. She lifted the silver lids and managed to react positively to the choice. "Copper River Salmon, a wonderful selection."

Lara was not about to reveal that she'd just had the same meal at lunch. It wouldn't kill her to enjoy the salmon for dinner and Sophia would be able to enjoy a Pacific Northwest treat.

"When I called down, this was highly recommended. I guess the Copper River Salmon only run for a short time in the spring. They assured me it was a Northwest specialty that I shouldn't miss."

Lara smiled. "They're right."

Lara re-focused her energies on her wife and opened the wine that Sophia had ordered to complement the meal. She poured two glasses and raised one in the air. When Sophia touched her glass, Lara offered a toast. "To my beautiful wife and delightful surprises."

Chapter Thirteen

Rachel slumped in the overstuffed chair. Disappointment was an understatement. With one phone call, Lara had blown her plans to smithereens.

Espresso jumped in her lap and rolled on his back, showing his stomach. Rachel rubbed his tummy and he started purring loudly.

"I guess it's just you and me tonight, my little furry buddy. I suppose I could start working on her surprise party, or…."

Rachel picked up Espresso and set him on the floor. She removed her shirt and unzipped her jeans. She kept her lace bra on. "I think mommy needs a little inspiration tonight."

Rachel shoved her hand into her jeans, picked up her phone from the side table, held her phone in front of her, posed seductively for a picture, and pressed the button. "That should do it. I'll bet I get a call tonight. I suppose phone sex is better than no sex."

She typed the short message and hit send.

Rachel walked into the master bedroom with her jeans still undone, and set the phone on the nightstand. After stepping out of her jeans, she tossed them on the chair across from the bed. She unfastened her bra and added it to the pile of clothes on the chair. The only item of clothing that remained was her blue thong.

Espresso followed her into the bedroom and jumped up on the bed.

"What do you think, Espresso, do you think stating, I wish her hand was here to take over, was too direct? Maybe I should have devised a more subtle message. I guess we'll have to wait patiently for her response. In the meantime, I think that book I started is calling to me."

Rachel read the same paragraph three times. Lara hadn't responded to her text and that was unusual. She never stayed overnight at the office, at least not when she was at her Seattle office. Granted, she had no idea what her work patterns were when she was in New York, but when she was in Seattle, she always came home eventually.

Rachel started to worry that something was drastically different. She decided that if Chelsea Martin was this demanding and it affected Rachel's limited time with her wife, perhaps she wasn't worth securing as a client.

Unfortunately, Rachel couldn't talk about this with her wife tonight because she was still at the office. She decided it would be a good time to make a surprise visit tomorrow in the hopes that she would catch her wife during lunch. Sometimes Rachel wasn't able to connect with Lara and she ended up taking the food back to the hospital where it always found a home with her hungry colleagues.

Rachel settled into the bed, now that she had a plan, and quickly acquiesced to the sudden drowsiness that hit her body. Since they hadn't gotten a lot of sleep the night before, she fell asleep with the reader resting on top of her body.

Espresso wormed his way under the covers and nestled against her bare midriff.

Rachel dreamed about Lara and all the delectable things she would do to her body when her wife finally came home.

†

Sophia moaned in appreciation as she took a final bite of her meal. "Mmm, the final perfect bite. If I'd known how wonderful Pacific salmon tasted, I would have traveled out here a lot earlier."

When Sophia first arrived, she had panicked when Lara's reaction was not what she had hoped for, but after the initial shock that her surprise arrival had caused, the look of love and desire returned. It was like when they'd first met. Sophia was looking forward to the rest of the evening.

Lara pushed the tray away, stood up, and pulled Sophia into her arms. Her movements were slow and precise as she led Sophia to the bedroom and undid each button on her blouse. Sophia's shirt hung loosely on her body until Lara carefully slipped it off her shoulders.

Sophia began to unzip her slacks, until Lara covered her hand. "Let me do the honors."

Sophia could feel Lara's hand brush lightly against her silk panties. It sent a rush of arousal through her body as goosebumps magically appeared on her arms.

Sophia stepped out of her pants and stood before Lara in her bra and underwear. As Lara moved each bra strap down Sophia's arms, her corresponding touch hit a few of Sophia's erogenous zones. The need to feel Lara move above her was overwhelming.

She thought it was odd that the bed covers seemed askew because Lara was such a stickler about making the bed every morning. Maybe housekeeping wasn't able to get to the room before her business meeting. She wrinkled her nose and thought she smelled an unfamiliar perfume in the room. Maybe the client she was entertaining at the penthouse bathed in the stuff and it somehow permeated into the bedroom.

Sophia smiled to herself as she noted another smell. The room smelled of sex. She wondered if Lara was also pleasuring herself. Maybe they were doing the exact same things thousands of miles away. She would have to remember that and perhaps coordinate their schedules so they might be able to video call one another to make it more exciting.

"I need to feel your naked body move on top of me," Sophia pleaded.

"Not yet. Who is in control here?" Lara asked.

"You are."

"Get in the bed, but leave your panties on," Lara directed.

Sophia pulled the covers down and positioned herself for her wife. She licked her lips as she saw the feral look on Lara's face. The lust in her eyes was evident. She missed that look and now that it was back, she was going to take full advantage.

"Aren't you afraid of ruining your outfit? I can smell your arousal and soon I'll be able to see the wet spot. You'd better take off your clothes before that happens," Sophia suggested.

"Cheeky little minx, aren't you? I thought I'd made it clear that I was in charge. If you aren't good, I'll make you wait longer," Lara threatened.

"I take it all back. I want to see the wet spot."

Lara laughed. "You are pushing it. Wait there and don't move. I need a few items."

Lara moved to the dresser and pulled out the leather and lambskin restraints and eye mask.

Sophia squirmed on the bed, waiting for Lara to secure her hands above her head. It was freeing to know that she could lay back and allow Lara to take control. There would be nothing to distract her. Although Sophia enjoyed the times when Lara and she would reach simultaneous orgasm as they stroked or licked one another at the same time, there was nothing like being the recipient of Lara's complete focus. She didn't have to worry about whether Lara was getting close.

Lara carefully secured the leather mask and restraints. Sophia felt vulnerable, yet excited. She ached to feel Lara's hands and mouth on her body. She didn't know what Lara was doing because the mask covered her eyes, but she heard the refrigerator door open.

After what seemed like an eternity, she felt a cool drop of something hit her nipple, then another hit her bellybutton.

"Mmm, dessert is served. I just needed to add some whipped cream," Lara murmured.

Sophia squirmed as she waited for Lara's inevitable tongue. She felt the tip lick her right nipple and circle it. A light bite sent her nearly over the edge. Her left breast ached for the same treatment and before long, Lara rewarded her with the same love bite.

Sophia's clit was throbbing in anticipation. She felt Lara's hands stroke her stomach and brush lightly across her panties. She could feel Lara make her way down to her sex with a momentary side trip to her bellybutton as Lara sucked the sticky cream that pooled in the small indent.

Finally, Lara brought her hands to Sophia's hips and Sophia could feel her move the silk underwear down her legs.

After Lara removed her panties, Sophia felt Lara sucking her toes and pressing down on her arches.

As Lara's hand made its way back up her calf and inner thigh, Sophia cried out. "Please, touch me where I need you."

"Where would that be, love? You have to be more specific."

"Oh, God, Lara. Stop teasing me," Sophia begged.

"You have to tell me and I'll walk out the door if you use overly clinical terms, my prim and proper professor. I'll give you a hint. It starts with a P."

Sophia could hear the smirk in Lara's words.

"My pussy, please, touch my pussy," Sophia cried out.

"Well, now that you've asked so nicely, I suppose I can do that," Lara responded.

It didn't take long for Sophia to buck in an effort to meet Lara's mouth. She needed to feel Lara's tongue on her clit. She wanted to feel Lara suck the engorged area and let her teeth graze across the hood. Sophia got her wish, but not until after an additional ten minutes of teasing.

When Sophia's orgasm hit, she was more than ready to feel the pulsations ripple up and down her body. She hoped that Lara would allow her to return the favor and she got her wish.

†

Lara was thankful that Sophia was in the throes of passion when she heard the buzz of her cellphone. It was enough to distract her, but fortunately, Lara had an uncanny ability to block out everything and narrowly focus her attentions on the task at hand. Not that she considered making love to her wife a task, but she was an expert in the art of making love.

A plan for how to deal with this new wrinkle began forming in her mind. There was no way she could allow Sophia to hang around Seattle. Even though Sophia indicated that she would not visit the office again, Joy might talk her into it. She assumed that Joy might try to hit on her receptionist, Chandra. The temptation was too great for Joy. She knew Joy would egg her on. She would probably say something like "Lara has to eat, so you might as well visit her at lunch". There was no way she would be able to keep her from visiting for the next three weeks and she wouldn't risk a chance meeting of her two wives.

Lara just needed a couple of days to set things up. She would tell Sophia that she needed to work hard and probably stay at the office for the next couple of days to get everything done and then she would take Sophia away for a second honeymoon. She would make reservations at Rosario Resort on Orcas Island and then whisk her away for another week in Victoria, the charming city on Vancouver Island in British Columbia. She'd spend the next few days with Rachel and explain that an emergency came up and she had to return to New York for a few weeks.

As Sophia slept soundly beside her, Lara slipped from her bed to respond to the message on her phone that she knew Rachel sent.

Lara creeped out to the living room and glanced at the message on her phone. She groaned as the picture of Rachel lounging in her chair with her hand in her pants popped up.

It was such an appealing picture she almost saved it, but thought better of it. It would be careless to keep it on the off chance that Sophia picked up her phone and read any of the messages. Sophia wasn't one to nose around on her phone or her private affairs, but Lara wasn't willing to take the risk. She'd managed to keep her two lives separate thus far mainly because she was excruciatingly careful not to let the two worlds collide.

She would call Rachel first thing in the morning and ask her to come to the office so they could have lunch together. That should appease Rachel. She imagined that she might suffer a few consequences for not returning the text message right away. In her experience, Rachel was not someone you toyed with. She demanded her fair share of attention and this recent turn of events would not sit well with her. In many ways, Sophia was a lot easier to manage, because she accepted things more readily and was far less demanding.

Chapter Fourteen

Sophia blinked her eyes when she felt the warmth of the sun sweep across her face. The empty space beside her was cold. She must have been tired after their night of making love because she hadn't woken once, even when Lara got up to shower and get ready. She wondered what time it was and if Lara was still in the penthouse. It seemed quiet— too quiet.

Sophia stretched in bed, yawned, and pushed the covers aside. Evidence of their night of passion was evident with the various articles of clothing and leather restraints littered across the bedroom floor. None of the clothing was Lara's. She'd apparently gathered her clothes and sent them out to the dry cleaners. No doubt the wet spot would have required special attention.

Sophia strolled into the brightly lit kitchen and found a note attached to the fancy espresso/coffee machine.

Good Morning Lover,

I had to get an early start, but I'll call a little later. I have a surprise for you. Unfortunately, there may be a down side to the surprise during the next couple of days. I'll explain later. Next time you need to take instructions a little better and not tease with your cheeky suggestions.

All my love,

Lara

Sophia laughed at Lara's quip in the note. She walked to her bag and pulled out her cell phone. She noted the time was a little later than she thought and worried that Joy would tease her mercilessly. There was a text and a voicemail message from Joy and a voicemail from Lara. Although she was anxious to learn about the surprise in Lara's note, she decided to call Joy first to set up the day. She pushed the button to reply to the voicemail.

"Hey, trouble. Now, shush, it's not that late... Just give me a half an hour and then we can head downtown. Maybe. Okay, we can talk about it when I come to get you. Yes, I most certainly want to hear about your night, because I know after I dropped you off, you went to a lesbian bar. Can you call down to the desk and have them bring my bags up while I jump in the shower?"

Sophia took a quick shower and donned the fluffy white robe hanging on the hook next to the brass and glass shower equipped with two showerheads on each end and one hanging from the ceiling right smack in the middle. Just as she tied the robe, she heard the knock on the door.

A young man in a uniform brought her luggage into the room and Joy walked briskly behind him.

"I saw him coming up the hall and thought I'd follow him to your suite. I'll tell you about my night if you give me all the details on yours." Joy winked.

"Why don't you make yourself useful and give this nice young man a tip," Sophia said.

"Oh no, ma'am, Ms. Beck takes excellent care of the staff and has already taken care of me."

"Damn, I got to get me a sugar momma who has the smarts to anticipate my every need. I was coming here to tell you that he was already on his way up to bring your bags. When I called down, they let me know that. How do you think she knew when to have them deliver the bags?" Joy asked.

Sophia shrugged. "I guess after ten years of marriage, you know the other person's habits so well, including when they normally get up after…"

Joy raised her eyebrow. "After? Oh, I need to hear every single detail. Let's wait until Archie here leaves and then tell me everything."

The young man blushed and made a quick exit.

"I'm not telling you every detail, you smarmy voyeur," Sophia exclaimed.

Joy pouted. "You're no fun. I'll give you every detail about my night."

"That's because you are a shameless exhibitionist and that extends to the vocalization of every single detail of your extensive sexploits," Sophia quipped.

"Sexploits, I like that. So, I take it from the expression on your face that you finally got some and boy, it sure looks good on you."

Sophia was glowing in the aftermath of her evening with her wife. "Yes, I did and that's all the details you'll get from me. Come on into the bedroom and tell me all about your night while I get dressed.

"I'd love to. I never miss a chance to see you naked."

"Oh, shush now. So, did you meet someone?" Sophia asked.

"Indeed I did. A leggy brunette who I swear fucked me raw. You know that I don't often let someone top me, but damn she was hot. The vision of her long hair hovering above me while she expertly used her strap on is almost enough to made me come again just sitting here telling you about it."

"God, Joy, the way you talk about your liaisons, one would think you're an uneducated, low rent hussy, instead of a highly educated professor of English literature. Do you save it all up just for me to see whether you can get a rise out of me?"

"You've discovered my secret. See, I know that deep down there is this wildly passionate, throw caution to the wind hellcat simmering underneath your well-put together veneer."

Sophia winked. "You could be right and for the right person, that hellcat comes out to play. My wife used to cajole it from me on a regular basis and based on last night's activities...." Sophia peeked around the partially closed bathroom door. "I'm back."

"Oh yes, I love you in those jeans. Your ass looks especially pinchable," Joy remarked.

Sophia climbed into her comfortable jeans and leaned toward the makeup mirror to apply a little eyeliner, mascara, and blush. She blew out her long wavy hair and let it settle loosely on her shoulders. "Okay I'm ready. Listen, Lara mentioned a surprise for me and I'm dying to find out what it is. Do you mind if I make a quick call?"

"Not at all. Go ahead."

Sophia grabbed her phone and dialed the number to Lara's Seattle office. "Yes, may I please speak to Lara. This is Sophia. Oh, okay. No, I'll try to catch up with her later."

"The business tycoon is not available, huh? We should just march down to her office and make her come to lunch with us. I'd like to visit with her cute assistant. Maybe she'll join us."

"I don't think that's such a good idea. It sounds like she's busy. I'm sure she'll call again later," Sophia reasoned.

Joy batted her eyes. "Please. How much can it hurt to simply stop by and just see if she's available and if her lovely assistant is free as well?"

"Oh, all right, you big baby, but we better hurry if we want to see a bit more of the city before stopping by her office. It's a little after ten already."

†

Rachel smiled when her assistant told her that her wife had called and wanted her to call her right back when she got in. Rachel was running late again and forgot to check her phone. After learning that Lara had called, she glanced at her phone and noted the text message and voicemail from Lara.

The text was brief. You're evil. Call me.

"Thanks," she said over her shoulder as she rushed into her office and shut the door so she could talk privately with her wife. It was already eight thirty and if she knew her wife, which she did, Lara was probably already embroiled in some account. However, Lara had asked her to call back and even tried to track her down at the hospital where she worked as the executive director of the foundation, so it must be important enough to interrupt her.

Rachel thought back to the night she'd met Lara two and a half years ago at the annual children's hospital foundation dinner. She remembered glancing up and seeing a striking woman in a tuxedo. Not too many women dared to wear a tux—even in the liberal city of Seattle. Later she would learn that Lara felt equally comfortable in a sexy black dress or a full tuxedo. It depended on her mood, regarding which she would choose for these types of events. Rachel noted she looked equally scrumptious in both.

Rachel picked up the receiver on the phone that sat next to her computer and punched in the number she knew by heart. "Hi Chandra, it's Rachel. Is Lara available? She did? Great. Well, hello yourself. I'm flattered that you directed Chandra to interrupt you if I called. So what's up, did you get my message?" Rachel laughed as she listened to Lara's response. "Sure. I have a light day today, so no problem. I'll swing by around noon if that works. Oh yes, I am most definitely looking forward to seeing you. I missed you last night. I love you, too. See you in a bit."

Rachel hung up the phone and debated whether she should remove her underwear and go commando for her lunch date with her wife. She nodded to herself and walked around the corner to sneak off to the bathroom and remove the potential barrier to a little afternoon delight. Lunch was always a double entendre in her world. Rachel had a definite spring in her step for the remainder of the morning and an ear-to-ear grin. Meeting her wife for lunch never got old for her, but it was especially desirable today since she'd had to sleep alone last night.

†

Lara paced inside her office. She practiced in her head what she would say to Rachel. Maybe her wife would be too distracted to worry about hearing that Lara needed to travel back to New York so soon. She'd decided to mention it in an off-handed manner so as not to draw too much attention to the situation. Perhaps she would wait until Rachel was on her way back to her own office after lunch and then she would say something like, *I know I just got back, but an emergency came up and I need to head back to New York for a couple of weeks. I'll just catch a limo to the airport, so don't bother to re-arrange your work schedule.*

Yes, that ought to do it.

Rachel had a fiery temper and Lara knew that if she wasn't careful she would set off the powder keg. She'd been successfully managing Rachel since she'd won her, but it always took just the right words to handle her. She had a good thing going with Rachel and didn't want to chance screwing that up.

It was eleven forty five and if Rachel wasn't too late, she would be here any minute. Lara didn't want to waste any of her precious time, so she sat back down at her desk and studied a new contract that her new CFO, Carrie, sent in with the interoffice mail. Time was money, after all, and soon she'd lose two whole weeks. It would be good to reconnect with her wife, but this was a precarious time for Lara as she oriented the new CFO. She decided she would take her tablet and laptop and sneak in a few hours each day of work while

Sophia was sleeping. The financial world did not stop just because she had a delicate situation to resolve.

The commotion she heard outside of her office did not register with her at the time as she focused on the contract in front of her.

†

Rachel was so anxious to see her wife that for once she was not only on time for their lunch date, but she'd made it to the office a few minutes early. When she burst through the doors, she noticed two very attractive women standing in front of Chandra.

"Hi, Chandra." Rachel held up her hand. "I know can you believe it, I'm early for our lunch date. Is the boss ready?"

"I was just explaining to these women that Lara has a previous engagement and isn't available for lunch." Chandra motioned to the women standing in front of her.

Rachel turned her head to look directly at the stunning brunette. The other woman looked like pure trouble. "Hi. I don't think we've met before. Are you one of Lara's new clients? I'm Rachel."

Rachel extended her hand and when the elegant hand met hers, a sizzle of energy traveled up her arm. *Hmm, interesting.* She looked into the most compelling chocolate brown eyes she'd ever seen. A reaction like this had only happened to her once before and that was the night she'd met Lara.

The woman chuckled. "Lord, no, we don't even live in this city. I'm Sophia and this is my surprisingly mute friend, Joy."

Joy was standing there with her mouth agape.

"Sophia and Joy are friends of Lara's from New York. They made a surprise visit yesterday, but seem to keep missing her," Chandra disclosed.

The woman looked puzzled by Chandra's remark.

"I'm so sorry you haven't been able to connect. I'll bet you've come all the way to Seattle under false pretenses. I'm afraid Lara is a horrible friend and tour guide, but you both are in luck because I'm a fabulous tour guide. While Lara is doing her boring financial stuff, I'd be happy to show you around. I would feel horrible about you coming this whole way and not getting an insider's view of our beautiful city," Rachel offered.

Finally, Joy found her voice and Rachel reluctantly turned her attention to the other woman. "Well, I'm not sure that my stick in the mud friend here will want to take advantage of your generous offer, because I think seeing your city is secondary to her primary reason for visiting. However, I would love a personal tour and whatever else you have to offer. I can't seem to convince Chandra to play hooky today and join us for lunch and more, but you seem to be a person who would jump at the chance for a little fun and adventure." Joy pulled a card out from her purse and handed it to Rachel. "My cell is on the back."

Rachel was incredulous at Joy's boldness. "Are you hitting on me, Joy?"

"I most certainly am. Are any of my hits landing?" Joy asked.

Sophia tugged on her friend's arm. "Stop it right now. I'm sure Rachel and Lara have important things to discuss." Sophia looked back at Chandra. "Can you just tell Lara that we stopped by again? I suppose our timing is terrible since we continue to keep missing her. Please have her call me."

"My offer stands." Rachel pulled out her own card, scribbled a number on the back, and handed it to Sophia. "That's my office number and also my personal cell number on the back. I would really love to show you the city. Maybe we can have lunch tomorrow and I can take off the afternoon."

Sophia hesitantly took the card. "All right, if you're sure it's not an imposition on you."

"Absolutely not. I don't want you heading back to New York with stories about the barbaric, rude Seattlelites. We pride ourselves on our friendly and welcoming nature."

Rachel chuckled to herself as she heard Joy whisper. "Why do you always have to shut down my fun? Just because you're taken, doesn't mean I am and if the delightful receptionist Chandra won't bite maybe the stunning Rachel will."

Rachel couldn't help herself as she watched Sophia's lovely backside walk out the door, tugging on her outspoken friend's arm. Nothing wrong with being friendly. She could look as long as she didn't touch and look she did. It was hard to miss that delectable ass.

Rachel didn't spend a lot of time analyzing the offer she'd made to tour around Lara's friends from New York. A part of her wanted to know and understand that part of Lara's life because Lara was so close mouthed about the time she spent in New York. Lara never mentioned any friends and Rachel had to admit she was more than a little curious. Rachel refused to acknowledge that a bigger part of the offer had to do with how the exquisite woman had inexplicably drawn her in.

†

"Ouch. I can walk on my own you know. You don't have to drag me out the door," Joy cried out.

"You need a leash. I swear if I didn't know any better, I'd think you were just like a dog in heat. You seem to squat everywhere leaving your scent," Sophia complained.

"So what? I'm single. I can do that. You, on the other hand, are very married. Don't think I missed the look you gave Rachel. Too bad you have a ball and chain because I swear I detected a whole lot of chemistry between the two of you. I could also feel the electricity when you shook her hand. I didn't fail to notice that she never offered her hand to me. She only had eyes for yooouu," Joy crooned.

"Don't be ridiculous. I was being polite. She's nice. I wonder if she works for Lara or is a client?"

Sophia wasn't about to admit it to her best friend, but she did find Rachel extremely attractive. A person would have to be dead not to notice the beautiful young woman.

Sophia wondered if Lara instructed Chandra to make sure that she kept Lara's marital status to a woman under wraps. She didn't know a lot about Washington State politics. Maybe they were not as progressive as New York. She didn't think so, based on what she'd heard, but that was the only possible reason for referring to her as a friend from New York.

Rachel seemed to take Joy's advances with a grain of salt and Sophia was one hundred percent positive that she was a lesbian. The intensity of her eye contact with Sophia was a dead giveaway. She had to admit that it felt flattering.

She would call Rachel. What would be the harm— especially with Joy tagging along—that is if she could get Joy to behave just a little?

†

Lara heard the assertive knock on her door and glanced at her watch. Rachel was early. She must be anxious to see her. Lara debated whether to have Chandra bring in lunch or take her wife to their favorite restaurant.

Her initial plan to make the proclamation after she'd satisfied her wife, making her a bit more pliable, would require lunch in, but taking her out had some advantages as well. Rachel would never start an argument in public.

Lara opted for lunch in. That would be more fun. She opened the door to her grinning wife and kissed her soundly on the lips. When she broke apart from the kiss, she stepped into the reception area to ask Chandra for a favor.

"Chandra, would you mind calling the bistro and ordering lunch for us. Just get our standard order," Lara directed.

"Sure thing. By the way, your friends from New York stopped by again. Sophia wanted you to call her back."

Lara could feel the color drain from her face. "Were they just here?" she managed to squeak out.

"Are you all right, Ms. Beck? You look like you've seen a ghost."

Lara composed herself. "Yes, I'm fine. I guess I stood up too quickly and since I missed breakfast, I just felt a little light headed for a second. Did Rachel run into them?"

"Yes, they were out here chatting for a short while. Your friend Joy hit on Rachel. I think Rachel was shocked by that, but she handled it well." Chandra chuckled.

No, no, no, no. Time to take control of the situation. I need to make arrangements pronto. I can't take the chance that they'll meet again.

Lara managed to formulate an appropriate response. "Joy is a bit of a wild child."

She walked back into her office and tried to control her shaking hands. For the first time, unplanned events were challenging her carefully erected double life and she didn't like the added complication.

"Hey, are you okay? You look a little pale. Come sit on the couch with me. My poor baby. I'll bet you worked well into the night and hardly got any sleep. Look, I had every intention of seducing you at lunch, but you look positively exhausted. Why don't we just have some lunch and tonight I'll give you a nice massage guaranteed to ease your stress?"

"That sounds like the best offer I've had all day. Lunch should arrive shortly. I had Chandra get our usual from the bistro," Lara said.

"You never talk much about New York. I don't know any of your friends. Joy and Sophia seem nice," Rachel probed.

Lara knew she had to change the subject. It probably wasn't the most opportune time to bring up that she would be away for the next couple of weeks, but at least it would side track the discussion from Sophia. "Hon, I need to talk to you about something and I'm afraid you're not going to be too happy, but I promise I'll make it up to you."

Rachel narrowed her eyes. "Okay, tell me what it is that is going to piss me off, because I know that look. Unhappy is an understatement. Am I correct?"

"The New York office has an emergency that I have no choice about. I have to return there in the next couple of days to straighten things out. I'll be gone for at least a week, maybe more. I won't know until I get there and try to unravel the mess," Lara hedged.

"Fuck, Lara, you just got back. If your time there extends by a few weeks, you're going to miss your birthday. I had something special planned. Can't you at least try to get back for that?" Rachel asked.

"I'll try and I promise when I get back, I'm going to see about scheduling us some time to get away for a week or two."

"Now you're just trying to butter me up," Rachel huffed.

"Is it working?"

"No," Rachel pouted.

"Aw, come on. A week away—just you, me, and a romantic bed and breakfast wherever you want to go. I'll even cross the ocean for you," Lara pleaded.

"When do you need to leave?" Rachel asked.

"I'll see to making the arrangements tomorrow, but probably day after tomorrow."

"Please take care of yourself and FaceTime me every night. You know all this money doesn't mean shit if you keel over from a heart attack. I read about women having heart attacks more and more each year due to the stress of busting through that glass ceiling into the previously dominated male domain of high finance." Rachel gently kissed Lara. "I love you and don't want to lose you."

"You're not going to lose me. I promise I'll try to slow down after I get this situation under control."

†

After her disappointing lunch with her wife, Rachel returned to her office and sifted through the hundreds of e-mails waiting for her.

"I swear these e-mails multiple like rabbits. How is it possible that in only a few short hours I have more than a hundred new e-mails?" Rachel grumbled.

Rachel wasn't able to concentrate because her thoughts kept returning to Sophia. The woman was intriguing and this uncharacteristic reaction was interesting. It was as if her brain was taking a major side trip from the main road. She wondered if she would call and take her up on the offer of lunch and a tour of the city.

She chuckled to herself about Joy's blatant flirting. She would be fun to get to know, but she'd have to make it clear that she was off limits.

Rachel wondered if maybe Joy and Sophia had something going. She didn't get that vibe. They seemed more like close friends. Sophia seemed like the type of person her wife would befriend, but not Joy. She'd get the scoop from Sophia if she ever phoned her. For some unknown reason, she really wanted her to call. Maybe it was a connection to her wife's mysterious life in New York, or maybe it was something else entirely, but Rachel had an obsessive need to learn more about the woman.

Rachel decided to stay a little late to catch up on some work, just in case Sophia called. She wanted to be able to take the afternoon off and ensure that Sophia had a proper introduction to Seattle.

†

Sophia decided it would be fun to take an afternoon trip to the famed Experience Music Project. Joy wasn't as interested in the attraction, but she went along with her best friend.

While Sophia was looking at the guitar sculpture made up of more than five hundred musical instruments, her smart phone buzzed in her pocket. It was difficult to hear in the large space so she walked to a corner to try to get some privacy as she swiped her phone to answer the call.

"Hi, honey. Yes, I know, but I was dying to find out what the big surprise was. I'll take the bad news first. Oh, yes, I understand. I'll drag Joy out tonight and we'll find something to occupy us for the next two evenings. Although I'll probably be crimping Joy's style if she drags me to a bar. Really? Oh baby, that is the best news I've heard all day. I can't wait to take that trip with you. Don't worry, Joy will understand. She's never had problems finding companionship, no matter what city she visits. Ok, I love you, too. Get back to work so that you get everything done in the next few days. I'll miss you tonight."

Sophia watched while Joy began chatting up an attractive young woman looking at the sculpture. She traveled back to give Joy an update.

"Hey. Who's your new friend?" Sophia asked.

"Oh this is—honey, what's your name again? I am so bad with names, but I have other attributes that absolutely make up for it and I never forget a face, or any other part of a woman's body." Joy winked at the young woman.

The woman waved at Sophia. "I'm Bonnie. Joy was just telling me that you guys are here visiting for a few weeks and she wanted to know where all the hot lesbians go for entertainment. My friends and I will be at the Wild Rose tonight. If you want a one hundred percent lesbian venue, it's the only one in Seattle. The other bars have a mixed crowd."

"It's good to know I found the right place on my first night in town," Joy replied.

"Well, it looks like you and I will be on our own tonight and tomorrow night, so I'll go with you to this Rose place. By the way, I'm Sophia."

"Okay, who are you and where did you stash my best friend? You never want to go out to the bars with me. Why are you trying to butter me up?" Joy asked.

Sophia felt bad. She'd dragged her best friend across the country with her and now she was going to abandon her in a few days to take a romantic vacation with her wife. "Well, um, Lara has this romantic vacation planned after she finishes tying up a few loose ends during the next couple of days. Are you mad?"

Joy smiled at the young woman. "Will you be my personal tour guide after my best friend leaves me to languish in this terribly overwhelming big city? You'll be helping to preserve our friendship if you agree."

"I'd love to. You seem like a kick in the pants," Bonnie answered.

"Don't let her snow you. We're from New York and this city is not at all overwhelming to her, but she can be charming and entertaining. I'll give you that," Sophia interjected.

"I don't know if I'm a kick in the pants, but I know exactly what to do in someone's pants."

Sophia smacked her arm. "Settle down. She's already agreed to tour you around, don't scare the poor woman off."

"Oh, I'm definitely not scared. Where are you staying?" Bonnie asked.

"We're at Hotel 1000," Joy answered.

Bonnie whistled. "Wow, nice place. How about if I come pick you up in the lobby at around nine?"

"Perfect. I am so glad we bumped into one another today. Seattle has been such a friendly city. I may have to put this on my radar as a nice place to periodically visit," Joy declared.

"Can we see some of the exhibits now? It is why we came here. I might have to come back again. There is just so much to see," Sophia enthused.

"Oh, all right. See you tonight, Bonnie." Joy waved her hand and followed Sophia when she turned to visit the Nirvana exhibition.

†

Sophia decided she wanted to go out to dinner with Joy and called the Canlis restaurant on the off chance they would be able to get a table. She figured that if they went early, like five or five thirty, the likelihood of getting a reservation might increase. She'd heard Lara rave about the food and decided to treat her best friend for being such a good sport.

When they arrived at the restaurant, a man showed them to a table by the window and she wondered if Lara had something to do with the location. She'd called her wife earlier to let her know what she planned to do for dinner. It seemed that Lara had connections everywhere.

Sophia let her thoughts wander as they landed on the intriguing woman she met at Lara's office. She wondered who this woman was. She seemed to know Lara well. Sophia was suddenly very curious about Rachel. She would call her tonight to see if she might want to join Joy and her for lunch.

"You're going to call Rachel, aren't you?" Joy asked.

"How in the hell do you do that? It's like you just read my mind," Sophia asserted.

"I've known you since grade school. What kind of best friend would I be if I didn't recognize the signs? Look, I'm no angel and lord knows I act on instinct all the time, but you need to be careful," Joy warned.

"What do you mean?" Sophia asked.

"I've seen you look at someone like you looked at Rachel today only once in your life. Six months later you were married to her."

"You can't possibly be suggesting that I would cheat on Lara?"

"Some people hit a rough patch around the seven year mark. In your case, I think it's the ten-year mark. I'm glad you and Lara are reconnecting, because you need to. I don't think you've been happy these past few years and I worry about you. It might be time to have a serious conversation with your wife about her work-life balance. I've seen too many relationships go kaput when they aren't able to manage that," Joy explained.

"You're right. We do need to talk. Honestly, I'm not sure how much I can take of her absence for more than half of the year and it's gotten a lot worse these past two years. I'm glad I came to visit. The first night was almost like when we first met."

"I know I haven't expressed any interest in settling down, but honestly I envy what you have. If I could ever find the right woman, I'd give up my carousing in the blink of an eye," Joy admitted.

"You'd have to start presenting who you are in a completely different manner. All anyone ever sees is that wall of promiscuity you portray to the world. Why would anyone take the chance if they believe you'll never settle down? You need to stop screwing your way through the entire lesbian population. I love you, hon, but you are your own worst enemy," Sophia admonished.

"Hey, how did we go from talking about you to my pathetic love life?" Joy asked.

"Because you finally admitted that your life is lacking an essential ingredient—love."

"Just don't let Rachel charm the pants off you."

"Not a chance, especially since I'll be heading off to my second honeymoon in a few days. I do plan to call. It would be rude of me to ignore her generous offer. Besides, I'm dying to learn how Lara knows her," Sophia explained.

"Uh huh."

Chapter Fifteen

Rachel walked into her office the next morning and grumbled a quick hello to her assistant. She was in a foul mood. Even though Lara had tried to make it up to her last night, she couldn't help being irritated about Lara's return trip to New York so soon after coming back to Seattle. Normally, she was able to forgive her after Lara paid special attention to her in the bedroom, but she was getting irritated with the back and forth and was ready to put her foot down concerning the amount of time they spent apart.

Since Lara had distracted her again with a fiery night of passion and Rachel kept pressing the snooze button, making her late for work. Lara left for work before Rachel had a chance to talk with her and insist that some things change if she expected their marriage to stay on stable ground. Even if the emergency in New York was weighing heavy on her mind, Rachel banked on the fact that they would have tonight to work things out before she had to leave for New York. Rachel wanted to take her to the airport and skip out on work, but Lara insisted that she would catch a limo so Rachel didn't have to interrupt her workday.

Rachel didn't know why she hadn't told Lara that she had invited Sophia and Joy to lunch, offering to take them around the city. Sophia hadn't called and that was another reason she was crabby today.

Rachel stared at the computer screen trying to focus on her fifty e-mails when she heard her office phone ring. It wasn't usual for the CEO to call the first thing in the morning—he was an early riser and tended to call his direct reports early in the day when he needed something.

"Development and communications, this is Rachel. How can I help you?"

Rachel was surprised to hear the sexy alto voice of Sophia on the other end.

"Yes, I was serious. I'd love to meet you for lunch… No, of course not. It sounds like your friend found her own personal tour guide. Seattlelites can be a charming bunch. I'm sure she'll have a blast. You can either meet me at my office or I can come get you. I'm at Seattle Children's Hospital. Do you know how to get here?" Rachel chuckled. "Yeah, I guess the limo service will know where to go. I'll meet you at the courtesy desk in the front lobby of the hospital. I cleared my afternoon so no worries. Yes, me too. I look forward to the afternoon."

Rachel leaned back in her chair and a smile finally appeared on her face. She was looking forward to her lunch date with Sophia. The day was looking up.

†

Sophia tipped the limousine driver and walked into the lobby of the hospital. She hadn't been inside too many hospitals, but it seemed like they made a concerted effort to create a cheery atmosphere for the kids.

She spotted Rachel right away and the sensual way she moved in her direction caused her breath to hitch. She should not be having this kind a reaction to a total stranger, but her body was rebelling. It would react in whatever bloody manner it wanted to and there was not a damn thing she could do about it.

Rachel smiled at her and she felt like a bright ray of sunshine just emerged from behind a tall tree.

"Right on time. I'm afraid that I am a perpetually late kind of gal, so you should be flattered that I made it to the lobby on time and the volunteer didn't have to track me down," Rachel said.

"Okay. Thanks, I think," Sophia responded.

"Come on, let's get a move on. We've people to see, places to go, and a ruckus to start. Just kidding, but I do guarantee a good time and I'm dying to hear all about your impressions of Seattle so far."

"Well, so far so good. Everyone has been extremely friendly. I really appreciate you making the offer for lunch since Lara can't seem to get away," Sophia replied.

"I want to hear all about how you know Lara, but first I want to know a bit more about you. New York seems like such an exciting place to live. I've only been there once when I was much younger and I remember the city never shutting down," Rachel said.

"I suppose that's true, but not everyone partakes in the endless nightlife. Maybe I'm letting my age direct my social life too much, but I rarely take advantage of the vast culture laid out for those who have the energy and desire."

Sophia walked beside Rachel and was surprised when she clicked open the locks to an expensive Tesla in the parking garage.

Rachel opened the passenger door for Sophia. "Your carriage awaits."

"Wow, hospitals must pay very well."

"Heavens no, and hospitals don't pay all that well, this is a birthday present from my wife. She's the rich one in the family." Rachel grinned.

"So what do you do that allows you the flexibility to take an afternoon off during the workweek?" Sophia asked.

"I'm the development and communications director for the hospital. It's a fancy way of saying that I plan all the fundraising activities for the hospital. It's how I met Lara," Rachel answered.

"Oh right, yes, I heard you answer the phone "development and communications" earlier. Yes, Lara is big on fundraisers. I met her at one, as well," Sophia stated.

"I am so curious about Lara's life in New York. I had no idea Lara even had friends there. I thought everyone was a client or potential client," Rachel offered.

Sophia was thinking the very same thing, but Rachel seemed to know Lara a little more intimately than just a client. Perhaps they'd become friends, but if they were friends she wondered why Rachel didn't seem to know that she was married to Sophia.

Sophia thought that it was such a short distance to the Sand Point Grill, they probably could have walked, but maybe Rachel's plans for the afternoon required a car. She'd learned that parking in Seattle could be quite challenging. She was glad she had a limo driver at her disposal.

Rachel opened the door for Sophia and the hostess took them to a table right away. She assumed that Rachel had taken the time to make a reservation. Sophia sat across from Rachel at the table tucked away in a private corner of the restaurant. It was much quieter where they sat and Sophia assumed Rachel made those specific arrangements so they could easily talk to one another.

Rachel sat down and smiled at Sophia. "So, tell me. What was the fundraiser? I presume it has something to do with what you do for work."

"Mm hmm. It was a fundraiser for the college. I'm a professor at CUNY. I teach in the gay studies program," Sophia answered.

"That's wonderful. I didn't even realize they had a gay studies program at that university. That would have been a kick."

"Technically it's called the LGBTQ program, but that's kind of a mouthful so I shorten it sometimes to gay studies. It's easier than answering the inevitable question about what each letter stands for. You probably know, but sadly most people do not," Sophia explained.

A waitress in a crisp white shirt and black pants approached the table. "Can I get you ladies something to drink?"

"Would you like to share a bottle of wine?" Rachel asked.

"Sure, why not? I'm on vacation. Perhaps we can walk around a bit after lunch before driving anywhere."

"Sounds like a plan. White or red?" Rachel asked.

"I prefer white, but I'm not picky."

"I'm not picky either, but you're in luck because I prefer white as well. Would you mind if I ordered something on the sweeter side?" Rachel inquired.

"Not at all. It's what I prefer."

"Can we get a bottle of your Snoqualmie Riesling?" Rachel folded up the wine list and handed it back to the waitress.

"Good choice. I'll be right back with your wine and then I'll take your order."

"I'll bet you are a popular professor. Your students must love you. I probably would have signed up for every course you ever taught if I was a student at CUNY. I don't suppose you ever had an affair with one of your students," Rachel teased.

"Absolutely not. I'm a happily married woman and have been for nearly ten years now. Before that who had the time? I'd just finished my doctoral degree and was desperately trying to prove myself at the college. Getting tenure was a hard road and I sure wasn't about to mess that up by screwing a co-ed."

"Damn, you just popped my little fantasy bubble. I imagined you in the throes of passion with one of your adoring students begging for you to teach her the art of making love, academic style," Rachel added.

Sophia chuckled. "Just what exactly is academic style?"

Rachel leaned in. "I was hoping you could educate me on that."

Sophia leaned back. "Married, remember?"

"Well, duh, so am I, but I'm not dead, you know. Look but don't touch, always works for me," Rachel stated.

The waiter interrupted Rachel's flirtation when he arrived with their wine, poured two glasses, and set the bottle inside the bucket of ice. "What can I get for you today, ladies?"

Sophia glanced down at her menu and realized the harmless flirtation had completely engrossed her and she hadn't even looked at the list of options. Rachel grinned at her.

"We're sorry we haven't had a chance to look at the menus yet," Rachel answered.

"No problem, I'll come back in a few minutes."

"So, you're married too?" Sophia asked.

Rachel looked puzzled by Sophia's question and Sophia wondered if maybe she'd offended her by not flirting back.

"I thought you were close friends with Lara?" Rachel asked.

Sophia thought that was an interesting response. She knew that Lara could be closed off and suspected that she kept her private life very separate from work, but Lara never seemed like the kind of person to stay in the closet and certainly Rachel had seen her picture in the office before. Lara had several framed photos from their wedding in her office in New York. "Besides the fundraiser, how are you connected with Lara? Did she charm you into becoming one of her clients?"

Sophia picked up her glass of wine and started to take a sip.

"What, no. Lara's my wife. How exactly do you know Lara?" Rachel asked.

When Sophia heard Rachel's answer, wine spewed from her lips like spray from the ocean. "Did you just say Lara is *your* wife?"

Sophia began to cough and Rachel jumped from her chair. "Hey, are you okay?"

After Sophia's coughing fit, she looked up at Rachel and managed to squeak out a question. "When did you get married?"

"Almost two years ago, why?"

"I've been married to Lara for a little more than nine years. Well, legally coming up on four years, but we had a ceremony of sorts nine years ago before it was legal in New York. I guess that makes me the true wife and I'm not sure what the laws consider you," Sophia whispered.

Rachel stood next to Sophia, blinking her eyes rapidly. "You're not kidding, are you?"

"I'm afraid not."

Rachel leaned back into her chair, but didn't say a word. Her eyes narrowed in Sophia's direction and if looks could kill, Sophia would be dead by now.

The gravity of the situation suddenly hit Sophia. It all made sense now. The pieces finally shifted into place for her. A sucker punch to the gut would have felt better at this moment. Sophia felt like she was about to throw up all over the beautiful setting on the table. She slapped her hand to her mouth and rushed to the bathroom.

Pushing open the first stall door she came to, Sophia barely made it to the toilet. The acid in her stomach continued to churn. She heard someone enter the bathroom, but at this point, it didn't really matter. Her life was suddenly in a tailspin and nothing would make this feeling come to an end.

"I suppose you think that Lara is meant to be with you, but frankly if I was a betting woman, and I am, I would bet that your pathetic sex life does not compare with ours. She married me for a reason," Rachel snapped. "Our chemistry is undeniable."

Sophia was speechless and didn't have an immediate retort. Instead, she began to cry softly.

Rachel was probably correct. Sophia had felt Lara's distance during the past two years and almost felt resigned to the fate of her marriage.

"You know, you're probably right. I'm not sure I have what it takes to keep Lara." Sophia tried to muster some amount of self-respect. "I'd challenge you to consider that if Lara was able to so easily marry you while still staying married to me, what makes you think she won't do it again?"

Sophia looked up at Rachel and thought she saw her expression change. The cold hard stare she witnessed earlier was replaced with something new.

"Hmm, I guess you have a bit more gumption than I thought possible. Good point," Rachel acceded.

She felt a gentle hand touch her arm. Tears were streaming down her face and Sophia didn't have the strength in that moment to control her emotions. She needed to get out of here and it didn't help that Rachel looked at her as if she was ready for a one way ticket to an inpatient mental health facility. It surprised her that Rachel's actions seemed caring

"Aw, shit. I hate to see a woman cry. I'll probably get pissed later and you can talk me down from doing something I will most definitely regret, but right now I think you're the more urgent victim to attend to. Let's go take a walk. I'll take care of the bill," Rachel said soothingly.

Sophia stood up and Rachel brushed a lock of her hair back. Her gait was unsteady as she walked to the sink, ran cold water over her hands, and scooped it into her mouth. She looked at her reflection in the mirror. It wasn't a pretty picture. "I'm a mess."

"No, you're beautiful. Even distraught looks good on you," Rachel assured her.

"How can you be so calm?" Sophia asked.

"I just look calm on the outside. Inside I'm thinking up ways to torture that two timing, bigamist wife of ours. Do you want in on the devious plans in my head?"

"Is bloodshed involved? I'm a bit squeamish." Sophia gave Rachel a weak smile.

"Maybe? But I'm thinking more along the lines of her precious money and reputation. That's her true Achilles heel. Don't get mad, get even, right?"

"Right now, I am doing everything in my power not to completely break down in front of you. I'm nowhere near the anger stage yet," Sophia explained.

Rachel slipped her arm inside Sophia's, caught the eye of the waitress, handed her a hundred dollar bill, and gently led Sophia to the exit and out of the restaurant. "Come on, let me take you to one of my favorite places, Magnuson Park. It's right on the water and whenever I get a little down, it always cheers me up to walk to the park. It has such a calming influence on me," Rachel suggested.

†

Sophia kept brushing away each new tear as she walked arm in arm with Rachel to the park. It should have been an uncomfortable silence as they made the journey, but it wasn't. Rachel didn't interrupt her thoughts or try to tell her everything would be okay. Sophia supposed that Rachel was in a unique position to say, *I know exactly how you feel.* The irony of Rachel providing her comfort wasn't lost on her, but she didn't care because somehow Rachel was able to make the shocking news livable.

Finally, they reached the park and headed to the beach area. Sophia was surprised by the number of people that were out and about in their shorts, with dogs running around everywhere. In New York, everyone had to have a leash for his or her dogs. Sophia figured they didn't have leash laws in Seattle, because not one dog was on one.

Although it was partly cloudy, the sun kept trying to make an appearance and for that, she was grateful. She pointed to what looked like a mountain desperately trying to part the cloud cover in an effort to display its majestic beauty. "Is that Mount Rainier?"

"Beautiful, isn't it? The view of the mountain from this park is one of the best in the city. Too bad it's cloudy today. You can barely see her peeking through."

"How come they let all the dogs run around without leashes?" Sophia asked.

"That's why the park is my favorite. It's one of the few parks with a large off leash area for dogs. Dogs are so easy to please. Feed them, love them, provide a decent area for them to run and they'll stay by your side for all eternity—unlike people. Damn." Rachel angrily swiped at a tear.

Sophia spied a bench in a relatively private area and tugged on Rachel's arm to lead her to the perfect place to sit and let their emotions settle. Sophia sat down first and then tugged on Rachel's arm until she sat beside her. Without analyzing her motives, she clasped Rachel's hand and their fingers intertwined. "I suppose I've had my freak out moment—it's your turn now."

Rachel shook her head. "I don't want to feel sad right now, I want to stay angry. I can wallow in my sad place later with a full bottle of Jack Daniels."

"No, don't do that, all you'll get is a terrible hangover. I liked your earlier suggestion. Tell me more about those evil plans to get even."

Sophia watched as Rachel focused her bright blue eyes in her direction. She felt like she was under a microscope and Rachel was sizing her up.

"Are you serious? Because if you are—I am definitely game. What about your friend, Joy? Think we can get her to help us out?" Rachel asked.

"Oh, I don't think that will be a problem. The real challenge will be keeping Joy from tearing off Lara's head before we have a chance to execute the plan." Sophia smiled and she had to admit, thinking up a plan was far better than wallowing in a vat of pity soup.

"Okay, here's what we're going to do," Rachel began.

Chapter Sixteen

Lara decided to call her wife to let her know that she'd be home on time. It was the least she could do, considering that she was about to abandon her to take a romantic excursion with Sophia. She knew that Rachel had noticed her distraction the night before. She needed to pull herself together and manage the situation in the same manner she would manage an unruly client.

As she was walking out of her office, she started to punch the number on her phone to call Rachel. "Hey, honey, I just called to tell you that I'm coming home on time. I wanted to spend as much time as possible with you since I need to leave tomorrow. Oh, you are? Okay. Well, then when will you be home? That late? Um, no, I'm not mad. I just thought with me leaving, you'd want to spend the evening together. No, I understand. Yes, I know your work is just as important to you. Yes I would be a big hypocrite if I didn't understand. No, of course I'll wait up for you. No, it doesn't matter when you get home. Yes, wake me up if I've fallen asleep. Okay, I'll see you later tonight. Bye. I love you."

Lara frowned. Something wasn't quite right. Rachel hadn't even said goodbye. That was the first time she hadn't said I love you back. Maybe she was still angry about the lie she'd told to enable her to whisk Sophia away before the two could talk more.

She didn't know whether to head back to the office or head home and hope that Rachel was able to get away earlier than she had indicated. She couldn't remember Rachel ever having to work until midnight. What could she possibly need to do that required her to stay that late?

Something unthinkable passed through Lara's brain. Rachel wouldn't be cheating on her with someone else. Would she? Sure, Rachel was a very beautiful woman, but she was dedicated to Lara, wasn't she? That double standard that she felt should not apply to her was not something she believed should extend to her wife. She expected her to remain one hundred percent faithful.

Lara's heels echoed loudly on the sidewalk as she walked to her car. The angry staccato punctuated every distrustful thought Lara had.

Normally, Lara left much later, so when she eased into the Seattle traffic, she grumbled at the line of cars waiting to enter the freeway. The highway had an equally long queue as far as she could see. It would probably take her more than two hours to get home in this mess. So much for leaving on time. "Damn Seattle traffic. Why can't they approve a decent public transit system?" she grumbled.

By the time Lara arrived home, she was in a rotten mood. She was too tired to make anything for dinner—besides cooking for one was depressing—so she ordered a pizza and read the Wall Street Journal.

After several failed attempts to call Rachel back, Lara crumpled into her favorite recliner and tried to relax. The phone startled her from her thoughts and when she glanced at the screen she smiled. Maybe Rachel was on her way.

"Are you coming home now? Sophia and Joy? You offered to tour them around? You didn't tell me that. You shouldn't have felt obligated to do that. You took both of them to dinner? Sophia? So why are you still there? Joy is a shameless womanizer. I absolutely forbid you to have drinks with her tonight. I'm sorry I didn't quite mean it the way it sounded, but it's really not a good idea. I think we need to settle this right now. Right now you're acting like a petulant child—"

Lara heard the dial tone on the other end of the phone and ground her teeth. She and Rachel had argued in the past, but Rachel had never hung up on her before. She'd handled the situation all wrong. She knew that now.

Lara paced the floor after Rachel's disturbing phone call. She knew she had overreacted to Rachel's plans for the evening, but right at this moment she felt like she was playing Russian roulette and any moment that bullet would land in the chamber. She could take Sophia out of the equation, but Joy was a whole other wrinkle in desperate need of a hot iron.

Lara got up, fixed a drink, and then settled back into her chair. When midnight came and went, Lara's exhaustion from the past few days overtook her body and she fell asleep in her recliner.

†

Rachel couldn't remember a time when she'd felt so comfortable around someone she'd just met, especially when that someone was the *other woman*. It wasn't Sophia's fault that the two-timing female version of Warren Jeffs had hoodwinked her into marriage. Rachel didn't know the legal ramifications to her situation—she hadn't explored that with Sophia yet. She suspected that since Sophia married Lara first, her own marriage wasn't legal.

Miraculously, she managed to keep it together while Sophia had her emotional meltdown, and when Rachel's emotions finally poured from her soul, she felt Sophia's arms embrace her in a protective hold as she softly cried on her shoulder.

After Rachel explained phase one to Sophia, she was ready to fill Joy in on the plan. "I think it's time we called Joy and got her involved. Do you mind heading back to the hotel? We can have them send up an early dinner. You must be hungry by now, considering we missed lunch."

"I know I should eat something, but I just don't have much of an appetite right now. You haven't had anything to eat either. God, what a pair we are." Sophia sighed.

"I promise to eat something if you do. I'm glad we walked here. I think the fresh air and exercise has done both of us some good. You can tell me all about your life in New York while we walk back to the car. Just one rule."

"What's that?" Sophia asked.

"Until we get to the hotel and have to bring Joy into the mix, we follow the Harry Potter rule." Rachel clasped Sophia's hand and pulled her to her feet, but didn't let go when she began to walk back to the car. She needed the human connection of someone who could empathize with her.

Sophia scrunched up her nose. "The Harry Potter rule?"

"Yeah, we can only refer to the two timing bitch as she who shall not be named, because that is how evil she is. Better yet, I'd prefer to leave her completely out of the conversation until we get to the hotel."

Rachel saw Sophia glance at their intertwined hands, but didn't feel her pull away. She hoped Sophia needed the connection as much as she did.

"I think I can adhere to that rule," Sophia agreed.

†

The drive back to the hotel was relatively short and Rachel didn't learn nearly as much as she wanted to about Sophia. She racked her brain for a way to spend more time with Sophia.

Rachel tossed her keys to the parking attendant and strolled confidently into the lobby. She was anxious to bring Joy into the plan.

She kept stealing glances at Sophia in the elevator. It appeared as though Sophia's somber mood had returned and Rachel was desperate to get her to smile again.

"You can stop worrying that I'll jump out the window. I won't give her the satisfaction. I can feel you watching me," Sophia said as she stared straight ahead.

"I'm not worried," Rachel lied.

"Liar."

"Okay, I am worried about you, but that's not why I'm looking," Rachel blurted out.

Sophia turned her head and Rachel recognized the despair that Lara's betrayal caused. "Aren't you familiar with proper elevator behavior? Everyone is supposed to face forward and avoid eye contact at all costs," she teased.

"Where did you learn that? Don't tell me. You read Emily Post's, *Etiquette*. I don't remember a chapter on what to do in an elevator," Rachel noted.

"Holy cow. How do I know what's in that book? I don't see you as the type to have that book on your library shelf. Please tell me that's not in your collection or your street cred will take a dive and I'll have to reassess this plan of yours." Sophia grinned.

"My grandmother is from the South and that is practically the Bible down there. I don't have it in my library, but I might as well, because she made me memorize it. She was a tough one, every time she thought I wasn't paying attention, she'd say to me, *I'll knock you so hard you'll see tomorrow today.*"

Sophia laughed and it was music to Rachel's ears.

Sophia knocked on Joy's door and an extremely disheveled Joy greeted them.

Joy raised her eyebrow. "Well, well, well, look what the cat dragged in. Where have you two been all afternoon and why do you both look like shit?"

"We'll get to that, but first I need to know if you're alone or is your date, and I use that term lightly, still here?" Sophia asked.

"Why?"

"Because we have a situation and we need your help. I'd prefer things stay between just the three of us for now," Sophia responded.

"Yes, I'm alone, Bonnie had to go back to her place to get ready for work. She's a nurse at your hospital. You might know her. Cute redhead. Very flexible. I failed to get her last name, but this one might be worth calling again." Joy grinned.

"It's a big place, but that's probably Bonnie Harris. She's a real sweetheart, but I think she's just looking for some fun. Bad break up not too long ago," Rachel explained.

"Perfect. Just my type—for now. If I do break my pattern and settle down, I'd prefer to find someone closer to home. So, what's this situation? It sounds ominous." Joy waved her hand and stepped aside while Rachel and Sophia walked into the suite.

Rachel sat next to Sophia on the love seat and Joy sat in the chair across from them.

Rachel glanced at Sophia as she opened and closed her mouth. She jumped in and rescued Sophia from having to say the words. "Lara is a two-timing snake who is currently married to both of us."

"What? You're kidding, right?" Joy asked.

Sophia shook her head and started crying again.

Rachel gathered her in her arms and rubbed her back. She didn't take the time to realize that Joy, as her best friend, should be the one to comfort her. It was an automatic reaction to her distress.

"Oh, shit. I'm going to smack that woman like a Piñata until her teeth fall out as candy. Sophia, don't you worry because, if revenge is sweet and payback is a bitch, then I'm the sweetest bitch on the planet. I got this, darling." Joy jumped up from her chair.

Before Joy reached the door, Rachel ran to her and touched her arm. "Wait. We have a plan and we need your help."

"It better be as good as what is rolling around in my head right now," Joy bellowed.

"Oh, it is. Phase one is going to make her squirm more than a three year old in church," Rachel promised.

†

Joy had to admit the plan was ingenious. She couldn't help but appreciate Rachel's cleverness. Fortunately, she was able to direct all her anger at Lara. She didn't have any delusions about who the culprit was. It was clear to her that Rachel had previously had no idea who Sophia was. In Joy's mind, Rachel was as much a victim as Sophia.

Joy insisted that Sophia and Rachel have something to eat after she learned that the revelation earlier had interrupted their lunch. She felt bad for not being there for her best friend, but maybe if she had, they never would have learned the truth.

Joy watched, as Rachel seemed to coax a smile or two out of Sophia. It seemed like the focus on the plan was a godsend to both of them.

Joy was relishing her role in the scheme. She entered her cell phone number into Rachel's phone and grinned.

"We're charging this whole dinner to Lara and several bottles of their best wine," Sophia declared.

"That's a given," Joy interjected.

"Time to poke the fire a little," Rachel added.

Rachel grabbed her phone back from Joy and touched the screen. "Hi, baby. No, it looks like I'm going to be here a bit longer because I offered to tour your friends around today. Yeah, the ones I met in your office the other day. I felt bad that they came all this way and you weren't available for lunch. No, I thought for sure I'd told you that I made the offer to take them to lunch and then tour them around. It was fun, but it really ate into my work time and then I took one of them out to dinner."

Joy listened to Rachel setting things up and had to work hard to control her laughter.

Rachel waved her hand in the air and then covered her mouth before answering. "No, just one of them."

Joy began making faces at Rachel.

Rachel mouthed the word stop.

Joy thought she could almost hear Lara's stress level kick up on the other end of the phone. She wondered what would be the most disturbing, Rachel having dinner with Sophia or her.

"No, Sophia decided to head back to the hotel. She mentioned something about a headache, so it was just Joy and me. Sorry, I also promised to meet Joy for drinks after I finish up here. Tell me you did not just forbid me to have drinks with Joy. I am not having this conversation with you right now. Just go to bed and I'll talk to you in the morning. I don't want to fight about this right now. Bye."

Rachel abruptly ended the call and Joy saw her turn off her ringer.

Joy grinned at Rachel. "Okay, this is fun. I need to be subtle with my texts, huh? Sophia, you need to help me with that. You know that I don't really do subtle."

Joy thought their plan was a little like the old game of Chinese water torture she played with her brothers, when you kept poking them until it became too much and they exploded.

"All right. Do you two mind if I hang out with you until about one? I want to stroll in late enough for her to conjure up all kinds of nasty possibilities," Rachel said.

"Not at all. There's good wine and great company. This is somewhat surreal to me. I don't know about you, but isn't this strange to team up with *the other woman*. I should hate you, but I don't at all," Sophia confessed.

"We've both been made fools of. I don't blame you at all for this. I knew right away that you were an innocent victim. No one could have possibly faked that reaction. I'm just glad you recognized that I had absolutely no knowledge of your existence. I swear I never would have gotten involved with Lara had I known. I'm so sorry for whatever part I've played in your pain," Rachel uttered.

Joy watched as Sophia lifted her eyes and locked onto Rachel's.

"There is something about you that is so genuine. I don't know. I guess I just trusted you from the very start— even after you sort of sniped at me being horrible in the bedroom," Sophia confessed.

Rachel groaned. "Oh God. I'm so sorry, that was not one of my finer moments. I let the hurt take control of my good sense."

"No need to apologize. You didn't have to go after me when I had my meltdown in the bathroom, but you were right there—comforting me—even though I knew how much you were in pain yourself. It was incredibly sweet," Sophia whispered.

"Damn. You two are just the cutest thing. Wouldn't it be karmic justice if the two of you were to fall in love and live happily ever after leaving that bitch Lara to dry up like an old prune," Joy announced.

"After this experience, I may never fall in love again," Rachel noted.

"Never say never is what I always say," Joy responded.

Chapter Seventeen

Lara felt the buzz on her watch and blinked her eyes. She'd fallen asleep in her recliner. Her back was killing her. She worried about the reason or reasons—plural—why Rachel hadn't woken her to go to bed when she'd returned the past night.

She heard the shower going and walked into the master bedroom. Rachel never got up this early. Rachel's phone buzzed on the dresser. She needed to know what was happening and if her luck had finally worn out. She didn't get as far in business as she had without the ability to siphon through every available clue. Without any sense of remorse about violating Rachel's privacy, Lara picked up her phone and looked at the string of text messages.

Had a blast last night. J

Me too.

Interested in a repeat?

Absolutely. Lara leaving for New York tonight.

When the cat's away....

Flirt.

Damn tooting I am

Careful I'm a married woman

And....

Ignoring you...Interested in breakfast?

You bet! Call me when you wake. A little bit of coffee and I'll perk right up, especially if I get to spend time with you.

Sweet dreams

Ditto

Can't wait to CU today...thirty and counting J

By the time Lara read the entire stream of text messages, she was fuming. Joy was a loose cannon and she had her sights set on her wife. At least it appeared as though they hadn't discussed her during their evening, but it was only a matter of time before Rachel discovered her secret. Joy was Sophia's best friend. It was bound to come up at some point if they kept hanging out. Her only hope was she knew that Joy wasn't the type to focus on learning anything personal about her next sexual liaison and she was a master at keeping things light. She needed to figure out how to manage this situation without Rachel knowing she'd read the texts.

Lara heard the shower shut off and walked into the master bath to talk to her wife.

"You didn't wake me up last night. I missed you," Lara stated. She was going for a conciliatory approach after her overbearing declaration absolutely forbidding Rachel to spend more time with Joy.

Rachel grabbed one of the fluffy white towels hanging on the brass hook next to the shower. "You were sound asleep in the chair and I didn't have the heart to wake you up. I didn't want to interrupt your sleep."

Lara saw her smile, but it didn't seem to reach her eyes. Something was definitely amiss.

"You're up early, especially for how late you were out last night. I thought we might have a nice leisurely breakfast before I have to leave for the airport today. I'm sorry I reacted the way I did last night. I have no right to control your social agenda."

"Apology accepted, but I'm sorry, I have a breakfast meeting this morning," Rachel answered.

Lara was seething on the inside, while maintaining her poker face on the outside. "Oh. Who with? Maybe you can cancel. I'm sure they would understand."

Rachel towel dried her hair and walked into the closet, selecting her clothes for the day. "Well, actually, I promised Joy I would go to breakfast with her. Sophia is abandoning her today. I think that's rude to drag your friend all the way across the country and then take off on a romantic getaway. I know you aren't able to spend time with your friends and now Sophia has deserted her. I feel bad for her."

Lara followed Rachel into the master bedroom. "Trust me, Joy can take care of herself. It's not that I'm jealous or anything, but Joy can be a bit of a stalker. That's the reason I reacted so strongly last night. You are a very beautiful woman and Joy has absolutely no morals. Even though we're friends, she will think nothing of making a play for you."

Rachel chuckled. "Oh, she already has. It's harmless flirtation. Besides, don't you trust me?"

Lara watched as Rachel pulled on her clothes, rushed around the bedroom, and got ready more quickly than usual.

Lara sat on the bed and Rachel continued to button her blouse. "I trust you, but Joy is a piranha."

"So, who is Sophia going off with? Does she have a love interest here in Seattle? Is that really why she came to visit, dragging her best friend across the country?" Rachel asked.

It took all of Lara's boardroom skills to control her reaction. "I don't really know. Sophia tends to keep things close to her chest." Working to keep control, Lara added, "Can't you please cancel your breakfast date with Joy? I won't see you for at least a whole week."

Rachel walked back into the master bathroom and grabbed her toothbrush.

As Lara followed her, she noticed that Rachel was using the manual brush. Normally she would use the electric toothbrush unless she was in a hurry.

"I can't. Really, I'm already running late. I told her I'd meet her at eight and she's probably on her way already," Rachel mumbled through her toothbrush.

Lara frowned. Things were definitely not going her way this morning. She needed to find out if the unthinkable had occurred. In her mind, she focused solely on Joy making a play for her wife—hoping their time together would not lead down the path of enlightenment for Rachel. Lara was at the edge of the volcano and she knew it. There wasn't much she could do about the precarious situation she found herself in without raising a red flag. She needed to find out more.

"I know you, Rachel, something is wrong. Talk to me."

Rachel rinsed out her mouth and began applying her make-up.

"Nothing is wrong. Well, sure, I'm not happy you have to leave again so shortly, but I'm used to it and I'll get over it. I also didn't appreciate your Neanderthal response to an innocent round of drinks with a friend that you are totally ignoring."

"I've already apologized for my behavior last night. Are you sure that's all?" Lara asked.

"Of course, what else could it possibly be? Just have a safe trip and take care of your business. I'll be here when you get back."

Lara sat on the edge of the Jacuzzi tub and watched her wife get ready. "I promise, when I get back, I'll make it up to you. Maybe we can plan a second honeymoon. You name the place and I'll take you there. Anywhere you want to go. Paris, Rome, Greece, you name it. I'll make the arrangements."

Rachel grabbed the hair dryer and plugged it into the outlet. Before turning on the dryer she answered. "We don't need to go far. I've always wanted to go to Rosario Resort on Orcas Island and then maybe a visit to Victoria."

It was a good thing that Rachel turned around and focused back on drying her hair as the hair dryer blocked out the sound Lara made when she reacted to Rachel's suggestion. She experienced a niggling in her brain that suggested this was not a coincidence. Her plans to take Sophia to Rosario and then to Victoria was a freaky link to Rachel's request.

After Rachel finished drying her hair, Lara attempted to lead Rachel in a new direction. "I'm sure they are nice places to visit, but wouldn't you rather go somewhere farther away?"

"No, I don't think so. Listen, I really have to go. Call me when you arrive in New York. Bye." Rachel pecked Lara's lips, then grabbed her keys and purse as she ran out the door.

Lara felt like she'd just been blindsided by something, but didn't exactly know what. *Is the honeymoon finally over?* Every other time an energetic romp in the bedroom would sway her passionate wife and forgiveness would soon follow. She didn't have any time to react or control the state of affairs before Rachel ran out the door. The situation was a bit more than unsettling to her and she didn't have the time to make a course correction with her wife, because she needed to get moving on her plans with Sophia. For the first time, Lara thought having two wives was far too exhausting to manage effectively. She was losing her tightly maintained control on everything and that was disconcerting to her.

She had to pray that neither Joy nor Rachel would spill the beans on her marital status. She was banking on Joy's self-centeredness.

†

Sophia yawned as she sat in the café with her best friend waiting for Rachel to arrive.

Rachel burst through the front door. "Sorry, sorry, I'm late. I know. Here's the good news. I am relatively confident she read the texts. Lara thinks she doesn't show emotion on her face, but I, no, we, definitely have her on the run. I could almost see the wheels in her head spinning and trying to find a way to control the situation. I left the phone on the dresser and if you sent the final text at the specific time I told you to, she would have found them all. I imagine she woke up in the chair when her alarm went off and then started searching for me. She would have entered the bedroom at just the right moment to hear the buzz. You know all about Lara's need to control every situation. We have her on the run right now and everywhere she turns is another obstacle."

Joy grinned. "How were my texts?"

"Perfect," Rachel said enthusiastically.

"So, now I just wait for her call. I'm getting nervous. I don't know if I can pull this off. Right now, I want to scratch her eyes out—not act like everything is hunky dory. I don't know if I can manage to let her kiss me without puking in her mouth," Sophia announced.

"Ew. That is definitely not a mental picture I want. I think I may be rubbing off on you. That's something I would say, not you," Joy said.

"Yeah well, a person changes when they learn they are married to a lying, cheating, manipulative, bitch," Sophia spit out.

"Ooh, you go girl. I think I like this new side of you," Joy said.

"Are you gals ready for the next phase? Sophia, can you do this? If you can't, I totally understand. I had a hard time not slapping her silly myself this morning. You have the hardest part," Rachel remarked.

Sophia felt Rachel's warm hand cover her own. She genuinely liked Rachel. She was such a good person. When she first learned about Lara's deceit, she had been bitchy and insensitive, but when she saw some of the light retreat from Rachel's expressive eyes, it was her undoing. Although they were still somewhat dull, what she saw in them this morning was compassion.

Rachel was a very beautiful woman and under different circumstances, she would have wanted to get to know her better and perhaps she would have tried to explore a relationship. That was out of the question now, but she couldn't help feeling the attraction. She felt a pull toward Rachel that she didn't have a lot of control of at this moment. The circumstances didn't matter. It was a strange, yet not an altogether unwelcome feeling. She'd have to tamp down that attraction, because the last thing Rachel needed was Sophia acting on her attraction to muddy the waters even further. Besides, Sophia was not about to jump into anything for oh, maybe ten years. That wasn't an unreasonable time to remain celibate.

"I can do this," Sophia responded.

†

After the confusing interchange with Rachel, Lara shook it off and concentrated on the need to focus on Sophia. She'd find some time to call Rachel and do whatever was necessary to repair the continental divide that had suddenly appeared between the two of them this morning.

Calling Sophia's phone, she found a new irritation when it went straight to voicemail. She tossed the phone on the dresser, not bothering to leave a message.

"Goddammit. What the hell is going on this morning? Which Goddess did I piss off? Sophia knew I would call her this morning to tell her the plans," Lara barked.

She stomped into the shower to try to let the warm water wash across her body. She felt tense. Rachel hadn't even stopped for one minute this morning while she got ready. Not only did she have to worry about Joy spilling the beans, but she'd also lost out on having sex with her wife last night. She'd hoped to have some intimate time with her before leaving for Rosario and now she had a bunch of pent up energy.

Lara soaped up her breasts and let her hand travel down to her treasure trove. She wanted to release the tension from her body, but everything was going wrong for her. None of her strokes had any effect on her. After several minutes of targeted caresses to her own body, she gave up and opened the shower door to find nothing hanging on the hook.

"Where the hell is the other towel? Fuck. How many more things can go wrong?"

Lara shivered as she walked out of the shower dripping wet.

Espresso poked his black furry head just inside the bathroom door.

Lara looked down at Rachel's cat. "What are you looking at? I'm entitled to a hissy fit now and again." She reached into the cabinet where the extra towels were stacked neatly on top of one another and pulled one from the top.

Sauntering naked into her bedroom, Lara considered what clothes she needed to pack for her week long get-away. She liked to do her pre-planning ahead of time. She would pack her suitcase after selecting clothes from her back up wardrobe that she left at the penthouse. By the time she went to pick Sophia up, she wouldn't have to waste her precious time deciding what would come with her on the trip.

She stepped into her comfortable pants and pulled her soft natural cotton shirt over her head. She looked at herself in the mirror and groaned. The tiny crow's feet at the corner of her eyes were starting to become more prominent. Vanity was beginning to get the best of her and she decided to consider some minor plastic surgery. She wasn't positive when she would be able to fit that in with her busy schedule, but she would just have to make some time. Turning forty was not a welcome milestone.

It was still relatively early, but certainly Sophia would be awake by now. Sophia tended to be an early riser, especially when she slept alone. Lara assumed that she was able to catch up on her sleep these past two nights. She wondered why the phone went straight to voicemail when she'd try to call earlier.

Espresso sprawled his long lean body across the bed and lifted his head when Lara sat on the bed next to him and put on her shoes.

"Meow."

"Well, excuse me. I guess I disturbed the king. I should have told Rachel I needed to leave yesterday. A lot of good it did me to stay one more night, I didn't even get to sleep with her, but you did, didn't you. Lucky bastard. I still can't believe she left me sleeping in the recliner. It'll take two days to work out the kinks in my back. Oh, what do you care? I've officially lost all my marbles—talking to a cat."

Lara picked up her phone from the dresser and called Sophia again. When a groggy Sophia finally answered the phone after four rings, Lara wondered why she was still in bed. "I'm sorry, babe, did I wake you up. Yes, I got everything done and I'm ready to pack a bag and be on our way. I'm not sure we'll make the eleven am flight, so I'll call and rearrange our flight for two. That should give you enough time to pack and be ready to leave by noon. I hope you are as excited as I am. I'll see you in a little while. I love you."

Lara decided she would call Rachel on her way to pick up Sophia. She wasn't sure when she would get a chance to break away and call her when she was on her way to Rosario, so she might as well take advantage of the shitty Seattle traffic that was sure to delay her drive to Hotel 1000 where Sophia was waiting at the penthouse.

Hopefully, she'd learn more about the breakfast date with Joy. There had to be a way to keep those two apart while she was out of town with Sophia. Maybe she could ask Chandra to keep Joy occupied. Chandra was exactly Joy's type. Chandra might even have some fun. Lara rationalized that everything would work out and she was just doing everything to keep all parties happy. What was the harm in that? She wasn't really pimping Chandra out. Joy was charming and beautiful. Chandra was single. It was the perfect solution to her current dilemma.

†

Rachel hugged Sophia, holding on a few seconds more than she would normally. "Lara is nothing if not punctual, so you better get back to the penthouse."

Her hands absently caressed the sides of Sophia's arms. "Listen, you're going to do just fine. I hate like hell to ask you to do this, but you have to act as though nothing at all is wrong. I'll take care of all the legal paperwork, but I may need you to respond to a text here and there as I work with your attorney. We'll see you tomorrow. All you have to do is make sure she doesn't whisk you to a new location. Lara is very clever—one change of venue is child's play to her, so two won't pose much of a challenge. We have to time it just right so she can't do a damn thing about the inevitable. I want her to see the train coming and know she's doomed."

Rachel felt Sophia pulling her in for another hug and she melted into her arms. After she broke away from Sophia, their hands remained linked together.

"Thank you for taking care of all the legal crap. I honestly don't have the energy for it. Do you think you might be interested in taking a short vacation after this is all over? I've always wanted to spend time in the Pacific Northwest and I'd hate to return home with my tail between my legs. I begged for this time off and I'll be damned if I'll let her ruin my vacation," Sophia announced.

"You know. There are an awful lot of places I've never visited. I'd love to hang out with you and Joy. I'm due a bit of vacation. Sure. I think that would be lovely. Count me in. We can make plans after the shit show is finished. You really better get going now. No more procrastination." Rachel broke away from Sophia and kissed her cheek. "Good luck."

"Thanks for your help too, Joy," Sophia said.

"Anytime. You know I'll always have your back."

Sophia started walking toward the exit.

"Come on kiddo, let's go meet with your attorney and wrap up the boring stuff and then we can have some more fun." Joy flung her arm over Rachel's shoulder and they followed Sophia out of the café.

†

Lara entered the penthouse and listened to the shower running. Having already planned which clothes she wanted to take to the islands, she began pulling out the various outfits to pack in her suitcase.

She found Sophia's bag open on the bed with a pair of casual pants and pullover top laid neatly next to the fully packed case.

Lara smiled as she noted the outfit. It was one of her favorites. The blouse clung to Sophia's shapely curves and accentuated her full round breasts. Sophia always knew how to select clothes that would complement her coloring. Her classic beauty was easy to showcase, but Sophia had a knack for choosing just the right style.

Lara lifted her head when she heard the shower turn off.

Sophia walked into the bedroom with a towel wrapped around her body and her long wet hair hanging loose in a disheveled manner. She oozed sensuality.

Lara gently loosened the towel. She watched the droplets of water make their way down Sophia's breast. Bunching the towel up, she pressed it against the ends of Sophia's hair. She leaned down and captured Sophia's lips in a slow torturous kiss. For a brief second she thought she felt Sophia tense in her arms before acquiescing to the kiss.

Sophia broke away, pulled the towel from Lara's hand, and vigorously rubbed her hair. "I don't think we have time to start anything if we plan on catching that plane."

"You just look so tantalizing right now. I better stop gawking at my beautiful wife and finish packing while you get dressed."

"Good idea. We'll have plenty of time for that when we get to the resort."

†

Sophia stepped up to the counter with her bag. She'd wanted to avoid raising any suspicion so she made sure to pack enough for a weeklong excursion. Unfortunately, she was unaware of the weight limit.

The young woman frowned as she hefted the bag onto the counter. "The bag is ten pounds more than the limit, ma'am. We'll have to wait to see if we'll be able to put this on the plane. How much do you weigh?"

"Excuse me?" Sophia asked.

"Your weight. I need to know how much you weigh so I can balance the plane."

"You're kidding, right?" Sophia glanced at Lara.

"No, hon, she's not. This is standard with small planes," Lara answered.

"Women never tell the truth about their weight and I'm supposed to get up in a plane that quite possibly is imbalanced?" Sophia asked.

"We know that, ma'am, it's why we usually add ten pounds to whatever number that is given to us," the woman whispered.

Sophia chuckled nervously. "You're sure this is safe? A lot of famous musicians have died in these tiny planes."

"If you're talking about Buddy Holly and Ritchie Valens—that was like fifty years ago. It's perfectly safe, hon. Kenmore Air has a stellar safety record," Lara soothed.

Sophia was already nervous enough about continuing to act as if nothing was wrong and now she had to squeeze into what felt like a tin can with wings. She tried to visualize Rachel's encouraging smile. She wished that Rachel was the one performing in this little one act play, but unfortunately, the situation didn't call for that particular rendition. She tried to imagine how Rachel would react. She was vibrant and adventurous. She would love going up in a floatplane. If only she was more like Rachel.

Joy always told her that opposites attract. *Wait, where did that come from?* She needed to stop having random thoughts about her co-conspirator

"Ma'am? Your weight?"

Sophia shook her head. "Um, sorry. I'm one hundred and twenty five pounds and you do not need to add ten pounds to that number."

The woman gazed across Sophia's body. "You may be the only woman to give her true weight, but I would say that looks about right."

"One thirty-five and don't even think about adding ten pounds to that number," Lara growled.

Sophia was grateful that in an effort to balance the plane, she did not have to sit next to Lara. She could enjoy the view from the window and mentally prepare for her role as the dutiful and loving wife. Her stomach churned thinking about what she might have to endure during the next couple of days. Oddly, she felt like a prostitute—or at least she would if she had to have sex with Lara. Sex for the sake of the plan was extremely distasteful to her, but she would do whatever she needed to do.

Rachel had promised that her forensic accountant would be able to uncover everything they needed within forty-eight hours. She'd doubled his fee in an attempt to get the report as quick as possible and he'd assured her that she would have most of the information she needed within twenty-four hours. Seattle Children's Hospital was about to receive a very generous donation to their foundation. At least something positive would come from this mess.

Four other passengers joined Sophia and Lara on their flight. The excited chatter filled the small cabin as the plane began its ascent into the air.

Sophia remained quiet in her seat. When the plane reached cruising altitude of eight thousand feet, she focused on the aerial view of Lake Union. What she saw from the tiny window took her breath away. Her fear of flying in the small plane floated away like tiny seeds from a dandelion flower. Could she make a wish like when she'd blown on the weed as a child? If only it were that simple, she would wish for this mess to all be finished.

In the distance, Sophia could see the snowcapped mountain peeking through the clouds. Mount Baker was every bit as awe-inspiring as Mount Rainer. Everywhere she looked, Sophia saw the lush landscape of Seattle and eventually, the San Juan Islands. It looked like a thousand diamonds sparkling on the dark blue water of the sound. Flourishing green forests peppered the water in an uneven pattern.

Sophia felt a calm come over her as she looked out at the famous archipelago of the northwest. Suddenly, she wished she could share this view with Rachel. It was an odd thought that she wasn't prepared to analyze at this particular moment.

As the plane began its descent into the harbor where the seaplane dock was located, Sophia took a deep breath.

Landing on water was a brand new experience for her. She could hear her mother's voice in her ears, *if you can't drive there, count me out.*

Too much of Sophia's ordered life was influenced by her cautious mother. Even during her college days, with Joy encouraging her wilder side, she remained more reserved. Her mother's death hadn't changed a thing. She'd broken away some when she met Lara, but deep down she was still that play by the rules, prudent young girl that her mother raised. If only her mother could see her now—scheming with her wife's mistress— or whatever you'd call Rachel— and landing on a speck of water.

Sophia chuckled to herself.

Lara turned around to look at Sophia and her quizzical expression screamed, *what are you laughing about?*

Sophia shook her head. She wasn't about to reveal her internal dialogue. She felt the buzz from her phone in her pocket and glanced quickly at the text message before deleting it.

Right on track. Hang in there, the cavalry will be there in a day or two.

Sophia smiled. The encouragement was just what the doctor ordered.

†

Rachel marched confidently into the reception area of Lara's office.

"Hey, Chandra. Lara asked me to come get something she left in her office. I know she won't be back in the office for at least another week, so when she returns she can look at those papers in her office at home. If I can't find them, I'll grab you to help, but I don't want to disturb you, so just give me some time to find everything," Rachel stated.

"Lara didn't tell me you were stopping by," Chandra wavered.

"I know. She's been so pre-occupied lately. I'm surprised she remembered to ask me to do this favor for her. I'm sure you've noticed how stressed she's been lately. It's the least I can do to help her out."

"Oh, okay. I suppose that's true. Let me know if you need my assistance," Chandra called out.

Rachel was already on her way to Lara's office as she heard Chandra capitulate.

The desk was completely devoid of any papers, folders, stray pens, or other items typically adorning most executive desks. Rachel knew that it was Lara's insane need for order that drove her to clear off her desk every evening prior to leaving the office. Lara constantly preached how everything had a place and after use, it ought to go right back where it belongs—it was one of the many obsessions that drove Rachel crazy sometimes, but today she was grateful for the quirk.

All Rachel had to do was find the keys to her file cabinets and she knew all of Lara's financial records were stored neatly in a file with her name on it. Lara didn't trust her money with anyone else, so she was both owner and client of Fortified Financials.

Rachel began rifling through the drawers looking for the set of small file cabinet keys. In the middle drawer in the desk, she found a cherry wood box with a combination keypad.

"Bingo, if I were a betting woman, and I am, I'd bet the keys were in this little box. Hmmm, I wonder what the combo is. Let's try my birthday."

Rachel punched in 0886.

"Nope, I guess I don't rate. Let's try her birthday."

Rachel selected 0575.

"Well, I guess you're not as narcissistic as I thought. How about our anniversary?"

After trying 0813, Rachel frowned and picked up her phone, sending a quick text to Sophia.

What's your birthday and anniversary?

Why?

Breaking into her office now and need to crack a keycode.

Ok it's 9/9/80 and 7/8/06

Libra. Nice. We're compatible. I'm a Leo. Whatcha doing now?

Waiting for our luggage, now stop texting. She's going to start asking questions.

Okay, good luck.

Rachel tried 0980 first, but that didn't work. She growled in frustration. On her final attempt after entering 0706, the lock popped open, and the tiny set of keys was the only item lying neatly in the box.

"I guess I know where I stand now in the pecking order of wives."

Rachel hurried to the large custom cherry file cabinet and started searching for the file she knew she would find. Finally, her thumb brushed across her wife's name. The neatly typed label stared up at her like a neon sign. She plucked the file from its home and brought it to the desk, flipping through the pages inside where Lara's neat print outlined every transaction, password, and current balance for each of her accounts. There were a surprising number of different accounts. Some were joint accounts with Lara and Sophia's name attached and others had her own name linked to Lara's. There were a fair number of individual accounts and those were the ones that Rachel focused on.

The forensic accountant was good, but even he didn't uncover all the accounts. It was a good thing that Rachel knew where to find the information. Rachel grinned when she discovered there were some accounts the accountant hadn't found that the file revealed. Rachel assumed there was a similar file set-up in Lara's New York office.

Rachel shrugged. It didn't matter. The attorney would address those accounts and they would just have to be satisfied with the fact that Lara might have some additional money squirreled away in individual accounts she'd set up in New York. This would have to do.

Rachel methodically snapped photos of each page and then carefully replaced the papers and returned the massive folder to the file cabinet.

She wanted to call Sophia and tell her the good news, but that was out of the question. If all went as planned, she would see Sophia in Victoria. She decided one more quick text wouldn't hurt.

Got them.

Rachel smiled when she received a smiley face in return.

Rachel looked around the office. She needed to take something with her so she wouldn't raise suspicion with Chandra. She found a stack of empty folders and some copy paper. Grabbing a folder and putting a half a dozen sheets of paper into the file, she walked out of the office.

Chandra looked up from her desk. "Did you find what you were looking for?"

"Yes. Thanks. It's all right here," Rachel replied.

"Oh, by the way, Lara asked me to try to get in touch with her friend, Joy. She mentioned that she felt bad about abandoning her after she came all this way to visit. She asked if I would entertain her while she's visiting. I'm not sure where the other friend went off to. That seems strange to me. Anyway, Lara said you don't need to keep her entertained anymore. She knows how busy you are. I assume she's still at Hotel 1000. Right?" Chandra asked.

Think you've figured out a way to keep us apart, have you? Rachel thought.

"Aren't you just the sweetest thing? Don't worry about it. I got it covered. I've got the whole tourist plan mapped out for Joy. I have plenty of vacation time and since it seems like Lara can never get away, I took the next week off. I didn't want to lose the time I have accrued. I'll let Lara know when I call her tonight. Bye, Chandra. Have a great weekend."

Rachel ran out the door before Chandra engaged her in more conversation. She heard Chandra say goodbye before the door closed and she was outside the suite on her way to meet Joy.

†

After retrieving their luggage, Lara looked for an opportunity to check on the situation with Joy and Rachel. She'd called Chandra earlier and asked her to entertain Joy while she was gone. She'd even suggested that Chandra could call in a temp to take her place at the office while she showed Joy around. Of course, she would pay Chandra for her time. She also needed to call Rachel.

"I'm sorry, babe, but will you be okay if I make a few business calls. I promise I won't be long and once they're out of the way, we can start our vacation." She pecked Sophia on the lips and strolled outside far away from the commotion at the sea dock.

The squawking of the seagulls was irritating as she tried to block out the noise.

"Hello. Yes, it's Lara. I'm sorry, Chandra, these damn gulls are making a lot of noise. You'll have to speak up. So, I was just checking to make sure you connected with Joy. What? No, no, I'll give her a call. Thanks, anyway. Yes, I'll touch base in a few days, okay?"

Lara resisted the urge to throw her phone at the seagulls. *Fuck, what on earth is going on?* She needed to calm down before she called Rachel. She wouldn't react well to a directive, as though she were one of her staff members just waiting for orders. When she'd first learned of Rachel's plans to have drinks with Joy, she'd blurted out the first thing that came to mind and that hadn't worked out too well for her.

When Lara tried to call Rachel, it went straight to voicemail.

"God dammit," she muttered.

Lara knew she'd have to try to get away again to call Rachel. She couldn't let that runaway train head down the tracks.

She plastered on a smile and started walking back to the dock where Sophia was patiently waiting with their luggage. She took a few seconds to admire her wife who was looking out across the clear blue waters of the sound. Sophia's hair was blowing in the wind and Lara thought it was one of those Kodak moments. Despite her earlier concerns, Lara couldn't help feeling blessed. She needed to make the most of this trip before the chaos of running her business, and keeping two women on opposite ends of the world satisfied, occupied all of her free time.

Lara wrapped her arms around her wife and nuzzled her neck. "I'm really glad you made a surprise visit to Seattle. I get to share a little of my world with you. There's not much that compares to the beauty of these islands. It's spectacular—isn't it?"

When Sophia didn't respond, Lara turned her around, pulled off her sunglasses and looked into her eyes. There was a depth of melancholy she'd not seen on Sophia since her grandfather had passed. "Oh, baby, what's wrong? You look so sad," Lara noted.

"Do you think we'll see the whales? That's definitely something on my bucket list," Sophia responded.

Lara decided to accept Sophia's change of subject. Obviously, whatever was bothering her was something she wasn't ready to discuss. It wasn't Lara's style to pry. If Sophia wanted to confide in her, she'd listen, but prodding her to talk was not in her repertoire.

"Mmm, it's possible. Sometimes the whales come in close to shore and you can see them dancing in the waves. We have a water view from our suite. We can have drinks on the deck. I reserved the Cliffhouse honeymoon suite because the deck overlooks the water," Lara answered.

"We should go check in now. I'd like to settle a bit before dinner. Maybe even take a nap. I didn't get much sleep last night and I'm a little tired," Sophia announced.

Now Lara wanted to pry. She was curious about why Sophia hadn't gotten much sleep. Something was obviously going on with her wife and she needed to know. "Sophia, you know I don't ever force you to talk about anything until you're ready, but obviously something is going on with you and now it's impacting your health. Please tell me what it is and I'll do my best to fix it."

Sophia waved her hand in the air, extended the handle on her bag, and began rolling it toward the resort. "Nothing's wrong, I'm just tired. Joy woke me up to tell me about her latest love interest. She has the hots for that client of yours, Rachel, but she's married. Of course, that never stopped Joy. I told her to leave it be, but you know Joy. I think the fact that this woman is married just makes her more appealing in Joy's eyes. That way she can have her little Seattle fling and go back home without any strings following her. I hate when Joy gets this way and I really hate when she pursues married women. There's nothing worse than an adulteress in my eyes. Why in the world would you get married if you're going to fuck around? No one is holding a gun to anyone's head. If you can't be monogamous, don't make that kind of commitment. Don't you agree?" Sophia asked.

Lara blanched at the question, but quickly controlled her expression and answered. "Yes, of course. I'm surprised you've remained friends with Joy since her moral compass is obviously one hundred and eighty degrees from yours."

Lara grabbed her own rolling bag and followed Sophia up the path to the resort. She was thankful that Sophia needed a nap because that would give her plenty of time to make a call to Rachel. She had to find a way to keep this situation from blowing up in front of her. If Sophia or Rachel discovered anything about her double existence, the shock would be of epic proportions.

†

Rachel kicked off her shoes and put her feet on the coffee table in the Corner Studio Water Suite while Joy lounged on the bed.

She took a sip of her wine and smiled at Joy. "I think it's time to kick up the heat now that all the legal stuff is well under way."

"She is going to pee her pants when you tell her that you plan on taking me to the islands and you booked a flight tomorrow to arrive at Rosario at half past noon." Joy laughed.

"Do you think Sophia will really get to rest while taking her nap?" Rachel asked.

Joy shrugged. "Doubtful. This whole thing is really taking an emotional toll on her. She's going to need a real vacation once this is finished. I might have to call her boss and fill her in on what's happening so that she arranges for someone to complete the semester for Sophia."

"Are you ready to have some fun?" Rachel asked.

"You bet your sweet ass, I am. And you do have a sweet ass, I might add," Joy quipped.

"I'm ignoring that comment. You have to be quiet. No snickering or anything because I'm going to put the call on speaker, okay?"

"Sure, sure. No problem," Joy responded.

"Oh, lookee here, missed call from Lara." Rachel laughed.

Rachel pushed the button on her favorites list to call Lara.

"Hi, babe, how's New York?" Rachel asked.

Joy made a face and Rachel shook her finger in warning.

"Lonely without you," Lara responded.

Joy stuck her finger in her mouth and pantomimed the universal gagging sign.

Rachel slapped her hand across her mouth to keep from laughing and managed to squeak out, "Hey, listen, I was talking to Joy and she mentioned she'd always wanted to visit the San Juan Islands, so I made us a reservation on the eleven o'clock float plane tomorrow. Remember, I wanted to visit there anyway. You didn't seem very excited about the location, so I thought I would take advantage of Joy's interest in going to the islands. That way, we can go wherever you want after you get back. It sounded like you might want to take a trip overseas."

Rachel could hear the strain in Lara's voice as she carefully responded.

"That's kind of a long way to go for a short weekend. I didn't mean to suggest that Rosario wouldn't be a good place for us to visit together. I'd like us to make that trip since Rosario is a romantic getaway place that's more suited to couples. Why don't you cancel and I'll make reservations for us to go there in a few weeks after I get this emergency taken care of?" Lara countered.

"Nonsense. I know a lot of friends at work that go to the islands to just hang out and relax. I heard Rosario has an amazing spa. Hey listen, I gotta go, Joy is going to be here any minute now. Don't work too hard, baby. Love ya, bye." Rachel pressed the end button before Lara had a chance to respond and offer another counter argument.

Joy rolled in the bed in a fit of giggles. "I'll bet she's looking for a way to get to Victoria as soon as they wake up tomorrow."

"Right about now she's pacing and trying to decide whether it's in her best interest to call me back and try to convince me to cancel, or to make other arrangements for her romantic getaway with Sophia. I sure wish I were a fly on the wall to witness her angst. Just in case she makes an attempt to call, I'm turning off my phone. Let her wonder what we're doing tonight," Rachel stated.

"Do you think she'll check to see if you made the reservations?" Joy asked.

"No, she wouldn't have any reason to believe I didn't."

"You know, I'm kinda glad we're going to Victoria tomorrow instead. I really have wanted to make a trip there. I've heard so many wonderful things about the city. Although, Rosario sounds like a lot of fun, as well. Maybe another time. Are you interested in heading to the Wild Rose tonight?" Joy asked.

"No, I want to get a good night's rest. This tormenting thing is exhausting." Rachel giggled.

"Maybe I'll give Bonnie a call. She was a lot of fun."

"Go right ahead, but make sure you're ready to go at ten tomorrow and I'm not responsible for whatever state you're in. However, if you hurl in that floatplane, I'll kick your ass when we touch down. They're nothing more than a tiny little sardine can with wings and the smell will cause a sympathy response from me. I refuse to puke right along with you when I haven't been out carousing the night before," Rachel warned.

"Spoilsport. Fine, I'll limit my alcohol intake to two drinks. I don't need alcohol to have a good time. Sex, yes. Alcohol, no." Joy smirked.

"Ten o'clock, Joy and you better be ready to go."

"I seem to recall that you are the chronically late type, not me," Joy retorted.

"Good point. I better set my alarm for an hour earlier. Call me at eight to make sure I'm up."

"Oh, honey, if I'm up at eight, I'll be too pre-occupied to call you. Bonnie works the night shift, so morning is likely to be a particularly active time for us. If I remember correctly, she wears that sexy just fucked look in the morning quite well. That's a bit too hard for me to resist." Joy smirked.

"I guess I'll have to set my watch, phone, *and* tablet. I'll put them each in a different place so I won't be tempted to just go back to sleep after I turn one off." Rachel stood up and waved at Joy as she left the suite. "See you tomorrow, sexapotamus."

†

Lara paced on the deck as Sophia slept. Immediately after Rachel ended the call, Lara considered her options. If she called Rachel back, she might piss her off and add to her problem. Lara wondered about the uncanny timing of Rachel's call. Leaving so shortly after just arriving at Rosario would be difficult. How would she explain to Sophia why they were leaving so soon? She needed to come up with something quick. *Think, think, think.*

She looked in at her wife who had just rolled to face the opposite side. It seemed like she was having a hard time getting to sleep. Was it possible she'd heard her on the phone just now? Lara discarded that notion. The glass door separating her from the room was heavy and Lara was speaking in a low tone. Maybe her pacing was disruptive. Lara sat down in one of the chairs to ponder her dilemma.

Lara snapped her fingers. A mix up with one of the rooms—that would be a good reason. The luxurious honeymoon suite had been double booked. If they insisted on staying, they would most likely ruin the young couple's wedding. Lara would explain to Sophia that she didn't have the heart to do that to them, so she made alternate arrangements for them to visit Victoria several days earlier than the original plans. She would tell Sophia that they could come back after the young couple left.

Lara sneaked into the room and exited to find a private location to make the alternate arrangements for the rest of their romantic getaway. She didn't want to take the chance that Sophia would wake up while she was on the phone. Besides she needed the excuse that while she was out making arrangements for dinner and a visit to the spa, she had learned about the resort's dilemma.

It's a good thing I have my travel agent on speed dial.

Lara walked outside and found a private spot on the grounds. A young male deer walked close to her, seeking a tasty treat. She'd heard that the deer were so tame they'd take a slice of apple out of your hand or even from your mouth if you strategically placed it there for them to nibble it away—not that she could ever see herself kneeling on the ground with an apple slice in her mouth waiting for the deer to approach. Rachel might, she thought. Sophia might even do that because she loved animals. Maybe she would take Sophia here again, just to see her joy while interacting with the deer.

"Sorry little one, you picked the wrong person to beg from."

She turned away and selected the button on her phone to connect with her travel agent.

"Hello Marlo, I need your assistance. No, the accommodations at Rosario are fine, but I'd like to get a flight out first thing tomorrow morning for Victoria. Please make arrangements for a suite at the Empress. Perhaps we can make it in time for high tea. We'll stay in Victoria for the rest of the time and keep our flight back the same. Thanks, Marlo, you're a doll."

With the new travel plans set, Lara relaxed and began to enjoy her walk around the grounds. She planned to arrange a private dinner in the suite, make love to her wife, and then head out first thing tomorrow to continue the quick vacation without any possible drama. Life was good again. Problem solved. Every problem in Lara's mind had a simple solution. The trick was not to panic and find that solution every time. She was a natural problem solver.

†

Sophia strained to hear Lara talking to Rachel. She began to smile as it appeared as though their plan was right on track. She couldn't let Sophia see her grinning from ear to ear, so she'd turned away. Lara had been pacing, which was a sure sign of agitation. Sophia wondered what lie she would tell to get them away from Rosario and heading to Victoria a few days early.

She really needed to sleep a little bit. Despite the knowledge that everything had gone just as planned, her emotions were raw and sleep evaded her. Concentrating on slowing her breathing and taking deep even breaths, she finally fell into a light sleep.

Sophia heard the door open and realized that she had managed to get a few hours rest. She turned to look at her wife and noticed the smug look on her face.

"Well, good morning, sleepy head? Did you have a nice nap?" Lara asked.

"I did. Thanks for letting me sleep. Sorry to leave you on your own. Did you explore the resort and make dinner or spa reservations for us? I could use a nice massage."

Lara approached and sat on the edge of the bed. "I know this isn't going to be the best news, but I just couldn't ruin that young couple's wedding. Unfortunately, the resort double booked this room and they don't have anything else available. I hope you don't mind going to Victoria a few days early. The resort has a nice atmosphere and we could have had some relaxing spa treatments and enjoyed walking around the grounds, but Victoria will have a lot more to offer us anyway. You're not disappointed, are you?" Lara asked.

Sophia sat up in bed. "Well, I could have used a few more days of rest and relaxation, but if I understand correctly, this room was booked to newlyweds. I agree, we shouldn't disturb their honeymoon. Marriages should always start out without any hiccups. Too often, they come later without warning. You owe me a spa day in Victoria, though."

"Deal. I've arranged for the chef to prepare a special meal for us—to be delivered and served right in our suite. I plan on doting on you for the next ten days until you have to return to New York." Lara stroked the side of Sophia's face. "You're still the most beautiful woman I've ever laid eyes on. I love you."

"Oh, you sweet talker. I still feel bad about leaving Joy all alone. I did drag her across the country to keep me company while you were working. Maybe I should call her up and have her meet us in Victoria. Knowing her, she'll have convinced that married woman to come along. Joy can be very persuasive when she turns on the charm. I'll try not to judge her too harshly or the married woman. I know I don't ever have all the details. Maybe this woman is preparing to get divorced or something."

Lara frowned. "I wouldn't encourage her or support her carousing with a married woman. Someone always gets hurt in that scenario. Let's not talk about Joy and her oversexed libido," Lara snapped.

"You seem tense, hon. Joy's escapades have never bothered you in the past. I know you've seen her flirt with married women before and it never seemed to concern you. What's going on?" Sophia asked.

"I just think that marriage is sacrosanct and should always be revered as something special."

Oh, that's rich. Sophia did everything in her power to remain neutral with her response. "Mmm hmm. I suppose you're right."

Sophia pulled the covers away and slipped out of bed.

"Hey, where are you going?" Lara asked.

"Just because we're having dinner in the suite doesn't mean I shouldn't get dressed up in some sexy evening wear. Let me take a shower and get ready. I promise you won't be disappointed," Sophia vowed.

"I never am," Lara responded.

Sophia made a hasty retreat into the bathroom. She needed to collect herself and avoid revealing the revulsion she felt toward her wife at this moment. If they were giving out Oscars for her performance as the loving, faithful, wife, Lara would win hands down. The bile in her throat threatened to make an appearance all over the lovely marble tiled bathroom vanity.

Sophia thought losing it again might solve her present dilemma. She could feign having a twenty-four hour flu bug and that would surely get her out of a romantic evening with her wife. However, that might also wreck the plans to meet up with Rachel and Joy in Victoria. She'd have to think of something else.

Maybe it was time for one of her infrequent migraines to appear. That would be a plausible reason to end the evening without too much intimacy. She would still have to endure Lara's arms wrapped around her body in a protective, loving gesture. As much as she hated Lara right now, she was always very sweet and caring whenever Sophia got one of her debilitating migraines.

She'd work that out later. Right now, she would get dressed and leave Lara with a final remembrance of just what she lost, because by this time tomorrow their marriage would have already taken its last breath and died a dramatic death.

Chapter Eighteen

Rachel tossed and turned all night. She couldn't get the vision of Lara and Sophia making love out of her head. She knew that a romantic getaway to Rosario Resort would probably mean that Sophia really didn't have a choice if she didn't want to ruin their plans to make Lara squirm before slapping her with the multitude of unpleasant documents.

Rachel didn't know what bothered her more, the realization that Lara would be making love to Sophia or that Sophia would have to endure the intimacy that was clearly repulsive to her.

She finally admitted to herself that she cared about Sophia and didn't want her to feel any more pain than she'd already clearly suffered.

Rachel began to second-guess the plan. Perhaps they should have just confronted Lara straight away. It had been her idea to prolong the agony and make Lara uncomfortable. They could have gotten the legal documents written up without sending Lara on a wild goose chase in an effort to keep Rachel and Sophia apart. Too late now, but the guilt began to nibble at her subconscious.

Rachel vowed to make it up to Sophia. She would whisk her away to get some much needed rest and relaxation. *Would going back to Rosario be a painful memory?* she wondered. Maybe they could stay in Victoria and enjoy the city for the remainder of her visit to the Pacific Northwest.

Rachel felt a spasm of pain at the realization that Sophia would be returning to New York. She would have liked to get to know her better. She already felt somewhat connected to her. A long distance friendship could work. She had a feeling that Sophia would make a good friend. Rachel had many acquaintances, but no one she could call a friend. She could use a confidant right about now. Rachel didn't think her family would let her live this down. They already hated the fact that she'd married a woman and now that the marriage wasn't even legal—well, that would be the cherry to push the cream over the top. She might as well find a private island to hide away on. Her life would suck now. An endless string of phone calls from her oh, so helpful, family would consume her life for the next several months. The *I told you so* would come in various forms—directly from her mother and indirectly from everyone else.

Rachel shook away her negative thoughts and headed off to the shower. For once, she would be on time. Just in case, she'd carefully rolled clothes that would last for at least two weeks into her trusty backpack. Rachel never liked the fancy luggage Lara bought for her—always preferring her comfortable pack.

Getting time off from work was a piece of cake since she had a boatload of vacation accrued. Convincing Sophia to stay and join her on a little rest and relaxation journey was an entirely different ball of wax.

Espresso was lounging on the bed when she came out of the shower with a towel wrapped around her body. He placed a paw on her arm.

"Sorry, little bad boy, I have to go out of town for a little while. Damn, I know that you love your other mommy, too, but you are coming with me no matter what. Shit, it's always the kids that get hurt the worst in adult transgressions." Rachel stroked his soft fur as he stretched and then placed his paws over her shoulders in a kitty version of a hug. He began to lick the water drops on her neck as she giggled.

"Stop it you lickapotamis. I swear you have some kind of oral fixation. Probably weaned too early from your mom. You can give your aunty all the kisses you want. She likes it. Now, be a good boy for her, okay?"

"Meow."

Rachel pushed Espresso off her shoulders and continued to get ready. She'd already picked out a comfortable pullover and her soft worn out jeans. She wanted to be comfortable in the floatplane.

Lara always preferred her in the fancier casual clothing she'd purchased for her when they first starting dating. It never felt completely right to her, but it was a small compromise if it made Lara happy. Well, now she would dress however she bloody well pleased. To hell with what Lara preferred. The more she thought about it, the more she felt like she'd been losing that part of herself that made her who she was. She felt like she'd somehow managed to change into something she was never entirely comfortable with. It was somewhat freeing to go back to her comfort zone again.

Rachel glanced at her watch. Perfect timing. She couldn't believe that she was right on time. She grabbed her keys, threw the backpack over both shoulders, and walked out the door to pick up Joy. They would have time to spare.

†

Lara rolled and reached out for Sophia, but the space was empty. She opened her eyes and spied Sophia looking out the glass doors leading to the deck.

"Morning, honey. Are you feeling better?" Lara asked.

"Mmm hmmm," Sophia responded without turning around.

"Listen, something seems to be off about your health lately. I think you ought to make an appointment with the doctor to check you out when you return to New York. I can't put my finger on it, but I'm concerned."

Sophia waved her hand. "Pssh. It was just a migraine. You know I get them on occasion." She smiled. "I'm really looking forward to our trip to Victoria. I just have this feeling that everything is going to turn out perfectly."

"I'm so glad you aren't disappointed that we had to make a course correction mid-vacation. We can come back here another time," Lara offered.

Lara kept feeling like something was slightly off-kilter, but now that she looked upon her wife's smiling face, she decided she was probably imagining things or projecting her own stress as a result of the situation with Joy and Rachel. One problem at a time. First, she would wine and dine Sophia. Then, she would send her packing back to New York. After Sophia returned to New York, she would put things back on track with Rachel. It was a simple task of putting puzzle pieces into place to complete the picture the way she wanted it.

"It's a good thing we didn't fully unpack when we first got to the room. We should have plenty of time to have a nice breakfast and make it to the seaplane dock in time for our flight to Victoria. Unless…." Lara wiggled her eyebrows. "I suppose there are other things we could do to occupy our time."

"You don't mind if we have a nice big breakfast, do you. I didn't eat much last night because my migraine made an early appearance, so I'm really starving right now."

Lara tried not to sound too disappointed as she answered her wife. "No, of course I don't mind. Would you rather eat here or go to the restaurant?"

"Let's hit the restaurant. I heard they have a spectacular brunch. Do you mind if I shower first?"

Lara heard her phone buzz on the dresser and scrambled to retrieve the text message that she knew was from Rachel.

"No, go ahead. I'll answer my text and try to get my staff to limit their communication with me. Sorry about that."

Sophia waved her hand and walked into the bathroom.

Lara turned her phone and stared at the cryptic message.

Change of plans. Running late, I'll fill you in when we arrive at our new destination.

"Well, fuck me, all that plotting and planning and now it looks like I didn't even have to make those new arrangements," Lara grumbled.

Lara had a fleeting thought that maybe she should just cancel those new plans and tell Sophia that the resort was able to work things out after all. She discarded that notion immediately. She'd had to scramble too much already and she wasn't going to change things again at the last minute. Sophia might think she was going crazy. Hell, she thought she might be going crazy with all the impossible maneuvering during the past couple of days.

Oh the tangled webs we weave, when first we practice to deceive, whipped through her brain like an angry wind. She needed to get on the other side of this chaos and everything would return to normal. Recently her lying had reached a frenzied peak and it was exhausting keeping everything straight.

When Sophia exited the bathroom, Lara plastered a smile across her face and turned to focus on her wife. It was time to pour on the charm.

†

Rachel was enjoying the view from the front seat on the floatplane. Instead of one tiny window to look out, she got a one hundred and eighty degree panoramic of the vista before her. She smiled knowing that Sophia probably experienced the same exhilaration on her trip. She wondered if New York had the same breathtaking views that the Pacific Northwest offered. She didn't think so, but she'd never been to New York as an adult and couldn't quite remember the family vacation of her youth. All she had to go on was how Hollywood depicted the busy city. So many people chose to live there, so it must hold some appeal, she thought.

She turned around and looked at Joy who had her head leaning against the window with her eyes closed. Rachel chuckled. The plane was so loud that she couldn't imagine anyone taking a nap on the short forty-five minute trip, especially when such a mind-blowing landscape appeared in all its glorious finery.

Rachel appreciated how much of a trooper that Joy had been this morning. Despite coming in at a late hour, she was ready to go when Rachel came by to pick her up. Not only was she ready, but Rachel sensed that she was eager to go on this journey if it meant ensuring that Lara got her just desserts.

She laughed to herself, thinking about the first time she'd heard that expression. She was ten years old and wondered why getting your just desserts was a bad thing, because she loved dessert. Her mom patiently explained the archaic expression desserts was a derivative of deserve and not her favorite tasty sweet.

As the floatplane landed, Rachel retrieved her phone so that she would be ready to send a quick text message. This would be the final droplet in their Chinese torture scheme before tracking Sophia and Lara down to finally confront her on her deception.

Once the pilot placed the bags on the dock, Rachel shot Joy an evil grin. "God, I wish I had a camera pointed at Lara in about ten seconds. I'd love to see her expression when she peeks at my text message."

"I don't suppose it would work to send a text to Sophia and have her discreetly use her phone to tape this historical moment," Joy quipped.

"I wonder how she's doing? It won't be long now. I don't envy what she had to endure last night—knowing what a conniving, two-timing skank Lara is," Rachel remarked.

"If I know Sophia, she found a way to avoid that bitch."

Rachel pushed the button to open her text message app and thumbed in the final jab.

Hey, babe. Landed in Victoria. That was our change in plans. Took Monday off. Heading to the Empress. Call me and I'll fill you in.

"Done. Now we have to hightail it to the hotel. If Sophia is successful and was able to get her to high tea and keep her there, we'll end the torture. If not, I can think up several new ways to yank her chain as long as Sophia is able to feed us updated information on their whereabouts. Lara might try to whisk her away to their room and keep her there, but that won't fly too long. It would seem odd not to enjoy the city, especially since Sophia has never been to Victoria."

"I'd vote for more torture, but then Sophia would have to endure further pain and I don't want that for her," Joy explained.

"Agreed. I'd rather get to the Empress and end the game." Rachel frowned. "Do you think we should have just confronted her right away? I feel bad now."

"No. We all agreed to make her squirm a little. Besides, we needed more time to get all the legal mumbo jumbo squared away. Sophia will be fine. You can cheer her up when we all finally intersect with one another."

"We can cheer her up. It will be our job to get her to loosen up and enjoy a vacation in a beautiful city," Rachel declared.

Rachel felt the buzz from her phone and looked down. Lara was calling. She decided to ignore the call for now. "Oh darn, cell reception is so persnickety here in Victoria."

"Is that Lara?" Joy asked.

"Oh yeah, the rat is calling and most likely looking for a way to abandon ship."

Rachel felt another buzz in her hand, looked down, smiled, and retrieved the text message from Sophia.

Direct hit. She's in the bathroom now. Hopefully puking her guts out, but probably trying to devise an exit strategy. Hurry.

"Come on, oh faithful side kick, we have to hurry if we want to catch them." Rachel began running toward the enormous hotel covered in lush green ivy.

"You should have told me to wear running shoes, not high heels," Joy grumbled as she hastened to catch up.

†

Sophia walked into the elegant Empress Hotel and marveled at its old world charm. She insisted that they check in and then immediately return for afternoon tea which was served in the lobby until four.

As she sat across from Lara in the elegant wing backed chair, she looked around the room and marveled at the antique furniture, rich tapestries, and hand carved tables. She'd read that this British, time honored tradition, brought to Victoria had served famed royalty, celebrities, and other various dignitaries. However, this wasn't what impressed Sophia. What she enjoyed was the warmth of the place. A sense of peace and relaxation permeated her body despite the angst of the past few days.

Sophia looked directly at Lara when she heard the buzz of her phone. "Go ahead. I know you want to look. I'm enjoying the ambiance, so if you need to take a quick call, I don't mind."

"It's a text message, just let me read it and if it's urgent I promise I'll deal with it quickly. I won't even leave the table," Lara promised.

Sophia nodded and watched carefully as her wife read the message.

Lara turned white and shoved the phone in her pocket.

"Lara. Are you all right? Bad news?" Sophia asked.

"No, no. I do feel a little queasy. Maybe I have a delayed response to the flight. If you'll excuse me for a moment, I need to visit the washroom. I'm sure it's nothing."

"Do you need me to come with you?" Sophia tried desperately not to smirk while she asked the question.

"No. You stay here and order a nice calming tea for me. Peppermint is supposed to settle a person's stomach." Lara abruptly rose and marched in the direction of the public restroom.

It was now or never. Sophia sent a quick text to Rachel, and prayed that they had arrived and were on their way. She didn't know how much longer she could stomach playing the adoring wife.

†

Lara considered her options as she paced back and forth in the washroom. Victoria was a big city and the chances of them running into one another were slim— especially if she kept Sophia in the room most of the time—at least until Monday.

She could call Rachel, get a general idea of their plans, and then arrange to visit the various tourist activities located in the opposite direction of where Joy and Rachel might be.

The most pressing issue at this moment was her need to speed up afternoon tea. Lara supposed that her reaction to the text and feigning illness provided her with the perfect excuse to retire to their room for a short while. She figured she still had a few minutes since she'd just received the text and they still needed to check into the hotel before making their way around and possibly deciding to have afternoon tea.

Lara stopped pacing and threw her shoulders back. She could do this. After all, she was the owner of a billion dollar company. This was just a small wrinkle that required her special Lara iron. She was hot and ready to smooth it all out.

When she dialed Rachel's cell phone and wasn't able to connect with her, it was Lara's undoing. "Where the fuck are you, Rachel? You just texted me and now you aren't answering!" Lara shouted in the empty bathroom.

Lara's cool collected manner was unraveling. She would have to find time a little later to contact Rachel and discover her plans for the weekend. One of the things she loved about Rachel was her spontaneity. Unfortunately, this did not work in her favor. She needed to find a way to stay a step ahead and that would be challenging given Rachel's propensity to change her plans at the last minute. She'd have to make frequent calls to her wife to get the most updated information on their plans.

Lara walked briskly back to the table where Sophia sat facing the water view. Steam rose from the two cups sitting innocently on the table awaiting her return.

Sophia looked up. "How are you feeling? It was an unusual request, but they were able to track down some peppermint tea. I don't think too many people order that particular flavor. I got the feeling it was an insult to the queen."

"I'm sorry, darling, but would you mind terribly if we went back to our room. I'm not feeling better. Perhaps a short nap will help and then I'll be ready to go again. I'll make reservations for afternoon tea tomorrow. Okay?" Lara asked.

Sophia glanced out the window and Lara got the distinct impression she was looking for something. "Are you sure you don't want to sit down for a minute and have some tea? It might settle your stomach and then we can head back to the room."

Lara's forehead wrinkled as her displeasure snuck into her expression. "I don't think the tea will do the trick. I really think I need to lie down for just a little bit if you don't mind. You can stay and finish your tea if you wish."

"No, No, that's all right. I'll come with you. Let me get the waiter so that we can pay him."

Lara pulled two hundred dollar bills from her purse and laid it on the table. "That should more than cover the bill."

Lara had the uncomfortable feeling that Sophia was using deliberate delay tactics. She watched as Sophia slowly rose from her chair. When Sophia's eyes rested on a location over Lara's shoulder and a smile spread on her face, Lara turned around to see what caught her wife's attention.

Lara turned around and suddenly all the small clues shifted into place. Now she understood Rachel's odd behavior before she left for Rosario and all the change of travel plans that Rachel kept feeding her. The sudden realization that the trio had played her the past two days was like a neon sign in front of her face. Lara locked eyes with a smirking Rachel and a scowling Joy.

"Hello, Lara. Fancy meeting you here. Did your business in New York take a sudden turn in the opposite direction? If I had known, we could have shared a cab or something," Rachel snapped.

The exhaustion of maintaining her deception finally caught up with Lara as she crumpled into the chair with her head in her hands. She absently ran her fingers through her hair in a last minute attempt to massage her brain into coming up with a solution, but it was no use trying to salvage anything at this point. She recognized defeat. The bitter pill they forced her to swallow sat heavily in her stomach.

Lara lifted her head to meet Rachel's cold blue eyes. "I'm sure you have a pretty speech prepared. Get on with it. I'd like to know exactly what I'll be dealing with." She looked at Sophia. "If it's any consolation—I'm sorry. I couldn't choose. I loved you both too much. I know you don't understand. How could you? I'm not even sure I understand, but I swear it is possible to be deeply in love with two different women."

Lara thought she saw Sophia's eyes soften to her confession, but Rachel's eyes held the steel glint of pure hatred. She honestly had not intended to hurt either of them and she was genuinely sorry it had come to this. The cool ice in her veins melted as she noticed Sophia's eyes well up with unshed tears. She imagined the past few days had been pure hell on her.

Lara reached out to touch Sophia. She meant to comfort her, but Sophia slapped her hand away. "No, you don't get to comfort me and make it all better. You lost that right when you married Rachel."

Lara cringed when Rachel walked to Sophia and embraced her as her tears finally found a final destination in the fabric of Rachel's shirt.

Joy stomped to her and slapped Lara across the face. "If I didn't think that Sophia needed me more by her side than in jail right now, I'd shoot you."

"I guess I deserved that," Lara stated.

Lara directed her attention to her two wives. A small part of her thought that maybe she could still salvage something. As she pondered her dilemma, she realized that in a forced choice, Sophia would rise to the top. Rachel was fun and exciting, but she had to admit to herself that Sophia would always be the one for her. She had loved Rachel, but Sophia was her one true love. This realization hit her hard.

"I fucked up. I know that now. Sophia, can we please talk about this? Without an audience."

Lara glanced at Rachel.

"Rachel, I'm sorry I know this is callous of me, but Sophia is legally my wife and although I care about you, I've realized I need to repair my relationship with my wife. I don't know of a gracious way to end our relationship. This is very awkward for everyone, but if I can just have a few minutes alone with Sophia," Lara pleaded.

"Are you fucking kidding me?" Rachel still had her arm draped on Sophia. "Sophia, I'll do whatever you want, but please tell me you are not about to listen to this piece of shit. I have all the papers here in my pack."

"Don't you dare listen to one word that comes out of her mendacious mouth. She's like a politician. How do you know she's lying? Her lips are moving. I'll slap some sense into you myself if you give her one second of your precious time," Joy exclaimed.

Sophia slipped from beneath Rachel's embrace and stood up. "We might have had a chance if you hadn't married Rachel. I would have forgiven an affair and tried to work through the trust issues in counseling. You don't get to simply apologize and receive a blank slate. I want a divorce and if you fight me on anything, I'll have your ass in jail faster than you can call your lawyer. You do realize that bigamy is a felony in both states. Feel free to look at the papers that our attorneys have drawn up and take them to your fancy lawyer to review, but we will only make this offer once. Fight either one of us on this and I swear neither of us will stop until we see you behind bars. If you agree to all of the terms, you can continue to rebuild your business without the threat of jail time hanging over your head."

Rachel opened her pack and removed four sets of legal papers. She handed the documents to Lara. "Divorce papers for Sophia, financial settlement that I deemed appropriate for my pain and suffering, a separate financial settlement for Sophia's pain and suffering, and a rather large donation to Seattle Children's Hospital. We left you more than you deserve. You should be able to rebuild some of the wealth within a few years' time. Knowing you and your propensity to work twenty-four seven, you'll probably rebuild your financial dynasty in less than five years."

Lara took the papers and resisted fighting back. She couldn't risk provoking Rachel. Sophia might allow some leeway, but Rachel never would. She could see that in her cold eyes. Lara knew that she'd obliterated any ounce of love that Rachel once felt for her. It was time to graciously accept this setback. She would give Sophia some time while she considered her next move. Sophia might be a bit more malleable if she let some of the hurt subside. She'd give her a month to lick her wounds and then perhaps she would be open to counseling and a reconciliation.

"I can see those wheels turning in your delirious mind. Sophia is going to spend a few weeks with Joy and me, so I would advise you not to make any attempt to contact her. I swear, Lara, you will be sorry you ever crossed my path if you ever contact either of us again. You can take that threat to the bank," Rachel declared.

Rachel zipped up her backpack, slung it back over her shoulders, stood up, and wrapped her arm around Sophia. Lara heard her whisper in Sophia's ear. "Damn that was hot when you told her about the felony bigamy laws."

"What about the execution of these papers? I'm going to have to connect with both of you on that," Lara pronounced.

"No, you won't. Contact our attorneys if you have any questions. Everything from here on out can be settled through them. I mean it, Lara—don't contact either of us. I think we're done here." Rachel turned around, leading Sophia out of the beautiful parlor. The steam from the tea no longer existed, but Lara could almost feel the steam from Rachel.

Joy cast upon Lara one final angry glare before following her best friend.

Lara wasn't accustomed to losing. Although this was a particularly challenging problem, every problem inevitably had a solution. She always did like the line, *tomorrow is another day*, from *Gone with the Wind*. That was so much better than, *it isn't over until the fat lady sings.*

Chapter Nineteen

Sophia felt comforted by Rachel's arm casually draped on her shoulder. It was endearing to her that Rachel felt the need to protect her. At least that's what it felt like to Sophia. At first, she stumbled when Lara made her emotional outburst. She sensed that Lara was genuine in her confession and ultimate awakening, but it was too late and she'd been proud of herself for making that clear. A small part of her feared that if Joy and Rachel had not been there to lend moral support she might have crumbled and given Lara another chance. That would have been a monumental error. She knew that, but the heart hears what it wants to hear. You can't just turn off your feelings like a spigot—especially if you've been married to someone for nearly ten years.

Joy was pulling her luggage behind her and scrunched up her face. "Okay, now that we've disposed of that unpleasantness, can we please check into our rooms? I'm about done dragging around my suitcase."

"I'm not sure we can check in this early. That's what you get for packing so much. I always pack light, just in case I have to lug my pack around for a while. I got used to that when I traveled around Europe. I learned how to roll my clothes, leaving plenty of room in my backpack for gifts and trinkets. Do you need me to drag your luggage around until we can check in, princess?" Rachel teased.

"Nope, I don't need you to carry my books, unless it means something. Like maybe we'll start going steady with all the side benefits. Of course I will expect sex, if that's the case," Joy quipped.

Rachel shook her head and chuckled.

"We were able to check in early, so I'm sure you can as well. Oh shit, my luggage is back in the room. It's not even been ten minutes and already I'm going to have to face Lara again." Sophia teared up. "Damn, I can't do it. I feel like buying new everything and leaving my case exactly where it is, but then I'll have to give up my favorite shirt. Fuck it." Sophia slapped her hand against her mouth. "I can't believe I'm conversing like an ignorant sailor. I promise I am college educated, but those cuss words keep sneaking out of my mouth."

"You can swear all you want. We won't think any less of you. Will we, Joy?"

"Hell, no. Cuss away, girlfriend. It's about time you let your hair down a little," Joy assured her. "I have no problem storming the fort and liberating your luggage. Just give me ten minutes and I'll have your bags for you."

Joy glanced back in Lara's direction. "Don't turn around, but Lara is still in the parlor on her cell phone. You two just head out into the sunshine and wait for me. Okay?"

Sophia hugged her friend. "Thank you. I don't know what I would do without you and Rachel to help me through this little Greek tragedy."

Sophia had forgotten her sunglasses and as they made their way outside on their way to the Inner Harbor, she squinted in the sunshine. The bright light felt like an omen to her. After two days in hell, she looked up and welcomed the warm sun on her face.

Rachel pulled her pack off her back and placed it next to one of the outside benches near the rose garden. She led Sophia to the bench and motioned for her to sit. When Sophia sat down, Rachel pulled her close and let Sophia rest her head on her shoulder.

"How are you doing? Really?" Rachel asked.

The tenderness that accompanied her question caused Sophia to shed more tears. She felt more care and concern from this near stranger than she had ever felt with her wife of almost ten years. Sophia marveled at the combination of strength and gentleness that exuded from every one of Rachel's pores.

"How is it possible that you are doing so well and I'm falling apart every other minute? I can't seem to get my emotions under control."

"Anger is fueling me at this particular moment," Rachel replied. "Plus, I've always felt the need to make things right. Middle child syndrome, I suppose. I have a hard time not playing the peacemaker or protector, whichever the situation calls for. At this point, that's what is monopolizing my attention. I don't have time to feel sadness. Not many people have seen me cry. You should feel honored, you are one of the few that was privileged enough to have a ring side seat at my mini breakdown when we were at the park."

"Well, maybe when I'm done emoting all over you, I can give you the support you need to come out the other side of this fucked up tunnel," Sophia offered.

"I might take you up on that, but only when I'm sure you've made it to the other side and can help lead me to the promised land." Rachel brushed her hand through Sophia's hair and caressed her back as Sophia continued to lay her head on Rachel's shoulder.

Sophia relaxed against Rachel. She guessed that they both needed to spend a few moments with their own thoughts without speaking. The silence was like a salve and Sophia appreciated how she could just sit without talking.

†

When a half an hour had passed, Sophia began to worry that Lara was somehow starting to weave another web of lies that would put her at an advantage.

Finally, she heard the distinctive clip clop of Joy's heels and turned around to see her grinning best friend.

"I checked us in and deposited my bag and yours. Mighty mouse can lug around her back pack since she's such an accomplished traveler." Joy bowed in front of Rachel.

"No problems?" Rachel asked.

"Oh, I wouldn't say that, but Lara is no match for me. Let's just say we came to an understanding and she won't be looking to me as an ally."

"Mighty mouse, huh?" Rachel laughed.

"Before I forget, I meant to tell you that I am so fucking proud of you, hon," Joy exclaimed. "I saw you waver for a second and then the powerful, independent Sophia I know came out to play. I couldn't have done it better. When you threatened to have her ass thrown in jail, I wanted to bump fists like those silly boys do all the time."

"You do know this isn't over for Lara?" Rachel asked.

"Hey, don't rain on my parade. It's a sunny day. I have a second wind thanks to you, Rachel. I'll be ready to deal with Lara when she crawls out from under whatever rock she slithers until she's ready to make her move. Don't worry, by then I'm sure I will have enough inner strength on my own to deal with her in the same fashion as today," Sophia assured them.

"Just so you know, I had the lawyers specify how she is allowed to get her shit from your place in New York and the house here in Seattle. She is supposed to make those arrangements through the attorneys and she has the next three weeks to accomplish that. During that time, we will be vacationing together and having ourselves a grand old time, compliments of her generous funding. In case she doesn't sign right away, I liberated some of her funds and established individual accounts in our names," Rachel explained.

Sophia looked at Rachel with renewed appreciation. In her eyes, Rachel was a pillar of strength when she felt lacking. Rachel talked a good game, but she suspected that Rachel had her own emotions to deal with. She was grateful that for now while she was still a little shaky, Rachel appeared to stuff those feelings deep inside in order to take charge and attend to all the little details.

"Thank you for thinking of absolutely everything. I was going to crawl back to New York with my tail between my legs and stay at a hotel until Lara cleared out the penthouse, but you know I deserve this vacation and screw it, I'm taking it," Sophia declared.

"That's the spirit. Let the debauchery begin," Joy exclaimed.

"Well, I'm not sure I thought of everything. I'm sure Lara is pondering her next move right now. It's what makes her such a great chess player. She always has several contingencies that I'm sure I haven't thought about, but thanks for your faith in me. I agree with Joy, let the debauchery begin. Let's see what kind of trouble three single, hot, women can get into. Have you noticed how delightfully gorgeous these Canadian women are? They have that wholesome natural beauty thing going for them. I say we check out all the artists performing on Inner Harbor, then order some mojito's at Milestones. They make some of the best mixed drinks in Victoria, or so I've heard," Rachel suggested.

Sophia watched as the corners of Rachel's lips lifted. Her brilliant smile caused Sophia to surmise that the sunshine was no match for how dazzling Rachel looked when her genuine smile came through.

Sophia couldn't help thinking that it was no wonder Lara fell for Rachel. She would be an easy person to fall in love with. Her lighthearted spirit and adventurous style was probably something that many women would gravitate to. Combine that with her stunning looks and her genuine down to earth aura, she could almost understand how she was irresistible to Lara. Maybe if she'd met her first, she might have been the one who started an affair. Sophia shook her head to toss the thought away. Who was she kidding? Sophia was not the type to ever stray from a committed relationship. She would move heaven and earth to work things out before she would ever cheat on her wife or girlfriend. She never had and she never would.

Sophia wondered why she wasn't prepared to do everything possible to fix her marriage. Some things were just too broken to mend. It would never be the same and she knew it. She also knew that even if she was able to temporarily repair the relationship through counseling, it was only a matter of time before it would break again. No, she was better off not trying, even though it went against everything she fundamentally believed in. You didn't just walk away from a marriage that you vowed for better or worse, but that was exactly what she was planning to do. She stopped in her tracks as this realization hit her.

Rachel turned around and looked at Sophia. A quizzical expression formed in her eyes and mouth.

Joy frowned. "Oh, no, you don't. I know you and you think that you should try to work this out with Lara because after all you did make a vow to her. Nope, she broke that contract when she broke the law and married Rachel. Lara is a felony bigamist. Don't you dare think that you owe it to her to stick with her no matter what. There is a limit to reasonable loyalty. I won't let you go back to her. Back me up here, Rachel."

Rachel looked at Sophia with such sadness in her eyes—it broke Sophia's heart. "I can't tell you what to do and I won't judge, but I really wish you wouldn't consider that a viable option. I don't know you all that well, but what I do know is that you are better than that. She doesn't deserve someone like you and she sure as hell does not deserve your forgiveness," Rachel implored.

"Sorry, it was just a temporary moment of weakness. I guess I let some empathy slip through as I realized how hard it would be to resist falling in love with you," Sophia confessed.

Rachel's eyes went wide and Sophia turned bright red as she realized what she just confessed to.

"I can tell you without reservation that if I was married to you, there is not one single person on this planet, including Angelia Jolie—who I think is totally smoking—that would turn my head enough to risk losing you," Rachel responded.

Sophia was taken aback at the raw honesty she saw in Rachel's eyes. She realized at that very moment that she wanted Rachel in her life. Rachel could be a good friend, a lifelong friend like Joy. She needed more people like Rachel in her life.

Sophia linked arms with Joy and Rachel and they started walking to the Inner Harbor.

†

Victoria's Inner Harbor was a menagerie of street performers, local artists, boats, seagulls, and tourists from across the world. The moon shaped walkway stretched around the harbor, giving a home to the eclectic people camping alongside the greenery, flowers, and vivid blue backdrop from the water splashing against the docks.

Rachel had a warm feeling as she felt Sophia's arm link with her own. As they strolled along the Inner Harbor, she noticed a large crowd encircling two street performers. She tugged Sophia along when she saw the fire torches tossed above the crowd.

"Now this looks interesting and dangerous," Rachel shouted over the *oohs* and *aahs* from the swarm of people enraptured by the performance.

"Who wants to help me out here? I need a brave assistant," one of the artists called out.

Rachel nudged Sophia through the crowd and pointed at her head when they were close enough for the performers to notice.

"Well, hello, pretty lady. We like our assistants to be beautiful. It attracts more attention. Come on over here. We won't bite and we'll try not to set you on fire, mostly because you're already hot enough."

Rachel laughed when she noticed Sophia looking around to see who they were talking to. She whispered in Sophia's ear. "They're talking to you, silly."

Sophia shook her head, "Uh uh, I think I've been burned enough lately, don't you?"

Rachel noticed the smirk on Sophia's face and was glad she could joke about her recent heartbreak.

Joy stepped forward. "Well, hell, if little Ms. Wussy Pants won't step up, I will. Whatcha need, boys?"

"See that big bucket of torches?"

"You mean the unlit ones? That doesn't seem too exciting for you to juggle. Where'd the fire go?" Joy asked.

"So you like to play with fire, do you?" the young man with shaggy blond hair asked. He wiggled his eyebrows. "My kind of woman."

"Barking up the wrong tree, Shaggy, but I do like to play with fire, you're just not quite my type."

"Too young for you?" he asked.

"Nope. Too male for me," Joy answered. "But if you have a sister?"

"Beautiful lesbians—just my luck. Oh well, you can still play with my fire." The blond man took a lighter out of his board shorts and tossed it to Joy. "All you gotta do it light those torches and keep handing them to me until the bucket is empty."

"I can handle that," Joy answered.

Rachel grabbed Sophia's hand and pulled her forward. "This I gotta see." When Sophia made no move to release her hand, Rachel continued to hold it as they enjoyed a front row view of the show.

Joy looked at Rachel and Sophia, and her grin was positively wicked. She winked. As she proceeded to light the torches and hand them to the blond performer, an artful game of juggling began. Rachel suspected that Joy was trying her darndest to light the torches quickly in an attempt to make it more challenging and interesting for the audience, but the performers were far too skilled for her to trip them up.

The artists started singing. "Love is a burning thing, it makes a fiery ring...."

Rachel burst out laughing. "Oh, that is freaking hilarious, *Ring of Fire* by Johnny Cash."

Sophia began singing along. "Bound by wild desire, I fell into a ring of fire."

Rachel looked at Sophia with renewed interest. She noted Sophia's sultry singing voice and thought she would follow that voice anywhere. "Damn, girl, you can sing."

The performers waved her on between catching their burning torches. As they turned, performing their increasingly intricate tosses into the air, around their backs, and under their legs, they continued to sing *Ring of Fire*.

The audience began clapping and cheering. Johnny Cash's song never sounded so good with the blend of voices.

Sophia stopped singing and giggled. "Gosh, that feels good. It's how I paid for college," she explained.

The street performers juggled the twenty torches for another couple of minutes and then one by one extinguished each torch.

Joy playfully pulled the young man's hat off his head and began working the crowd to get them to toss their money into the hat.

Rachel retrieved a hundred dollar bill and tossed it into the collection. Sophia pulled a wad of bills from her purse and added to the bounty. Joy gave the hat loaded with bills back to the young man and handed him a twenty.

"What are you doing for, say, the next three or four months?" the young performer asked. "We could use a third person who can actually sing. It gives our act a little more oompf."

Sophia waved him away. "I'm on vacation. Good luck, boys."

"Have a nice day, Shaggy and friend." Joy waved, too, as they walked away.

"Well, that was fun. We should go find a karaoke bar. This woman's got game. I just discovered her hidden talent. Anything else up that beautiful sleeve of yours?" Rachel asked.

Rachel took Sophia's hand again and led her to the rows of artists showing their handmade wares.

"Ooh, these miniature watercolors are incredible," Sophia exclaimed. "I want something to remember this afternoon. It's been the bright spot of my day and I want to focus on the positive. How much?" she asked.

"Twenty-five," the vendor answered.

Sophia smiled broadly. "I'll take it. The fish are so colorful. I love it."

Rachel marveled at the childlike wonder in Sophia's eyes and it was one more thing that endeared her to Sophia.

There was no sense in denying that she was attracted to Sophia, but to act on that would be the very worst thing possible. Friends. They needed to stay friends—nothing more. They could share their common experience. Maybe form a support group for victims of lesbian bigamists. Rachel wondered if such a thing existed and couldn't help finding humor at the absurdity of such thoughts.

She would enjoy spending time with her new friends, but Sophia was strictly off-limits. Frankly, at this point, every woman was strictly off-limits. She desperately needed a break from love and sex. No good would come from either one until she had time to get a handle on her anger.

Joy shook Rachel from her musings. "Okay, now that we've tasted the requisite Inner Harbor festivities—I say it's time for some alcohol therapy. Mojitos, bellinis, margaritas, pick your poison, because they have them all at Milestones. At least that's what I heard from a scrumptious Canadian woman that I ran across while I was checking us in. I think the food there is decent as well. We can have an early dinner."

"Do they have an outside patio? The day is too nice to spend locked inside a restaurant. I'd like to spent a few more minutes just relaxing and looking out at the water, if it's okay. A room packed with merry tourists might be a bit too much for me just yet. Can we ease into it, please?" Sophia pleaded.

"I wouldn't mind a few minutes of peace myself, but not here where all the crowds are gathered. I'm sure if we walk along the water we can find something a little less occupied," Rachel suggested.

"Oh, all right, but can we hit the gay bar tonight?" Joy asked.

Rachel looked at Sophia for confirmation that she was up for an evening out on the town.

Sophia nodded.

"I'll bet you know exactly where to go," Rachel remarked.

"Yes, indeed, I do," Joy answered.

Chapter Twenty

Lara's worst nightmare had just come true. She'd lost the love of her life and the woman she simply could not resist. This was unacceptable. She'd been surprised at Rachel's protectiveness toward Sophia. She'd expected Joy to be a pit-bull, but Rachel's reaction was a bit alarming. None of them were stupid women, that's what she most admired about them, and they'd certainly boxed her into a very neat corner.

She needed time to think. For now, she would let them think they'd won. She would sign all the papers without a fuss and then she would consider her options. She saw Sophia soften for a moment and that was her glimmer of hope. Certainly, her error was not fatal.

Lara honestly believed she would be able to get Sophia back. She would have to give up Rachel, but she could do that.

I guess it's true you never know what you have until you lose it, she mused.

Lara would allow Sophia her three-week vacation and give her time to process everything before she made a move. It made sense to Lara that Sophia would want to discuss what they needed to do about Fawn. After all, Fawn was as much her cat as Sophia's. They didn't have children, but it was common knowledge that lesbians considered their pets their furbabies. Joint custody arrangements were not unheard of. This would be her foot in the door. A medical emergency might even cause Sophia to come home early and she could work on her reconciliation plan. In reality, she did love the little furball. She loved them both, Fawn and Espresso. Lara had a surprising soft spot for her cats.

As Lara was pondering her dilemma, her phone rang. She was surprised to see who was calling her.

"Hello, Chelsea. Yes, it is a surprise to hear from you so soon. I wasn't expecting you to call. No, not an inconvenient time, but I'm not in Seattle at the moment. No, Victoria. Yes in British Columbia. Actually, I am available because my plans were suddenly altered. Yes, I can meet you for lunch tomorrow. I look forward to seeing you as well. All right, I'll meet you there."

Lara sighed. Would this day of surprises never end?

Lara pressed the buttons on her phone to connect with her travel agent. There was no sense in staying in Victoria now that everything had blown up in her face. She'd make sure her travel advisor got a large bonus this year. Perhaps she would be able to get some work done tonight. She grimaced as she remembered scanning through the legal papers delivered today. She would need to work hard to restore her fortune.

"Hey, sorry to bother you again, but I need a flight out as soon as possible. Yes, that should work. Can you also arrange for the limo to pick me up and bring me back to my house? No, Rachel will not be traveling back with me at this time. Thanks, you're a lifesaver."

At least when she got home, Espresso would be happy to see her. Cuddling up to her cat was not what she expected to be doing this evening, but Lara was flexible and adaptable. She would turn this lemon into lemonade.

†

Paparazzi Nightclub was the only gay club in Victoria. Throughout the years, other clubs had come and gone and now, this was the only game in town— the new rage for the LGBT crowd. Men seemed to outnumber the women by two to one and as a result, the music was the typical loud bass found in mostly gay clubs. The term butt-fucking music was often used to describe the repetitive beat that seemed to go on forever with each new song. While the songs may have been contemporary, none of them were familiar to Sophia. The songs just ran together, one right after another, and Sophia could barely tell them apart.

The mirrored ball rotating above their heads was so cliché for a dance club. The cheesiness of the club struck a funny bone with Sophia.

Immediately upon their arrival, Sophia made a beeline to the bar to obtain drinks for everyone. She wanted to hide in a corner and drink wine. After chugging her first glass, Rachel sauntered to the bar to get her another. The loud music made it difficult to have a conversation so Sophia was content to do a little people watching from her tiny real estate against the wall.

She was sipping her second glass of wine because she needed to slow down or she'd end up intoxicated and that was not something she wanted to do. Joy was on the dance floor with a beautiful Canadian woman. Tara or Tanya, Sophia couldn't remember her name, but did register her as the woman who suggested Milestones for drinks and Paparazzi as the only gay nightclub in Victoria.

Rachel had asked her to dance a few times, but Sophia felt self-conscious, so she just shook her head and made some excuse. Sophia couldn't remember the last time she'd danced in a nightclub. She would have danced to a slower song if Rachel had asked, but she worried that Rachel might somehow notice her growing attraction. Fortunately, the club didn't play too many slow songs.

Joy danced to her with her latest infatuation and pulled both Rachel and Sophia to the dance floor. "Come on, you two. Dance with us. You'd think you were at a funeral instead of a club."

Sophia let the music flow through her and began to sway as she watched Rachel move her body to the music. Rachel was an exceptional dancer as she let the beat dictate her moves and her raw sexual energy burst out onto the dance floor.

Rachel's movements put Sophia in a trance. She began to match the sway of her hips until she felt like she was in a syncopated rhythm with Rachel.

"Damn. You two look hot together. How long have you been together?" Tanya or Tara asked.

Rachel laughed.

Sophia stuttered a response. "Um… we're… not… uh… together."

"Coulda fooled me. You should be then, you know, together."

The music slowed down and before Sophia could exit the dance floor, Rachel pulled her close and whispered in her ear. "Don't leave. Please, dance with me."

Sophia nodded and let her body melt into Rachel's. She could feel Rachel's breasts meet her own and a shiver traveled up her back. She let her arms wrap around Rachel's neck as Rachel's hands traveled across her back, coming to a rest just above her ass. A few more inches and she would feel the caress on her behind. She worked hard to keep herself in shape and this was the one part of her body she felt good about.

This is innocent—one slow dance won't kill me, even if I am drawn to her, she reasoned.

It felt so good to have Rachel's arms wrapped around her that Sophia failed to notice the change in the music beat.

Joy tapped her shoulder and smirked. "Um, I think slow dance time is over."

Sophia pulled away. "Sorry."

"Don't be." Rachel's eyes bore into Sophia and ignited a fire inside. The words to *Ring of Fire*, burned inside Sophia's head.

Sophia needed to distance herself from Rachel. All of a sudden all the flashing lights, the aroma of sweat and arousal mixed with Rachel's unique sweet smell of lavender and lemongrass, and the loud bass sounds, were too much for Sophia. She ran for the bathroom in an attempt to escape her growing feelings.

Sophia looked in the mirror and grimaced at the dark circles under her eyes. It was no wonder, she thought, that Lara ran to the arms of beautiful, lively, Rachel. "Shit, shit, shit, why couldn't I have politely declined that dance?"

Sophia jumped when she heard Rachel answer. "It doesn't have to mean anything more than a dance if you don't want it to. I know it's far too early and our emotions are too raw to be thinking of anything else for either of us. I would never do anything to make you feel uncomfortable.

I'm sorry. We can go now if you want. I'll walk back to the hotel with you."

"I didn't hear you come in." Sophia sighed. "I need a friend right now, more than a lover, but God, I wish that weren't the case."

"I can be a good friend, Sophia. I want to be a good friend. Timing is everything and unfortunately, the timing sucks. You do know that if either of us had met before Lara, things might have been very different."

"Maybe, or this might be a result of our shared drama. We can relate to one another's pain like no-one else. That's probably what's causing this," Sophia waved her hand between herself and Rachel. "This, between the two of us."

Rachel laughed. "It's good to know that I'm not the only one with totally inappropriate thoughts and feelings."

"Come on, *friend*. Let's blow this popsicle stand. There is far too much stimuli out there for me. We should let Joy know we're leaving but I'm sure she won't mind." Sophia grabbed Rachel's hand and pulled her from the washroom back into the grinding couples, free flowing alcohol, and madness of the club. She told herself that sometimes friends held hands.

†

As far as anyone else knew, Joy was a happy go lucky club dweller, but she hadn't missed Sophia's abrupt departure after her slow dance with Rachel. Joy's shrewd eyes did not miss how much her best friend seemed to gravitate toward the stunning woman.

Joy wasn't sure whether this was a good or bad thing for her friend, but she decided she better stop all her innocent flirtations with Rachel just in case something positive developed between the two. She could see them together. They would be good for one another.

She watched them emerge from the bathroom with their hands linked together and smiled. Perhaps the timing sucked, but all was fair in love and war. Timing be damned. If they were meant to be, then so be it. Joy vowed to stand by Sophia, no matter what.

As Rachel and Sophia approached Joy, she separated from her pseudo date. "Why do I get the feeling that the two of you are about to abandon me?"

"I'm sure you'll survive. You seem to have your own personal tour guide slash companion to keep you company if you decide to stay a little longer, but I'm beat and Rachel offered to walk back with me. You don't mind if we take off now, do you?" Sophia asked.

What the hell. Joy decided a little nudge in the right direction wouldn't hurt. She whispered in Rachel's ear. "Hey, I don't suppose you would mind switching rooms with me tonight. I got you a room with a king bed and Sophia and I were supposed to share the double queen room. Tanya's lived here her whole life and never stayed at the Empress. I thought maybe I could take her back to my room, but Sophia might cramp my style a little."

Rachel chuckled. "Give me your key and you can keep mine. Knock yourself out. I'm glad someone is riding the love train tonight."

"You're all right, Rachel. Just so you know—you have my blessing to pursue anything you want tonight. Sophia's the best. I love her like a sister, so you best treat her with respect if you do decide to jump on *that* love train. Be warned, though, I'll cut off your clit if you hurt her."

"You don't have to worry. We're just friends. So you can stop your match-making. Rest assured if it ever did develop into something more, I wouldn't be stupid enough to fuck it up like Lara."

"Hey, no whispering behind my back. I'll get a complex," Sophia interjected.

Joy pulled the hotel key cards from her purse and handed one to Sophia and the other to Rachel. She grinned at Sophia. "See you later, little Miss Boring."

"Hey don't stay up all night. Remember we have our whale watching excursion tomorrow and I wouldn't want you to fall out of the boat and become a tasty meal for the Orcas," Rachel reminded Joy.

"I'm too full of piss and vinegar for them to want me," Joy countered.

Rachel chuckled and waved at Joy, then took Sophia's hand and led her out of the club.

†

On the way back to the hotel, the full moon reflected off the glass like surface of the water. The hustle and bustle that had been a prominent part of the Inner Harbor was invisible now. Rachel and Sophia were the only two people walking along the path. The stillness of the night only served to emphasize the strong beating of Rachel's heart as they meandered back to their final destination for the evening.

Rachel hadn't shared with Sophia the sleeping arrangements. She wondered if it would be an issue and didn't want to disturb the peacefulness of the night.

If this had been a date, Rachel would already have swept Sophia in her arms and kissed her against the backdrop of the moon as it shimmered just for them. The temptation to do just that was overwhelming and it took every ounce of Rachel's willpower to stop herself from tasting Sophia's sweet lips.

As they reached the entrance of the Empress, Rachel broke the silence. "I hope you won't be angry, but I agreed to switch rooms with Joy so she can entertain Tanya this evening. I'll be your roomy for tonight, unless you'd prefer to have your own room."

Sophia turned to look at Rachel and captured her eyes. "I'll probably regret this, but no, I don't want my own room. I'd rather not be alone tonight. If it won't make you too uncomfortable, I'd really like you to stay with me."

Rachel hadn't released Sophia's hand as they waited for the elevator that would take them to their floor.

"No, it won't make me uncomfortable at all. Oh crap, I just thought of something. My backpack is in the other room. You wouldn't happen to have an extra t-shirt I can borrow. I'll call down to the lobby to get a toothbrush and toothpaste, but unless you don't mind seeing me prance around naked, I'll need to borrow something to sleep in."

Sophia blushed and bit her lip. "Um, I normally sleep in the nude, but I did pack a couple of t-shirts. They aren't terribly long and I suspect they won't even cover your ass."

Rachel shrugged. "Well, I guess they will just have to do." She wiggled her eyebrows. "Will they cover your ass?"

"Unfortunately, no."

"Why unfortunately? I would say my luck just changed," Rachel teased.

"Friends. Remember?"

"Oh yeah, that's right. You'll have to forgive me. The older I get, the more forgetful I become."

Sophia bumped her shoulder. "Be good."

"I'm always good," Rachel answered.

"Stop flirting."

Rachel released Sophia's hand and held up her palms. "Okay, okay. I'll try to be good, but flirting with you is just so easy."

Rachel pulled the key card from her back pocket and slipped it into the door. She smiled as she took in the solid mahogany furniture representative of the hotel's old world charm. The suite came complete with a fireplace, sitting area, and small kitchen. The room was nearly as cozy as her home in Seattle. The only evidence that this was a hotel room was the prominent queen beds side by side separated by a healthy amount of space.

The distance wasn't going to be wide enough to keep Rachel from thinking about the beautiful woman who would occupy the bed beside her. So close, yet so far away.

Sophia blushed. "Uh, I think I'll change into my t-shirt and brush my teeth first if you don't mind." She rummaged through her expensive suitcase and tossed a bright blue shirt to Rachel.

Rachel smiled as she caught the shirt and noted that the royal blue color was one of her favorites. Women had often told her that the color looked especially nice on her and brought out her deep blue eyes.

After Sophia shut the door to the expansive bathroom with the enormous soaking tub, Rachel called up room service to have toothpaste and a toothbrush delivered. She pulled down her jeans and carefully folded them on the wingback chair. She'd only managed to get her shirt halfway undone when Sophia emerged from the washroom. The snug t-shirt clung to Sophia's body like a second skin and Rachel could see her nipples protruding as if they were standing at attention awaiting her orders. Rachel couldn't help herself as she stared at Sophia who seemed to be equally engrossed in her own state of mid-dress.

Rachel was glad she had selected the matching lilac purple bra and panties set. It wasn't her usual attire, but for some reason she'd decided to bring the surprise gift that Lara had bought her the previous year.

Rachel turned around and slipped off her bra and shirt, quickly pulling the blue t-shirt over her head.

The knock on the door startled them and Rachel chuckled when she noticed that neither of them was dressed and ready to answer the door. She walked into the bathroom and grabbed both robes hanging on the hooks by the tub. She smiled at Sophia. "Unless you want to give the poor bellhop a very exciting show, I suggest you put on this robe."

Sophia laughed and pointed at Rachel. "Ditto."

Rachel threw the robe on her half-dressed body, glanced over her shoulder to make sure Sophia had her own robe on, and opened the door.

A young woman offered Rachel the needed toiletries.

Rachel stuck them in the large pocket on the robe and held up her finger. "Wait one second." She dug into her jeans and found a ten dollar bill, handing it to the woman who thanked her and stepped away from the door as Rachel closed it behind her.

Sophia blinked once and then seemed to snap out of her trancelike state. "The bathroom's all yours."

As Sophia started to walk toward one of the beds, Rachel passed her on her way to the washroom. In an effort to avoid colliding with Sophia she stepped to the right just as Sophia was stepping to the left.

"Oh, sorry. Excuse me." Sophia touched Rachel's arm and started to move away.

"Now, Sophia, you're not angling for another slow dance, are you?" Rachel asked.

Sophia shrugged and looked directly into Rachel's eyes.

Rachel had never wanted to kiss someone so badly in all her life. She placed both hands on each side of Sophia and looked at her plump lips just begging to be kissed. "I shouldn't do this. We shouldn't do this. Shit, you're still legally married."

"Stop talking." Sophia brought their lips together.

Rachel felt the silky softness of Sophia's mouth and returned the kiss. Her tongue tentatively sought entrance into Sophia's mouth. The kiss had a level of sensuousness that she'd never experienced before. Normally, Rachel kissed a woman with passion and energy. She felt her body relax into Sophia's as her hands untied the robe and caressed Sophia's back.

When Sophia pushed away, she felt the loss instantly.

"I wanted to do that all night long, but as much as my body tells me I want to make love to you, I just can't. You're right, we shouldn't be doing this. I'm sorry. Can we re-wind? I don't want to fuck up what will probably turn into a great friendship."

"Okay." Rachel hesitated before continuing. "But...I reserve the right to change the rules somewhere down the line."

"That's a fair compromise."

Sophia scrubbed her hand on her face. "Would it be completely inappropriate if I asked you to sleep with me to just have someone to hold me?"

"Not exactly inappropriate, but you are testing my willpower," Rachel answered.

"Forget I asked that. Stupid idea."

"Wait. I was kidding. I am an adult and believe I can control myself enough. I could use a little innocent cuddling myself."

Sophia raised her eyebrow. "Somehow innocent doesn't really spring to mind when I think of you."

"Perhaps, but there is always time to learn something new."

Chapter Twenty-one

The small puffs of clouds dotted the sky, but at least it wasn't overcast or raining. Joy reveled in their good fortune, as the weather seemed to attempt to put its best foot forward as if they were in the beginning stages of a new relationship. All she'd ever heard about Seattle and the surrounding area was that it always rained. They'd only experienced the famous Seattle drizzle once since they'd arrived.

Joy walked gingerly to the small shop where they were about to receive instructions on their whale watching adventure. She'd almost talked Sophia into letting her sleep in this morning, but for whatever reason, Sophia insisted she come along with them. When she learned they would all have to don those disgusting orange jumpsuits she was even more inclined to pass on the quest for whales. Joy could sense that something had happened between Sophia and Rachel and she was dying to corner her best friend to find out. She hoped they just did the nasty and got it out of the way. All the sexual tension was spilling over and since Tanya had to return to work today, she had no one to play with.

"All right let's get this party started. Lead the way, Rachel. I can't wait to put on the fashionable orange jumpsuits," Sophia quipped.

"And I can't wait to see Joy here slip her lithe body into a suit some guy has sweated in all afternoon."

"The suits aren't cleaned between use?" Joy remarked, aghast at the implication.

"This I can't wait to see. Who's got the popcorn? You can't buy better entertainment than this." Rachel burst into laughter.

"Why do I think you selected this particular company at my expense? I noted in the brochures at the desk there were other options for a whale watching excursion, including large covered boats. I thought you were my friend," Joy grumbled.

"Where's the fun in that?"

"Come on, Joy. We'll all stink together. It can be a bonding experience," Sophia added good-naturedly.

"I think I would rather bond in another manner. A bellini, mojito or margarita would be my preference." Joy turned her wrist. "Oh look, it's cocktail hour in New York."

"I did instruct you to dress casually." Rachel grinned.

"Sophia, you promised we would take a luxury excursion, not this tiny raft with these smelly things," Joy pouted.

"These inflatables guarantee the best views. Those other boats are too high on the water. Don't be such a pansy," Rachel taunted.

†

Joy crinkled her nose as she stepped her legs into the sweat soaked jumpsuit. There was a decidedly unpleasant odor in all of the suits. As the tallest member of the group, she was obliged to wear a man's jumpsuit. Hers was by far the most rancid.

Rachel grinned as she retrieved her smart phone and snapped a quick picture. "We should get a picture of us all together in our high fashion garments." Rachel handed the phone to the tour guide and asked. "You don't mind do you?"

"Not at all." He pressed the button and handed the phone back to Rachel.

Rachel looked quickly at the screen and turned the phone around so the others could view the picture. "Not bad. I'll send you all a text with the picture attached."

The three women found seats in the front of the boat with Rachel's insistence that it was the best spot. Eleven other men and women joined the tour and they sped out of the bay. The radio crackled to life as the tour guide obtained the location of a pod surfacing on the west side of the island. Excitement built as everyone prepared for the first sighting. The boat slowed and the tour guide cut the motor. "We are required to stay at least one hundred yards from the whales. We let them come to us. They should be coming up on the starboard side soon. Get your cameras ready."

"Holy shit. Look, that whale is just sticking his head up and starting a staring contest with me. It's kind of creepy but fascinating at the same time." Rachel reached for her phone to try to get a good picture.

"That's called spy-hopping. Orcas can be very curious and scientists have noted that they actually do this more often around tour boats. They want to check us out as much as we want to check them out. Spy-hopping is kind of like treading water. They can actually do this for several minutes. We'll give them a few minutes to migrate farther north of us and then we can head out again."

"I've lived here all my life and have seen Orcas before, but this is the first time I've seen one spy-hop," Rachel proclaimed.

"I must admit it was worth it to put on this noxious suit. The Orcas are truly magnificent creatures," Joy conceded.

"Thank you, Rachel, for arranging this trip. I'm really glad I decided to stay and spend this time in Victoria," Sophia said.

"Hey look, there's a little seal playing in the waves. I know it's not as exciting as the Orcas but I think they're adorable. Kind of like a hairless puppy. They're fun to watch." Rachel pointed to the playful sea creature.

"The fishermen don't always appreciate the seals when they steal salmon but the tourists sure love them," the guide explained.

The bright yellow inflatable raft raced back to the dock as the tourists leaned back and enjoyed their journey across the crystal blue waters. Everyone was smiling as they crawled out of the boat.

"All right, I believe a mojito is calling my name right now. Ladies, shall we head to Milestones? I told Tanya we would meet her there after our whale watching excursion," Joy clarified.

Joy noted the smile on her best friend's face and the equally enamored look that Rachel was tossing quite naturally in Sophia's direction. They looked good together. Joy wondered what would transpire after the three week vacation was done. Rachel seemed entrenched in the Pacific Northwest. She grew up here and wasn't likely to make a drastic change. Sophia was a New York gal and Joy didn't want to lose her best friend to the unruly West. She had to admit that Sophia was more relaxed here in Victoria than she'd ever witnessed and the Pacific Northwest seemed to suit her more than the somewhat pretentious East coast. Right now, it was time for fun and games with Tanya and alcohol—she would ponder this dilemma later on.

Chapter Twenty-two

Two long weeks had passed since the big reveal and Lara was starting to get restless waiting until she gave Sophia enough time to settle. Chelsea had turned out a surprising distraction. She'd spend a few days and nights in the pleasure of her company and wondered how it was possible that Chelsea bent her own rules regarding intimate liaisons with women within her circle of business.

Discussing things and straightening out exactly what was the nature of their relationship was not high on Chelsea's list of priorities when they came together. Lara chuckled at the phrase *came together* because that is exactly what they'd spent most of their time doing in-between extraordinary lunches and dinners. Chelsea had good taste in food, music, wine, and women. If Lara really thought long and hard about it, Chelsea was a far better match than Sophia, but Sophia was who she wanted. Lara always did enjoy a challenge and now that Sophia had left her, the gauntlet was down.

As Lara was pondering her next move, Fawn wove through her legs and reminded her of the first idea she'd had which was to call Sophia because she was concerned about Fawn and the fact that he seemed listless lately. She could later explain that he wasn't sick, but probably just missing Sophia. It would be her foot in the door. Sophia loved that cat and might even fly home early.

Her cell phone startled her and when she looked at the caller ID, she frowned. Talking to Sophia's acerbic older sister was not something she was looking forward to, but if she ever hoped to win Sophia back, she had to play nice in the sandbox. She decided to risk getting verbally bitch slapped by Marie.

"Marie, to what do I owe the pleasure of this call? No, I'm sorry Sophia is not here. Why haven't you tried her on her cell phone? Oh, God, I am so sorry to hear that. I'll be right there and I'll try to get ahold of Sophia as well. She probably turned off her phone for some reason. Um, she isn't in New York right now. No, she hasn't talked to you and explained everything? Don't worry, Marie, I'll make sure she gets the first flight out as soon as we connect. I'll personally make the arrangements. You're welcome. In the meantime, I will be there in a jiffy."

Lara ended her call with Marie. She knew she shouldn't be happy by this recent turn of events, but she couldn't help thinking that maybe fate was intervening by giving her another opportunity with Sophia. Certainly, Sophia would need her strength as she dealt with her father's serious heart attack. Lara always knew that Dominick was one tiny step away from another heart attack. Everyone had been telling him for years he needed to lose weight and get more exercise. But since he'd lost his wife to cancer, he was slowly eating himself into an early grave. Moving to New York to be closer to his daughters had helped him with his profound grief, but not enough to overcome his addiction to food. Lara loved the tough old goat and prayed that this was her ticket back in. Dominick always favored her and he would at least be in her corner.

She quickly pressed the contact for Sophia and left a voice message. "Sophia, I know I promised not to contact you, but things have changed and no matter what, I still love you and want to be there for you. Please call as soon as you get this message, or call Marie, she's been trying to get ahold of you. This is an emergency and I need you to call me back as soon as you can."

Lara followed up her voice message with a text.

Call me. I've taken care of everything. Your flight leaves in two hours. If you don't make that flight, I've arranged for the next flight out. I'll pick you up at the airport.

†

It had been a glorious day and as they paddled back to shore. Rachel got a mischievous grin on her face as she dipped her paddle into the water and scooped up the fifty-five degree shock of liquid sending it in Sophia's direction.

"Ha ha, very funny. Are you trying to tell me I need a shower after kayaking?" Sophia asked.

"Nope, you were looking so hot there I thought I'd cool you off. The sporty lesbian look definitely suits you as much as the sultry Italian," Rachel responded.

"Well then, maybe I should return the favor because you look like you also need cooling off." Sophia used her paddle to splash Rachel back.

Rachel laughed as she emerged from her kayak and handed it off to the dock worker. She extended her hand to Sophia to assist her as she wiggled out of her Kayak. The kayak began to rotate from side to side as Sophia tried to step on to the dock. The movement of the kayak and Sophia's inexperience was just enough to flip the boat, sending both Sophia and Rachel into the freezing cold waters of the bay.

Rachel's head popped up first as she scrambled onto the dock.

Sophia sputtered as she surfaced next. Rachel quickly stretched her hand out and clasped Sophia's arm as she pulled her up onto the dock.

They were both rolling on the dock in a fit of laughter.

"Well, I suppose that's one way to cool off. Holy hell, that water is cold," Sophia noted.

Rachel looked at Sophia and noticed how her t-shirt clung nicely to her body. The cold water brought her nipples to the surface, protruding despite the two layers of clothing beneath.

"Cold is an understatement." Rachel pointed to Sophia. "Your breasts are saying hello to me. Friendly little buggers, aren't they."

Sophia playfully slapped her hand away. "Well, I'd say they were successful, because yours are waving back." Sophia grinned.

Rachel looked down at her chest. "Well, of course they are. I've taught them manners, you know. They would never ignore a friendly wave from a beautiful woman."

The female dock worker was laughing. "You two are hilarious. You make a beautiful couple. Did you have fun today?"

Sophia turned to the young woman and crossed her arms. "We had a blast. I didn't realize how big the Orcas were until one of them surfaced right in front of us. I barely managed not to flood the kayak with my pee."

"I wasn't as lucky. You may want to clean my kayak out more thoroughly," Rachel quipped.

Sophia giggled when the dock worker frowned.

"Oh, just kidding. Sorry, I have a sick sense of humor," Rachel clarified.

The woman smiled. "Have a great day, ladies."

Sophia shivered and her teeth began chattering uncontrollably.

Rachel slipped her arm around Sophia and pulled her close. "Come on, we better get back to the hotel to change before we both die of hypothermia. Unless you want to continue showing off how friendly our breasts are with one another. It's a good thing the weather is nice again today."

"I am definitely chilled to the bone. It's a darn good thing I didn't take my phone with me today. Having never experienced kayaking before, I do believe that was the right call to make. Joy is going to be so jealous she missed all the excitement."

Rachel picked up her pace and they walked quickly in silence back to the hotel. In a less than a week, Sophia would return to New York and this sobering thought saddened Rachel. They'd both danced around their attraction the past few weeks, never crossing the line again, but continuing the light flirtation. Although the line was invisible, it was always there.

Joy continued to spend time with Tanya, probably a record for her, Rachel thought. This gave Rachel more alone time with Sophia. The more time she spent with her, the more enamored she was with this incredible woman. She'd learned about Sophia's family, her work, and her life. She knew she'd fallen in love, but needed to keep that fact to herself. If friendship was all she would ever have with Sophia, well, then it had to be enough.

Not wanting to cause her any more distress, Rachel mustered up every ounce of willpower and kept her embraces to not much more than a friendship and just shy of enthusiastic lovers. It was damn near killing her not to take Sophia in her arms and make mad passionate love with her.

They reached the suite that had evolved into their joint dwelling for the past few days and Rachel pulled the Ziploc bag from her pocket and retrieved the key card. She waved Sophia into the room. "You go ahead and shower first. I clearly have more adipose tissue than you to keep me warm."

"Oookay. Th..thanks," Sophia chattered.

Rachel pulled off her wet shirt and bra and laid them out carefully on the drying rack she found in the closet. After removing her wet shorts, she pulled on a new pair of khaki shorts and soft t-shirt without bothering with a bra.

Rachel looked at the desk when Sophia's phone buzzed. She resisted the urge to walk to the phone and see who was calling when two minutes later it buzzed again. By the time Sophia emerged from the shower and walked into the common area toweling her hair, her phone had whirred on the desk six times.

"Your phone's been buzzing up a storm. I didn't look, but I admit I wanted to. If it's Lara, you should ignore it. I'm not sure why all of a sudden she's calling when she has so far adhered to our wishes."

Sophia stopped drying her hair and looked up at Rachel. "Do you think you can wait to take a shower while I check my phone? I think I might need encouragement to delete a few messages, or maybe to come up with a few witty retorts that will stop all the nonsense."

"Of course. If you want I'd be happy to respond to the big shithead," Rachel answered.

Sophia picked up the phone and grimaced. "Shit, there are twenty messages and a lot of them are from my sister." She put the phone to her ear and listened.

As Rachel watched Sophia's facial expression, she knew something was wrong. She crossed the room quickly and placed her hand on Sophia's arm as a measure of support.

Sophia pressed a button and began talking. "God, Marie, I'm sorry I was out kayaking and didn't want to dump my phone in the bay. I don't want to get into that right now. I'm in Victoria. Of course she did. No, everything's fine, I'll call her to get the details and be in New York as soon as possible. Yes, I love you too. I promise I'll bring you up to speed when I get there. No, it's okay, she loves him too, and I won't let our shit get in the middle of her relationship with him, especially right now. Bye."

Rachel was dying to ask what was going on, but waited patiently for Sophia to finish her calls. Clearly something big was happening.

Sophia pushed the phone again to connect another call. "I suppose I should thank you for making all the arrangements. Obviously, I didn't make the first flight, so I need the details for the next one. Don't, just don't. I won't ask you to leave, but don't think for one minute this changes anything between us. That's not necessary, I can get a limo to the hospital." Sophia sighed. "All right, fine. I'll see you at the airport. Thanks."

Sophia tossed her phone on the bed and several tears tracked down her cheeks. "My father's had a heart attack. He's in critical care. My flight leaves in less than two hours. I need to hurry."

"I'm coming with. I might not get on the same flight, but even if I have to take a later flight, I'll be there with you," Rachel declared.

"Oh, Rachel, that's incredibly sweet of you to offer, but it's not necessary. I've already disrupted your life enough."

"Sophia, I want to do this and you've been the best disruption in my whole life. Friends support one another during the tough times. It's what we do." Rachel pulled Sophia into her arms and let her rest her head on her shoulders and cry for a few minutes. She kissed her hair and soothed her as best she could.

"I've got to keep moving if I'm going to hope to catch that flight. You can do me a huge favor and bring Joy up to speed on what's happened. Tell her that Dad is at New York Presbyterian. I feel a little better knowing he's at one of the best cardiac hospitals in the nation. At least I have that to alleviate some of my fears."

"Look, I know that I'm just someone who's only known you a few short weeks, but I really care about you, Sophia, and I want to be there to help in any way I can. Besides, I work in a hospital and I know what to ask the caregivers. I can help make sure your dad gets the best care possible. Please let me do this for you—be there for you," Rachel implored.

Sophia kissed Rachel on the lips. It was a chaste kiss, but Rachel was pleased.

"I'm not going to argue with you. I'll just gracefully accept your support. Thank you."

"Is there anything you need in the meantime? Can I arrange transportation to Victoria International for you?" Rachel asked.

"No, Lara has taken care of everything. There should be a limo waiting right outside the Empress. I just need to pack my bags and get dressed."

"Go on, get dressed. I'll pack your bags, as long as you don't mind things in slight disarray."

Sophia caressed Rachel's cheek and kissed her again. "I am so blessed that you came into my life." She turned and walked back into the bathroom after snatching a pair of jeans, shirt, socks, underwear, and bra from the drawers.

Rachel touched her cheek, feeling the burn of Sophia's soft caress and then launched into action making her own flight arrangements as she put her phone on speaker and began to pack Sophia's clothes and personal items with loving precision, placing them into her suitcase. She figured that whatever Sophia left behind, Joy could grab and bring back with her.

By the time Sophia came out, everything was packed and ready to go.

"I got a ticket for the next flight out. I'll meet you at the hospital. I went ahead and arranged for another ticket for Joy. I figured she would want to return to New York as well." Rachel picked up Sophia's suitcase. "Come on, let's get you to your waiting limo."

Both women were quiet as they walked out of the Empress and headed straight for the transportation that Lara had arranged. Rachel didn't want to bring up the elephant that now stood directly in their path. She knew that Lara would be waiting for Sophia when the plane touched down in New York.

The driver opened the door to the back seat and before Sophia slid into the soft leather, she turned around to face Rachel. Rachel knew this wouldn't be the last time she ever saw Sophia, but she couldn't help feeling that something that never had a chance to develop and flourish was already ending. If there weren't so damn many complications, she would have told her that she was falling in love. Sophia didn't need any more shit piled on top of her, so she just told her she was right behind her and would be there for her to lend whatever support she needed.

Sophia smiled and Rachel pulled her close hugging her goodbye and kissing her one final time before she slid into the back of the limousine. The kiss was brief, but for Rachel it was a kiss filled with love—the love she knew she wasn't able to admit to. She thought she saw a flash of emotion in Sophia's chocolate brown eyes, but she turned away quickly without comment.

As the limo pulled away from the curb, Rachel watched until the car rounded the corner and disappeared from sight.

Rachel jogged back to the suite, mentally preparing herself for all the things she needed to attend to in order for her to make this trip. Work was the least of her worries, but she did owe it to her boss to let him know she would be out for an undetermined period. She worried that Lara would worm her way back into Sophia's heart, and that made her unreasonably concerned and if she was honest with herself— jealous. She knew that she didn't really have any business traipsing off to New York to be by Sophia's side in her hour of need, but she just couldn't help herself. It felt natural to do this and Rachel always trusted her instinct. Too bad there was some faulty wiring in her head when she'd met Lara. Lust must have taken control and dampened her impeccable instincts. However, she did want to thank the universe for sending Lara her way, because if that hadn't occurred she never would have met Sophia. Perhaps the universe knew things she did not.

Joy seemed disappointed that she would be leaving early, but Rachel thought she hid it well. Rachel surmised that Joy was not one to abandon her best friend, regardless of her growing affection for Tanya. She'd confessed to both Sophia and Rachel that she really clicked with Tanya and for the first time in her life, she was considering an actual relationship—even though it would require fancy logistics due to the distance between their respective homes.

Chapter Twenty-three

Sophia looked out the window and watched as the large fat droplets pounded against the window. She thought how ironic that, after leaving the Pacific Northwest and escaping the constant rain and drizzle that normally overpowered the area, she was returning to her home state and the pouring rain was her reception. Rain and Lara—she wasn't looking forward to either one.

Sophia let all the other passengers exit the plane before standing up, stretching, and retrieving her bag from the overhead bin. It was larger than the allotted dimensions, but since she was in first class, they'd discreetly looked the other way.

She walked into the busy airport and headed to the general area where travelers met their loved ones. Lara was waiting on the other side of the security area and Sophia suspected that her smile was genuine. The divorce wasn't final yet and her heart raced at the anxiety of seeing her wife after two stress free weeks of vacation. She marveled at how well she'd managed to ignore her complicated life during that time with Joy and Rachel. Every time she'd started to go down melancholy road, one of them distracted her enough to take away the pain.

Sophia didn't know why she'd allowed Lara to embrace her, stroke her hair, and murmur soothing words. She guessed that old habits died long, hard, deaths. In her head, she flashed to Rachel and her embrace right before she got into the limo that would take her back to the real world.

"It's okay, honey. I'm right here and I've been making sure that the very best doctors are tending to your father's care. I didn't tell him or Marie anything about what is going on with us because honestly I hope that after the urgency of the situation passes, that maybe we'll have a chance to talk."

Sophia was too tired and too numb to respond, so she just nodded. She hoped this wasn't a signal that she was willing to work things out, because she wasn't. She just wanted to get to the hospital and make sure her dad would survive this latest scare and then she would worry about her disastrous and confusing love life.

"If you have other bags to retrieve, I can send someone to get them so that we can go directly to the hospital right now without waiting at baggage claim," Lara offered.

Lara's small acts of kindness reminded Sophia of how attentive she could be. Lara was a first class bitch most of the time, but she had her moments. Sophia didn't even suspect her motives. Underneath Lara's cool exterior, she somehow knew that Lara actually cared and was genuinely worried about her father's health.

"I appreciate you taking care of that. Thank you. Let's just get to the hospital. I can't really think about anything else right now."

"Of course. The limo is just outside. They've been on hold for the past half hour just awaiting your arrival." Lara linked her arm in Sophia's and Sophia did not resist the connection.

On the way to the hospital, Lara held Sophia's hand, maintaining a gentle caress the whole way there. It felt natural to sit next to Lara while she held her hand and offered her unconditional support. At least Sophia thought it was unconditional.

Her vow to hold strong and not let Lara manipulate the situation began to wane as she sensed that Lara was genuinely sorry and contrite about her infidelity. Sophia began to wonder if it was possible to salvage her marriage and try again. Would she honestly be able to trust Lara? And what about her growing affection for Rachel? If she were truly honest with herself, she would admit that she wished Rachel were sitting next to her right now and not Lara. Rachel's pull was difficult to resist. Maybe she ought to be a little more understanding now that she knew what it felt like to travel in Rachel's orbit. She was honest when she'd blurted out how she could understand how difficult it might be to resist falling in love with Rachel. The sudden realization hit her like a Mack truck. That is exactly what had happened. She hadn't been able to resist falling in love with Rachel. She was in love and she didn't have the foggiest idea what she should do about that. She'd have to put those thoughts on the back burner for right now because she had much more important things to attend to.

†

The sterile white room with the space age equipment prominently displayed would have been enough to scare anyone. When Sophia looked down on her father's frail body attached to more wires than she remembered from the past heart attack, her own heart began to beat rapidly and it felt like she was having a mini heart attack of her own.

Her father's gray pallor was not encouraging.

Sophia's gasp caused his milky brown eyes to open.

Marie was holding their father's hand. She looked up, catching Sophia's eye.

"Hey, little sis. Glad you could join the party. I wanted it in a different location, but Dad insisted this place is the cat's meow. I'd ask you why the hell you were in Victoria without Lara, but we have bigger fish to fry right now. You didn't happen to bring any salmon back? I heard they are the best in the Pacific Northwest. We could start frying them up right now," Marie quipped.

"I see you haven't lost your sense of humor, Marie. I am so sorry I missed all your calls. How is he?" Sophia asked.

"I'm right here, you know. You could ask me and not your overbearing sister," Dominick answered.

"Okay, Dad, how are you feeling?" Sophia asked.

"A helluva lot better than before. You know, when they were rolling me in and the nurse ripped open my shirt to place those little shock thingies on my chest, she said, *Now that I have you like this, it will be easier to have my way with you.* Can you imagine me not taking that bait? But, I was in far too much pain to answer. This morning she came in and when I remembered her, I told her that I was ready for her to have her way now. She told me she wasn't in the mood anymore. Damn, another missed opportunity. How are you, girl? Give your old man a kiss."

Sophia raised her eyebrow and leaned forward to kiss her father on the cheek. "You look like shit, Dad. You best save your energy for when a serious offer comes your way."

Dominick winked. "What makes you think it wasn't a serious offer. Even flat on my back, I got game."

"Where the hell do you get those sayings? You got game? You're seventy, Dad, not seventeen." Marie chuckled.

"Your son is a wonderful wingman. We cruise chicks all the time. He's definitely got game and I think he learned it all from me."

Marie stuck her fingers in her ears. "La, la, la, la. I did not hear that and I definitely do not want to hear the details of your little jaunts with my son. Just remember that those so called *chicks* you both are cruising are someone's daughters. You need to teach my son to respect women."

"I guess you got a point there. How's my beautiful daughter-in-law doing? Lara, come give an old man some excitement and give me a kiss."

"You old goat. I married your daughter, not you, and you are definitely the wrong sex to use your charms on me." Lara kissed Dominick on the forehead.

"I am surrounded by gorgeous women. I can die happy now with my three beautiful daughters by my side." A tear snuck out of Dominick's eye. "I miss your mother so much, I would welcome passing on to the next dimension. I wish I believed in heaven because then I would be with her again, but I can only hope for my sorrow to end."

"Sshh, Dad, Mom would not want to hear you talk like that. You promised on Mom's memory to lose weight and all I've seen you do is eat yourself into a third heart attack," Sophia chastised.

Dominick started to cry. "You girls are all I have to live for. Your mom was too young to die."

"So are you. I haven't even had my kids yet. They'll need to know their grandfather," Sophia stated.

Dominick perked up. "You pregnant?"

"No, but I could be in the future, so toughen up and get well. I'll need a built in babysitter for when I'm too

Annette Mori

exhausted to care about anything else but getting away for the weekend," Sophia answered.

Sophia noted the quizzical expression on Lara's face. She hadn't realized until that very moment that she wasn't willing to wait much longer. She'd have a baby on her own without a partner's support if she had to. She smiled to herself when she recalled the conversation with Rachel about children. Rachel got a glint in her eye when Sophia mentioned her desire to have kids. Rachel had confessed to her that she'd already starting researching sperm banks and adoptions, but hadn't yet broached the subject with Lara. It seems that Rachel was on the same page as her regarding the desire to have kids. She suspected that Lara wasn't even in the same book.

"Well, get to it. I may die in the next year and I want to see another grandbaby pop out."

"Oh, that would be my primary reason for getting pregnant—making sure you have another grandbaby to play with," Sophia remarked wryly.

Dominick's eyes blinked a few times and it was evident that this small amount of banter had tired him.

"Dad, why don't you close your eyes? None of us is going anywhere. You can take a nap while Sophia, Lara, and I catch up on all the gossip in our lives," Marie directed.

"Ok, honey, but you all should go get something to eat while I nap. They can't screw up breakfast too much in here. I'm sure with all these wires hanging off every part of my body, except my penis, they'll know the minute my condition changes."

"God, Dad, do you have to make everything sound so—oh, I don't know, crass?" Marie exclaimed.

"What? They do have wires connected to everything. I'm surprised they didn't put one on my dick to tell them when I get an erection."

Sophia laughed. "It's no use, Marie. He's just trying to get a rise out of you and it worked."

At one point in Sophia's life, she had been very angry with her father. When she found her mother crying in the master bedroom about her dad's infidelity, it took a long time to separate Dominick the man, from Dominick the father. He'd always been a good father, but a terrible husband. Sophia suspected his infidelity stemmed from his deep-seated insecurity, or maybe he had a sex addiction like former president Bill Clinton, regardless, she learned that he was human. It was a devastating lesson to learn at the age of nine. She'd forgiven her father the indiscretions of youth, especially after he cleaned up his act.

Sophia wondered if this was ever something she could forgive in her own spouse. Monogamy was an important value to her, especially given the experiences she witnessed firsthand with her own parents. Her mother had forgiven her father and they went on to have a good marriage so she knew it was possible to mend those fragile threads of trust, but could she do it with her own marriage and achieve the same results? It was all so confusing to her at this moment.

†

Once they reached the cafeteria in the hospital, and had gotten an unappealing meal, they sat down in the uncomfortable chairs, Marie narrowed her eyes at her younger sister and asked, "Okay you two, spill. What the hell is going on?"

Lara had decided that if she had any chance of getting Sophia back, she needed to take full responsibility and hope that Sophia would give her a second chance like Sophia's mother had decided when she discovered Dominick's indiscretions.

"I made a monumental mistake that has forced me to do some serious soul-searching. Sophia filed for divorce and while I don't like it, I most definitely deserve it."

Marie raised her eyebrow. "So, what exactly is this monumental mistake?"

"I married another woman," Lara stated.

"Excuse me, but did you say you married another woman? What'd you do, adopt a new religion?" Marie barked. "I feel like I just got transported into one of those cheesy made for TV lifetime movies with an interesting lesbian twist. You can't be serious. Sophia, what the hell is going on?"

"I wish this was a joke. Lara met a woman named Rachel and married her two years ago. When I went to Seattle to surprise Lara for her fortieth birthday, instead of surprising Lara with a wonderful party, I met the other woman. I have to admit, Rachel is an easy person to fall in love with."

Lara didn't know what to make of the comment Sophia just made, it sounded like Sophia was enamored with Rachel. She'd noticed the overprotectiveness that Rachel showed toward Sophia and wondered if they'd become close during the preceding two weeks. She hadn't known exactly where Sophia had been, only that she had stayed away.

"Where exactly have you been the past couple of weeks?" Lara asked.

"Not that it's any of your damn business, but we stayed in Victoria. I got the time off and I wasn't about to squander my vacation brooding about our failed marriage," Sophia snapped.

"Who exactly is we?" Lara controlled the irritation in her voice, as she suspected she already knew the answer was Joy, Rachel, and Sophia.

"Rachel was kind enough to join us. Apparently, she was due a ton of vacation and decided she could use a break, as well. I know you think that we spent the whole time grousing about you, but to be honest, your name rarely came up. So relax, we did not spend the whole time lamenting our poor decisions."

"I don't give two shits about what is going on with you two right now because our concentration has to be on Dad. Lara, you seriously need some therapy if you thought you would get away with bigamy. Sophia, you need your own brand of counseling for hanging out with the other woman. Don't let your lesbian drama get in the way of focusing on Dad. I expect you to play the loving couple until Dad is well again and then by all means Sophia, scratch her fucking eyes out." Marie pushed out her chair and the wood scratching against the floor made a loud noise as she stomped out of the cafeteria.

Lara pinched the bridge of her nose. Nothing was going the way she wanted it to. "God, Sophia, I'm sorry. I have no right to question you and act like the jealous spouse. I sincerely hope you've been having a good time. You deserve it. Please don't make any decisions just yet. I've been trying to figure my shit out and I do want a chance to redeem myself—to make us work again. I'll sell the Seattle office. Hell, I'll sell the New York office and spend all my time doting on you if it means you'll give me another chance. I never stopped loving you. I'll do anything to repair what I've torn apart with my selfishness." Lara grabbed Sophia's hand and looked into her eyes. She was relieved when Sophia did not pull away.

"Lara, I never expected you to give up your life or spend one hundred percent of your time with me, but it would have been nice not to be apart so much. I don't know. I can't make any decisions right now. I need time and I need to focus on Dad." Sophia pushed away the tray of food. "I don't really know why we came down to get food because I'm not hungry."

"I suspect it was more a ploy for Marie to find out what was going on. I'm glad she's focused on your dad right now, because your sister scares the hell out of me."

Sophia laughed. "I know, right? She is scary. I'd like to go back to Dad's room now."

"Of course. Look, I know things are awkward right now, but I think that both of us can be adult enough to stay at the penthouse at least until your dad recovers and then we can decide where to go from there."

"I don't know if that is such a great idea. We can talk about it later," Sophia answered.

†

Joy and Rachel managed to catch a red eye back to New York that would arrive mid-morning.

Rachel was bouncing her knee up and down and squirming in her seat like a five year old needing to go to the bathroom. After multiple cups of coffee, she was jittery and nervous. She began to second-guess her decision to essentially crash Sophia's family emergency. Unsure of the exact nature of her relationship to Sophia, an outsider might question her sanity. Although Rachel tended to act impulsively on occasion, this went far beyond her impetuous nature. Something far more primal was motivating her to stand beside Sophia.

She knew that Lara would be right by her side and the thought that they might get back together was making her physically ill. There was no pretense anymore, Rachel was in love with Sophia and after the emergency with her father was resolved, she planned on declaring her feelings to see where she stood.

"Would you stop wriggling around? You're like a worm on a hook and it isn't at all attractive." Joy opened one eye. "You aren't going to be much help to Sophia if you crash and burn the minute we land in New York. I'll bet you haven't gotten one bit of sleep, which coincidentally, I usually wouldn't give two shits about, but you've kept me awake and that just pisses me off."

"I'm sorry, Joy. I'm worried that Lara will sink her meaty hooks back into Sophia using this tragedy as a springboard."

"Oh shit, I get it now. You've fallen in love with her, haven't you?" Joy asked.

"The timing sucks to confess that to her, huh?"

"You think."

Rachel made the sign of the cross over her heart. "I promise not to say a thing until this whole emergency situation is settled. I'm not even going to deny it. Yes, I love her. God, this whole situation is so fucked up. Her father and sister are probably going to hate me on sight. After all, I am the other woman."

"Oh you got that right. Marie is a real ball buster and her father is full-blooded Italian. He has a special bond with Lara that might save her ass, but you're toast. He will see you as the homewrecker."

"Not helping." Rachel groaned.

"If it's any consolation, I approve. I know this is a bit unconventional, but I think you two are good together. I also think that while Sophia may be confused, she cares for you. She may even think she's in love with you. Hard to say."

"Has she said anything to you?" Rachel asked.

"Even if she had, I wouldn't be breaking her confidence, but I can tell. It's all in the way she looks at you. I knew she was attracted to you from the very first moment she laid eyes on you. Can't say I blame her. As the vacation wore on, I could see something deeper develop between you two. I love Sophia like a sister and if you are the one for her, I won't throw any resistance your way. I might even try to smooth the waters with Papa Dominick. Marie's all hot air. More bark than bite. If she sees what I see—piece of cake. She loves her little sister and is very astute so she'll jump on board if it makes Sophia happy to be with you," Joy explained.

"Thanks, Joy. At least I'll be able to jump those hurdles with your support. I haven't quite figured out the distance issue yet. There are so many obstacles I must be crazy even contemplating a relationship with Sophia. Love definitely makes a person stupid."

"Maybe, but I would give my left tit for that feeling just once in my life."

"What about Tanya?" Rachel asked.

"A lot of fun, but definitely not move worthy. I would never consider moving across the country for her like I suspect you are considering right this minute."

"Guilty. They have hospitals in New York and now that I have a tidy sum from Lara I could take my time finding a position that suits me," Rachel acknowledged.

"You're a refreshing open book, Rachel. No matter the danger, you wear that heart of yours right on your sleeve. I admire that about you. I'm far too guarded for my own good. How about a speck of advice, if you don't mind?"

"Yes, please, I'll take any advice you want to share."

"Give Sophia time to realize her feelings. Don't rush things. She's likely to be confused and if you rush, you'll scare her away," Joy offered.

"You know that will be hard for me because honesty is fundamental to my nature, but that's good advice. Thanks for being in my corner."

†

Sophia felt grungy. It was coming up on nearly twenty-four hours since she'd had a shower. She swore she could feel the grease congealing in her hair. She pulled her hair back in a ponytail and laid her head back in the chair. She could feel Lara's eyes on her. To Lara's credit, she hadn't left her side since picking her up at the airport. Sophia wasn't sure if that was a good or bad thing. Her emotions were all over the map. Her father seemed pleased to have all three of them by his side as he went in and out of consciousness.

The doctor came by with the rest of the interdisciplinary team and explained the treatment plan in detail. The next twenty-four hours were critical to determine if another devastating heart attack might occur. He had explained all the options, including surgery. As with anything in life, there were risks attached to each option. Ultimately, it was her father's choice, but he wanted to know what they thought of each of his options.

"So, Pops, what do you think you'll decide?" Sophia asked.

Dominick smiled. "You haven't called me that in years. I think maybe I'll opt for the angioplasty. That seems to be a more conservative choice with less risk than surgery. I got the impression that it might take care of my issue for now. Quicker recovery time, too."

Sophia nodded. "I think that's a good choice. You need to stop clogging those arteries with all that rich food you eat. Maybe you should move in with me so I can monitor your food intake."

"No, thank you. All I have left is food. Haven't had sex in a while so don't take away my one pleasure in life. I'd rather die happy than deprived of my only vice."

Sophia frowned. "I'm not going to argue with you right now, but just think about it."

"It's not that I don't appreciate you girls visiting and all, but can you stop hovering. Go home and take a shower. I don't want you stinking up the room," Dominick joked.

Lara laughed. "You're an ungrateful old bastard, but you're right. I should take Sophia home to get a few hours rest because I'm sure she hasn't slept in more than twenty-four hours. She can get mean when she's cranky from lack of sleep."

"I can stay with Dad while you get some sleep," Marie offered. "You can take the evening shift tonight."

"Deal," Sophia responded. "Call me if anything changes and I can be back in a flash."

"Go, I got this," Marie answered.

"Come on, honey, I'll take you home and draw up a nice bath for you." Lara draped her arm over Sophia's shoulder and led her out of the room.

†

Rachel shifted the backpack to her other shoulder as she retrieved money from her jeans pocket to give to the limo driver.

Joy grabbed her rolling suitcase and walked quickly to the front of New York Presbyterian.

"Did you find out what room Sophia's father is in?" Rachel asked.

Joy walked up to the information desk. "No, but I bet this beautiful woman can tell us." Joy winked at the tiny woman sitting behind the huge desk. Her wrinkled skin stretched as a wide grin overtook her face.

"Can you tell us what room Dominick…?" Rachel looked over at Joy.

"Torre. Dominick Torre. He's probably in the cardiac care unit," Joy finished.

"Let me see. Ah yes, he's in room two fifteen. Let me give you a map of the hospital so you don't get lost." The old woman, who Rachel assumed was a volunteer, pointed to the map. "See, we're right here and you need to go to here. The elevator is right here."

"It's just like a supermall where they show you on the map how far away you are from where you need to go."

The volunteer smiled and Rachel thought she looked like one of those dried apples they made into dolls. She never did understand the appeal for those kinds of crafts. Whenever she went to the farmer's market, she would shake her head at the number of arts and crafts booths with items that would inevitably make it to some hoarder's home and turn into a big dust magnet. She had a hard enough time finding her keys and wallet—she didn't need more clutter to serve as a hidey-hole for her keys. Lara always used to grouse at her when she failed to use the key hook. That was a habit she would never learn and now it didn't really matter. She could take as much time as she wanted looking for her keys.

When Joy and Rachel reached the room, Joy strode confidently inside, but Rachel hovered just outside when she noticed that there was only one visitor in the room and it wasn't Sophia. The woman sitting next to the bed, holding the distinguished older man's hand was a carbon copy of Sophia—only older. Rachel guessed this was Sophia's older sister, Marie. She looked worried, but smiled when Joy entered.

Rachel stayed just outside the room, not wanting to interject herself into what appeared to be a fond reunion.

"Hey there, trouble. I hear you've been gallivanting around with Sophia," Marie whispered. "I haven't had time to rip Lara a new asshole yet. I assume you've already done that."

Rachel guessed that she didn't want to disturb her father who seemed to be sound asleep in his bed.

Joy turned around and waved her hand. Rachel shook her head and Joy waved again more vigorously.

Rachel timidly entered the room.

"We've been keeping Sophia company in Victoria. This is Rachel, who has become a good friend of Sophia's. Both of us took care of Sophia and sent Lara packing. Rachel arranged for all the legal crap and I was my usual entertaining self. Before you sharpen that acerbic wit of yours and take poor Rachel apart, let me share a few facts. One, she did not know Lara was married and is as much a victim as Sophia. Two, she didn't hesitate to jump on a plane to be with Sophia, and three, Sophia and Rachel have gotten close in the past two weeks and they care for one another."

Marie's eyes got wide. "Please don't tell me you're sleeping with my sister. Geez, you lesbians have more drama than those desperate housewives," she hissed.

"No, we are not sleeping together," Rachel responded.

"Not that you don't want to," Joy whispered.

"Shit, I heard that, Joy. I'm going to reserve my judgement, because at this particular moment—anyone but Lara is my mantra."

"Where are Lara and Sophia? I thought for sure Lara would take this opportunity to sweep in and play knight in shining armor," Joy asked.

"Oh, that she did. She took Sophia home to clean up and get some rest. I told them I would hold down the fort," Marie answered.

Rachel looked up when she heard a weak cough. The same chocolate brown eyes that melted Rachel's heart stared at her from the bed. The terminology, bedroom eyes, danced across her head. She was sure this man was a charmer.

"Well, well, well. What do we have here? Two more beautiful women have come to visit. I know one of you, but I'm afraid I've not had the pleasure of meeting you, my dear." He crooked his finger in a beckoning gesture.

Rachel stepped up to the bedside. "Hello Mr. Torre, I'm Rachel, a good friend of Sophia's." Rachel held out her hand.

Mr. Torre held her hand and kissed it. "Dominick, please call me Dominick. Mr. Torre is far too formal for my future wife."

Rachel laughed. "Sorry, Dominick." Rachel pointed to herself. "One hundred percent lesbian. I don't have an ounce of bi-sexual in me."

"Damn, just my luck. All the good ones are either taken or are lesbians. Hello, Joy. How are you, my dear? Is this your new girlfriend? I have to applaud your taste."

"No, Dominick, she's just a friend." Joy turned and murmured to Marie. "Sophia has a much better shot at the girlfriend status than I do."

"What was that you said?" Dominick inquired.

"Oh, nothing, I'm just being a bitch as always," Joy answered.

"Do you mind if we hang out here for a while before we grab some lunch and then maybe we can come back and wait for Sophia to return?" Rachel asked.

"Of course not, you brighten up this dreary room." Dominick smiled and showed off his perfect white teeth. "Pull up a chair and we can begin a game of strip poker. Marie, you can sit this one out."

"Dad, cut it out. You'll scare Rachel away."

Rachel laughed. "Sophia told me you were quite a character. You rival my grandmother. Too bad she's too old for you because you would make a great couple."

"How much older and is she a looker like you? Maybe she can teach me a few things. I always did like older women. To be honest, I like women of all ages. I'm probably older than I look and as long as your lovely grandmother is older than she looks, we might just make the perfect pair." He winked.

"Don't listen to him. He's more bluster than action." Marie waved her hand in the air.

"Don't be so sure of that, young lady. I still got it with the ladies—I just haven't acted on it since your mom died."

"So, poker anyone? I could use a new pair of shoes cause I plan on taking y'all to the cleaners." Rachel tossed out.

Chapter Twenty-four

Sophia rested her head on the foam pillow connected to the soaking tub as the bubbles of air circulated throughout the water gently massaging her aching muscles. After the three hours of kayaking yesterday and the long flight back to New York, she was exhausted.

Lara had taken control and drew up the bath just the way Sophia liked it. The lavender oil seeped into her pores and began its magical healing. It was her favorite scent and Lara knew that.

Sophia knew it was probably a bad idea to let Lara take care of her, but the mental energy it would take to right the situation was just too much to bear at the moment.

Sophia heard the light rap on the door and hesitated before inviting Lara inside. "Come in."

Lara had seen her naked thousands of times before, but for some reason this felt different.

"I ordered some take out from the bistro. I hope you don't mind, but I suspect you haven't eaten since yesterday when you got the call," Lara suggested.

"No, I don't mind. That was very thoughtful of you. God, the days are all merging together, I don't even know what the date is."

"It's May twenty first," Lara answered.

Sophia smacked her head against the pillow. "Shit, I forgot. I'm sorry, Lara. Happy Birthday. I'm sure you've got better things to do on your birthday than babysit your ex-wife on your fortieth birthday."

Lara sat on the ledge of the tub. "Sophia, there is nowhere else I would rather be. You are still my wife," Lara whispered. She extended her hand and Sophia felt sure that she was about to caress her in their old familiar way before she abruptly pulled back.

Sophia couldn't look at her just yet. She turned away before speaking, "Of course, I will always love you, Lara, but please don't misinterpret anything today. I just cannot promise you that I can forgive and forget enough to give our marriage another try."

"I'm not asking for a promise. I'll settle for you thinking about it a little longer before coming to a final decision," Lara said.

Too exhausted to argue, Sophia answered, "Okay."

"That's more than I could hope for. I'll leave you to your bath. The food will be here shortly."

Sophia felt bad for forgetting Lara's birthday, but things were different now. She had to keep reminding herself that Lara was the one who cheated. She didn't expect perfection. After all everyone has cracks—it's how the light gets inside. However in this instance, there was a big flippin' hole and that light had blinded her. It was time to move on and in the process, begin to sort out her feelings for Rachel.

Sophia closed her eyes for what she thought was only a moment, but when she felt the uncomfortable coolness of the water, she suspected that she'd fallen asleep in the tub. She stood up and grabbed the plush blue towel hanging on the brass hook next to the soaking tub. After toweling her body dry, she wrapped the towel around her hair and covered her body with the soft cotton robe dangling on the other hook. She needed to quickly eat and then try to limit her nap to no more than two hours. She knew Rachel and Joy would be on their way soon and she didn't want Rachel to endure any sort of awkwardness with her father and sister.

†

Marie had offered to get everyone some coffee and left Joy and Rachel alone with Dominick for a few minutes.

"Psst. Come here, beautiful." Dominick crooked his finger at Rachel. "I'd kill for a good cannoli right about now.

You wouldn't deny an old man his last wish before dying would you?"

"Why do I get the impression you timed this request right when your daughter left?" Rachel smiled.

"Aw, Marie's like a little Hitler. She won't let me have anything but rabbit food," Dominick griped.

"I'm probably going to get a lecture, but you've charmed me into going on this suicide mission. Where would you like me to procure this contraband?" Rachel asked.

"Carrot Top Pastries on Broadway," he enthused.

"Come on, Joy. You know your way around New York City. You can help me on this important mission."

"Un, uh. Not me. Why do you think he asked you? I know better than to cross Marie and Sophia." Joy smirked. "You're on your own, greenie."

Rachel looked from Joy to the smiling Dominick. "Nicely played, Dominick." She shrugged. "Trouble seems to follow me. Oh well, I like a little excitement now and again. How much grief can they give me if I plead ignorance?"

Joy chuckled. "Have you ever experienced a full-blown Italian lecture?" Joy glanced at Rachel who threw her hands up in defeat. "I didn't think so. I need to get me some popcorn, because the show tonight will be doubly entertaining."

"Quit scaring the poor girl. My girls aren't that bad. Now hurry up, Rachel, before Marie gets back."

Rachel could hear Joy laughing as she exited the room on her quest for the perfect cannoli. At least she would be in the father's good graces. She wondered who she had to impress more, Dominick or Marie? Rachel chuckled to herself as she realized that Joy had no idea that Rachel was Italian herself and was well aware of the passion and emotion of an Italian temper.

As she was walking out the door of the hospital, she saw Sophia and Lara walking from the parking lot. Lara had her arm draped possessively around Sophia's shoulder. Rachel thought they looked a bit too cozy for her comfort.

Rachel surveyed the situation as Lara turned and kissed Sophia on the temple. The gesture was both intimate and supportive. She didn't want to make a scene, so she continued to watch them enter the hospital unobserved. She feared that Lara was putting on the charm to try to salvage her failed marriage to Sophia. She wasn't sure which made her more depressed, the fact that Sophia was clearly Lara's choice or the possibility that she might lose Sophia before she even had a chance to declare her feelings. Rachel knew they could be amazing together, but she might never get the chance to explore that with Sophia if Lara managed to sink her claws back into Sophia.

Rachel had an errand to run and then she would decide what to do next. It might get a little uncomfortable for all involved if she stayed while Lara was present and that was not what she intended. She wanted her presence to help Sophia, not hurt her.

Her eyes followed Lara and Sophia until they entered the hospital and were no longer visible.

†

Sophia was uncomfortable with Lara's close proximity to her and what she really wanted to do was wriggle out of her embrace. The kiss on the temple was very close to crossing the line, but she didn't want to cause a scene in the hospital by confronting Lara.

When they reached the room her heart started to beat rapidly when she saw Joy and expected Rachel was close by. She looked around the room and noticed that Joy was the only one visiting her father.

"Hey, Joy, where's Marie?" Sophia asked. What she really wanted to know was where Rachel was.

"She stepped out to get us some coffee and Rachel went on a secret mission that I can't divulge. Don't be mad, but your dad conned her into getting something for him," Joy offered.

Sophia raised her eyebrow.

"What the hell is Rachel doing here?" Lara snapped.

"She offered to come and support me and I accepted," Sophia stated. She wasn't about to apologize for accepting Rachel's generous offer. Besides, she was delighted that Rachel was here.

"Don't tell me you two are friends now." Lara's expression was particularly dour.

"We are and please don't start an argument because you won't win. I'll just ask you to leave and visit Pops when I'm not here. I won't keep you from him, but that doesn't mean you can start a bunch of shit while Rachel is here," Sophia stated.

"This is a whole new kind of fucked up," Lara grumbled.

"And whose fault is that?" Joy interjected.

"What are you girls bickering about? Is my cannoli here yet? Is that why I'm hearing terse conversation? Don't blame Rachel, she couldn't resist my charm." Dominick grinned and he looked ten years younger.

"No, Dad, your contraband has not arrived yet. You should be ashamed of yourself—conning poor Rachel into getting you a cannoli. I'm not happy, but Marie is going to have a shit fit." Sophia grinned. "I think I'll just let her handle the situation. She's so much better at it than I am." Sophia couldn't really get too irritated at her father since he seemed to get so much joy from his favorite dessert.

"Did I hear my name? What situation?" Marie asked.

"Marie, why don't you go home and get some rest now that the other half of the armed guard has arrived?" Dominick suggested.

"Okay, what have you done? You're trying to get rid of me and that must mean you did something you weren't supposed to." Marie narrowed her eyes and looked around the room. "Okay where did your friend Rachel go and is she somehow involved in this subterfuge?"

Joy laughed. "I told you that you'd never get away with it. Poor Rachel, don't blame her. Dominick is as wily as a coyote."

"What exactly am I going to blame her for?" Marie asked.

"One little cannoli is not going to kill me, but I swear all your fussing just might," Dominick grumbled.

Sophia noted that Lara was wisely staying out of the controversy as she pouted in the corner.

"For fuck's sake, Dad, you just had a heart attack and I'm pretty sure that your daily intake of cannolis is one of the leading culprits," Marie chastised.

Dominick waved his hand in the air. "Bullshit. I had a heart attack because I'm old, fat, and out of shape. One little cannoli didn't cause this condition. A whole lifetime of rich foods may have been a factor, but it's far too late to change my ways now. They can just blow out the old pipes and I'll be good as new."

Marie rolled her eyes but didn't say anything more.

"So…shall we finish our game of poker? Dominick was losing so he conveniently used the excuse that he was tired and needed a nap. You big faker," Joy diverted.

"I suppose Rachel was winning," Lara complained quietly from her corner.

"Yep, she sure was. You should join us, Lara, when she returns. I'd love to see her clean your clock and liberate the remaining funds she generously left you," Joy countered.

Sophia glared at Joy as Dominick's questioning gaze penetrated Sophia. She knew he wouldn't ask anything while everyone was in his room, but realized he would definitely broach the subject when they were alone. She wasn't sure exactly what she would tell him because her father adored Lara. She was not looking forward to this conversation. It might break his heart to learn the depths of Lara's deception.

†

Rachel called a cabbie who was eager to take her to the bakery and wait while she procured the tasty treat. She decided to pick up a few more desserts while she was there. She reasoned that it might help if she came bearing gifts for everyone else. She was practically drooling on the chocolate torte prominently displayed in the glass case. Remembering that Sophia was partial to New York style cheesecake, she decided to buy the whole dessert rather than one piece. She also purchased several sauces to place on top. Armed with her bounty, she carried the two large shopping sacks out to the waiting cab and returned to the hospital. She was eager to see Sophia, but wasn't looking forward to the inevitable confrontation with Lara.

Rachel set one of the bags down and pressed the elevator button that would take her to the second floor. She took several deep breaths to calm herself before facing Lara.

There was a fine line between love and hate. As she analyzed the emotions surrounding Lara, she wondered if hate was what she was feeling or if she somehow still loved her. Thinking back on her time with Sophia during the past two weeks, there was no comparison. As she dug deeper into her feelings, she wondered if she had ever really loved Lara, or was she merely in deep lust the past two years. Her emotions ran deeper with Sophia than they ever had with Lara and they'd not even made love with one another.

The elevator doors opened and she picked up her bags, ready to face the situation and lend Sophia whatever support she needed.

Before she entered the room, a nurse came barreling down the hallway. "There should really only be two visitors at a time. I've made an exception up until this point, but now there will be five of you."

Rachel weighed her options and decided it was best not to anger the nurse. "All right. I understand, but can you please let them know I'm here and I brought the item that Dominick requested."

The nurse narrowed her eyes. "What exactly did you bring Mr. Torre?"

There was no sense in lying to the nurse so Rachel came clean. "He asked for a cannoli. I didn't think one cannoli would make a huge difference. You should have seen his face light up when I agreed."

"Let me just check with the doctor. It's probably okay, but I'm sure the dietitian will have some recommendations regarding Mr. Torre's future diet choices."

Rachel chuckled. "I imagine she will, so he might as well get a few final pleasures in before having to adhere to a strict diet. I brought back a variety of treats, can I interest you in something decadent. There's a chocolate torte in here that looks positively immoral."

"Are you attempting to butter me up, because if you are, it's working? Gimme the damn treat and I'll let you go in, but can you send one or two people out?" the nurse said.

"Thanks." Rachel reached in the bag and pulled out the torte, handing it to the smiling nurse.

†

As Rachel entered the room, she noticed how small it was with five visitors. Lara was sitting in the corner while the rest hovered around Dominick's bed.

"Ah, my savior has arrived," Dominick declared. "My mouth is literally watering in anticipation."

Rachel ignored Lara sitting in the corner, pulled out the cannoli, and handed it to Dominick. After giving him his dessert, she set down the bags.

"What'd you do? Buy the whole bakery?" Marie asked.

"As a matter of fact, yes, I practically did. There's a New York cheesecake for Sophia, Dutch apple pie for Joy, various chocolate treats—although I did have to bribe the nurse with a torte, so there is one less chocolate torte—and finally, various berry cobblers. By the way, I promised the nurse I would send a few people out because there's only supposed to be two visitors in the room at one time."

"That was very sweet of you, Rachel," Sophia said as she stroked her arm.

Rachel pulled Sophia into a hug and absently stroked her back. After several seconds, she pulled back. "How are you holding up?" she whispered.

"A little tired, but good," Sophia responded.

Rachel noticed Marie scrutinizing her interaction with Sophia.

"It sounds like a few of us need to rotate out for a little while. Dad already suggested I go home and get some rest so that he can eat his little dessert without me hovering and frankly I'm too tired to argue—so you win, Dad. Go for it." Marie peered into the bag. "I'll just take one of these little chocolate treats with me. Lara and Joy why don't you two hang out in the family waiting room for a bit and let Sophia and Rachel visit for a while."

Rachel thought Lara was going to protest, when she saw Sophia send her a pleading look.

Dominick was watching the interactions and Rachel thought he was trying to figure out all the subtle cues around him.

Rachel had yet to acknowledge Lara.

"I'll be right down the hallway, Sophia. Hello, Rachel. It was nice of you to come," Lara stated through gritted teeth.

"I'll catch up with you later, Lara," Rachel warned.

"I'll just help myself to one of these berry cobblers," Joy announced. "Lara, anything you want from Rachel's little bag of decadence?"

"No thanks, I'll pass." Lara stood up and exited the room.

Marie and Joy followed Lara after pulling their chosen treats from the bag.

†

Sophia looked back at her dad, who was licking his fingers. "Looks like you didn't waste any time gobbling up your cannoli."

"You didn't happen to get any more did you?" Dominick asked.

Rachel laughed. "I did, but I think we better save them for later. I'm sure you've already pushed your luck with Marie and Sophia."

Dominick smiled. "Okay, Sophia, out with it. Something is going on and I want to know what it is. The tension between you, Rachel, and Lara is so thick I could cut it with a knife."

"Dad, I don't even know where to begin. Can we talk about this later when you've had a chance to recover?"

"What's Lara done and how does Rachel fit into all of this?" Dominick asked.

"Why do you ask that?" Her father's question surprised Sophia.

"Give your old man some credit. I can spot a philanderer like myself a mile away. I just thought she truly does love you as much as I loved your mother and that eventually she would see the light like I did. I love Lara, but we're cut from the same stone," Dominick explained.

"Well, your prodigy may have taken it a bit further," Sophia bitterly replied.

"Oh, honey. I didn't mean to upset you by my observations. I also don't mean to excuse my behavior or Lara's. Rachel, how do you fit into this whole mess?"

"I'm the other woman, or more accurately, I was the other woman. I had no idea that Sophia existed before a couple of weeks ago or I never would have married Lara."

Dominick started coughing and the equipment starting beeping loudly.

"Shit, sorry. I didn't mean to upset you. The nurse is going to tan my hide," Rachel declared.

"See, this is why I didn't want to talk about this," Sophia added.

The nurse came bustling into the room. "What in tarnation is going on in here?"

Dominick waved his hand in the air. "Water down the wrong pipe. It's nothing to be concerned about. See? The crazy monitors are already starting to subside."

The nurse checked all the monitors and the leads attached to Dominick's body. She nodded. "Let me know if you need anything, I'll be right outside. Take your time when you take a sip of water."

The nurse left the room and Dominick looked from Rachel to Sophia. "Are you telling me that Lara is married to both of you?"

"Was married," Rachel corrected.

"Rachel helped me draw up legal papers. I served Lara with divorce papers two weeks ago. I remained in Victoria and spent the past two weeks vacationing and trying to take my mind off my disastrous marriage."

Dominick narrowed his eyes at Rachel. "Are you two friends now?"

Sophia watched the flicker of emotions pass across Rachel's face as she smiled.

"Yes, we've gotten close during the past two weeks," Rachel answered.

"Are you in love with my daughter?"

Sophia choked out her reply. "Dad, we're just friends. She has come to mean a lot to me. Rachel is as much a victim of Lara's infidelity as I am, so please don't judge her too harshly."

"Oh, I'm not judging anyone. I certainly don't have the right to do that, besides I like your Rachel. She brought me my cannoli so she just climbed up one more rung in the ladder. I was just asking the question. If it's any consolation, I do believe that Lara loves you. Probably both of you, but Sophia, you are her one and only, like your mother was for me. I'm sorry if that is painful for you, Rachel."

"You know, I've done a bit of soul searching lately and I wonder if I was blinded by something other than true love. Sure, I'm hurt, but honestly I'll survive. Maybe I wasn't as invested in the marriage as I thought I was. I think I understand more fully what truly being in love is really all about."

Rachel looked at Sophia and Sophia realized at that moment that Rachel's feelings for her had already evolved into something far deeper than friendship. This sudden realization knocked her off center. Was it possible that Rachel loved her—was in love with her?

"Why don't you two go out there and send in the other half of the visitor contingent. You should take a walk and visit with one another. From the looks of things, you need to talk," Dominick directed.

"Your father is a wise man," Rachel acknowledged.

†

Lara didn't like it one bit that Sophia and Rachel had become so close. She was on a mission to get her wife back and with Rachel in the picture it complicated things. She felt bad that she'd hurt both women, but she'd finally come to realize that her feelings for Rachel did not come close to her feelings for Sophia. She lusted after Rachel, but she loved and needed Sophia in her life. She might go as far as admitting that Sophia was the best thing that had ever happened to her and she feared she'd blown it.

She knew about Sophia's tentative relationship with her father because of his infidelity, but that might work to her advantage. In a rare confession from Dominick, Lara learned that Sophia's mom had forgiven Dominick and they ended up with a solid marriage until the day she died. Sophia had confessed to her that Dominick had been the loving, attentive, husband during her final days—taking much better care of her than either Marie or she thought possible, given his history.

Joy was glaring at her. Clearly, she might be an impediment. Marie had gone home to rest a bit before coming back and that left her all alone with Joy who was clearly declaring herself Sophia's guard dog.

She wasn't sure what she would do about Chelsea. She needed to nip that in the bud, and quick, if she had any chance at all. Chelsea had been a surprise. There was no pretense with Chelsea. It was all about sex with her and Lara had to admit the sex was fantastic, but not enough to risk her potential reuniting with Sophia.

"You can stop glaring at me, Joy. No matter what you think of me, what matters in the long run is what Sophia thinks and I'll be damned if I'll let you get in the way of our happiness. I admit I fucked up, but if we have a chance to repair this you need to back the fuck off," Lara warned.

"You think you're like Dominick, but you're not. He had the good sense to clean his act up. I don't think it's in your DNA to change. You think you can charm your way back into Sophia's good graces, but in my humble opinion you've already lost her to someone who is far more suited to her—someone who will treat her the way she deserves to be treated."

"Just stay out of this, Joy. I will crush you like a bug if you get in my way."

"Bring it on. Because you don't scare me one bit miss big shot financier. Don't forget that bigamy is a felony and I'm not quite as forgiving as Rachel or Sophia. In the historic words of Clint Eastwood, *go ahead, make my day*, I'd turn you in quicker than you can say *fuck you*."

Lara would have to rethink her approach. Joy was becoming a serious impediment that she might have underestimated as a potential enemy.

†

The Vivian and Seymour Milstein Family Heart Center, attached to New York Presbyterian Hospital had a stunning view of the Hudson River. Sophia led Rachel outside the center, hoping to find a way to the Hudson River greenway. It was one of the more beautiful parts of New York. Similar to Seattle, if you didn't live there you had numerous misperceptions about the city. To anyone who didn't live in Seattle the assumption was that Seattle was a small city lacking in culture. Likewise, Sophia imagined that Rachel viewed New York as a crime ridden, concrete jungle lacking compassion or community. Nothing could be further from the truth and Sophia wanted to show Rachel a small part of her world.

"Wow this is really beautiful. There's a lot more to New York than I originally thought, huh?" Rachel acknowledged.

"It may not have the same kind of beauty that Seattle has, but we have our own kind of magic."

"Sophia, New York will always be magical to me because it's where you live." Rachel sighed. "I promised Joy that I wouldn't rush in and tell you how I feel, but I just can't keep that promise. I know I'll probably scare you away, but you deserve to know how I feel. What you see is what you get with me and I can't be anything but honest with you no matter what the cost."

Rachel took both of Sophia's hands in hers. "See, the truth is that I've fallen in love with you and there's not a damn thing I can do about it because I understand that your emotions are all tied up in knots right now. I'm not expecting you to say anything back or even respond, but I just needed to lay my cards on the table and see where the chips fall. Shit, all that poker has got me using gambling analogies," Rachel confessed.

"I wish I had everything sorted out in my head, but I don't. I can't ask you to wait until I do, but if it's any consolation, I think I may have fallen for you, too. I have a long history with Lara and I owe it to myself to consider whether we can make it work. She's given me a few things to think about. Somewhere in the back of my head, I have to wonder whether we can make it work like my father and mother did so long ago. I know that's not what you want to hear right now, but it's the most honest answer I can give you."

"I understand. Really, I do. I wish it were different, but I can't fault you in any way. Regardless of what I feel, I want you to be happy and if Lara will make you happy, I will gracefully bow out of the equation. I think it may be time for me to exit sooner rather than later. If you and Lara have any chance at all, I have to let her be your support and stop mucking things up for you." Rachel brushed a tear away. "We'd better head back. I'll get the next flight out back to Seattle and let you get on with your life." Rachel gently kissed Sophia on the lips and started walking back to the hospital with her hands in her pockets.

Sophia swiped at her own tears which were falling freely now. She wasn't sure she'd made the right decision, but it was too late now. Rachel was going back to Seattle and she feared she'd never see her again. It hurt more than she thought possible.

Chapter Twenty-five

Life was good again for Lara. Although her marriage to Sophia was tenuous at best, she was confident that, in time, she would gain her trust back. She'd made good on her promise to Sophia and was actively looking for a buyer for her Seattle office. She had a backup plan if she wasn't able to sell the business. Although it was a stretch for her to give up control, she decided that it might be possible to keep the business and look for a partner who would run that office and let her concentrate one hundred percent of her time on the New York office. Yolanda, her VP of Marketing, was her first choice. She was intelligent, dedicated, and ruthless. That was a combination that Lara couldn't resist.

During the past couple of weeks, Dominick got stronger and was released from the hospital. He appeared to recover nicely. They scheduled his angioplasty and were optimistic about the results.

Lara was a little worried that despite the news about her father, Sophia appeared more melancholy than she'd ever seen before in her wife. She could understand her hesitancy to jump back into their marriage and the intimacy that they'd once enjoyed. They were working on that, but her sadness seemed much deeper than their fragile relationship.

Sophia was working on one of her lectures for the upcoming summer session. She'd volunteered to teach this summer. Lara suspected that she still needed some distance and a distraction to continue to work through her trust issues and the change in Lara's schedule that resulted in her spending a lot more time at home with Sophia. It was still awkward, but they were both trying to get the spark back.

Her cell phone buzzed on the counter while she worked on cutting up vegetables for their dinner. She frowned when she read the text message.

Just got in town. Meet me at the Times Square Hilton at seven. I'll have a bottle of champagne put on ice. Bring the strap on. I'll even play the submissive tonight.

Lara looked at her watch and wondered how she would manage slipping out of the penthouse to meet Chelsea. One final fuck and then she would find a way to let her down without losing her business. Lara rationalized that this wasn't really about cheating because it was just sex and business with Chelsea.

Need 2 push that back a few hours. How about 10?

Disappointed, but I guess I understand. This was a last minute trip. I've missed you.

Me 2. Now that I'm not in Seattle anymore, it's hard to arrange these meet-ups. CU soon.

Can't wait.

Lara sighed. She needed to make sure this didn't turn into another Rachel-like situation. She thought that Chelsea was all about meaningless sex, but she was starting to act differently and that worried Lara.

She set her phone back down on the counter and finished cutting up vegetables for the chicken stir fry she was making for dinner.

†

Sophia read the same sentence again. She was finding it hard to concentrate. Lara had been the model partner for the past two weeks. She was home every night by five-thirty and often the one who prepared their dinner when they didn't go out to eat. She couldn't fault her for a lack of effort, but Sophia could not stop thinking about Rachel. She wondered what she was doing. Was she forging ahead with her life? Had she met someone new?

Every time she picked up her phone to call, she'd stopped herself. It wasn't fair to anyone. She'd made her choice and now she had to live with it and make the best of her situation. It was time to meet Lara halfway. She knew her heart had not really been one hundred percent in it during the past couple of weeks. She vowed to change that tonight.

Sophia walked into the kitchen and swiped a red pepper, popping it into her mouth.

"Hey, that's for the stir fry. No stealing my ingredients before I put it all together," Lara joked.

Sophia smiled. "Surely you won't miss one little red pepper and...." She grabbed several snow peas. "A few snow peas."

Lara swatted Sophia with the dish towel draped over her shoulder. "Out of my kitchen. Oh, by the way, I have to go into the office tonight for a few hours. I'm really sorry. I've tried desperately to not revert to my old ways, but unfortunately this one is unavoidable. The account is large enough that I can't afford to neglect my duties. Is that okay with you?"

Alarm bells were ringing in Sophia's head, but she chose to ignore them. "It's fine. You've been especially attentive and one night away won't kill me. Go ahead. I never asked you to ignore your business to the point of causing you irreparable damage," Sophia answered.

Sophia was already thinking about calling Rachel— just to check to see if she was okay. She missed her. Weren't they friends and friends called to check on one another?

"What wine would you like tonight? I'll go get us a bottle from our wine cellar," Lara asked.

"Maybe a crisp Chardonnay. I like the one that reminds me of grapefruit. I know that's probably not the right description, but I never claimed to be a wine connoisseur," Sophia answered.

Lara walked out of the kitchen and Sophia sat on one of the stools situated next to the granite island in the center of the modern kitchen with its shiny stainless steel appliances.

When Lara's phone starting buzzing on the counter, Sophia picked it up, not even registering that it was not her phone. When she saw the text message, strung together with the previous text, the bile entered her throat and she barely made it to the sink.

Don't forget the strawberries and whipped cream. I particularly enjoyed that the last time. Anxious for your arrival tonight.

Sophia carefully laid her fancy cell phone—the one that Lara bought her—next to Lara's and walked out of the penthouse vowing never to return. It was time for a drastic change in her life. She felt like a huge weight was lifted from her shoulders and now she had the freedom to do what she should have done from the very start of this mess. This would be a clean break. She would leave Lara and her old life behind for good this time.

†

It had been three weeks, two hours and ten minutes since Rachel had seen or talked to Sophia, but who was counting?

She'd barely made it through each day and had to talk herself out of calling. She knew she was out of control when she'd attempted to drunk dial her, but her fingers wouldn't work properly and then she'd promptly passed out. Instead, she cried herself to sleep each night, lamenting what she knew she'd lost.

As long as Sophia was happy, she convinced herself that it was for the best. They lived thousands of miles away from one another, even if Lara was not in the picture, it probably would never have worked. Rachel knew that wasn't exactly true, because she would move in a heartbeat if only Sophia asked her to.

Rachel slumped down on her sofa and mindlessly clicked through the channels looking for something, anything, to take her mind off Sophia.

She wasn't expecting company, so when she heard the doorbell, she hesitated. She wasn't fit for visitors right now. Espresso was even avoiding her as he remained on his favorite chair, giving his mom a wide berth. Thank goodness Lara hadn't fought her for custody of their only furbaby.

When the doorbell rang a second time, she dragged herself to the door to see who was disturbing her solitude and perfectly righteous pity party. She wrenched open the door ready to let the person on the other end have it. She stopped mid-yell as she realized who was on the other side.

"Sophia." It was all she managed to say.

"May I come in?" Sophia asked.

"Of course. Not that I'm complaining, but what are you doing here?"

"Oh, God, Rachel. I've been a total fool. Can you forgive me?"

"Don't you know by now, Sophia, that I would forgive just about anything? I'm still madly in love with you. Although I'm not sure what I'm supposed to forgive."

"I don't have a single piece of clothing with me. I just walked out of the penthouse with my purse and the clothes on my back. All I could think of was you these past few weeks. I love you, Rachel and I can't imagine my life without you. I've made a mistake and I'm sorry that it took this long for me to realize it. The nail in Lara's coffin came via a text message last night from her newest girlfriend, but to be honest, I think I knew deep inside it wasn't going to work because I couldn't erase you from my mind. I've wanted to call you so many times."

Rachel pulled Sophia into her arms and crushed her lips against Sophia's. After thoroughly ravaging her lips, she broke apart but kept Sophia in her arms.

"I don't care what your reasons are. I'm just glad you're here. Everything else is just logistics and I'm very good at logistics. I love you, Sophia, and I will love you until I die. That's a promise I can easily make to you today and forever."

"You know they say that love the second time around is always better. I love you, too, and I'll never waver again on my feelings. Make love to me, Rachel."

†

Rachel took control of their lovemaking as she showed Sophia to the master bedroom. She began to undress Sophia and she knew she was going excruciatingly slow but she wanted to etch this moment in her memory for all eternity.

As Sophia's clothes tumbled to the floor, Rachel removed her pullover t-shirt in one swift movement and her pants soon followed. They stood before one another, naked and vulnerable.

"Beautiful," each said simultaneously.

Rachel took Sophia's hand as she pulled down the covers to the bed and guided her there.

She needed to feel Sophia's body against her own as she moved on top of her. Each inch of skin sent shivers up her body and she came undone when she heard Sophia moan beneath her.

Rachel was usually creative and inventive in bed, but tonight she wanted everything to be pure and gentle. She wanted to feel Sophia with her tongue and fingers without the aid of toys that often worked to distance the experience, turning it into something physical versus emotional. She knew that she would be able to introduce Sophia to her wilder side at a different time. Tonight she would show her just how deeply she'd fallen in love.

As she worked her tongue down Sophia's body, she stopped at her nipple and tugged gently with her teeth, pulling it in a playful, but sensuous manner.

"Oh, God that feels heavenly," Sophia uttered.

She felt Sophia's hands moving through her hair, noting their gentle caress on the back of her neck. This was one of Rachel's favorite erogenous zones. She made a mental note to herself that she would check this out with Sophia later on.

Sophia's musky smell alerted her to the level of Sophia's arousal. When she finally lapped up Sophia's glorious juices, the sweetness burst into her mouth like biting into a juicy berry.

Rachel could feel Sophia's clit enlarge as she teased and licked the sensitive bud. Sophia was bucking under her and moaning loudly.

"Please, don't stop. I'm so close. Go inside."

Rachel enjoyed how vocal and open Sophia was, not hesitating to direct Rachel. She obliged her by curving two fingers into her vagina and stroking inside with a slow in and out movement.

Ten seconds later Rachel felt the walls of Sophia's vagina contract around her fingers as Sophia called out.

"Yes, oh God, yes."

"Why is it that when I make love to women, they want to rename me and give me a much higher rank in the spiritual world. When I'm just going about my business, I get called an angel, but when my fingers are inside all of a sudden I'm the creator," Rachel joked.

Sophia flipped Rachel. "I better be the only one who from now on gets to elevate your rank. Just give me a few moments and pretty soon I'll be getting that promotion, but it will probably take the form of a chant more than a declaration."

"Absolutely, you will be the only one calling out my name from this day forward." Rachel moaned as Sophia started to kiss her neck and collarbone as she worked her way down. If anything, Rachel felt worshipped by Sophia. However, she had no doubt she would begin screaming in delight as she experienced Sophia's slow ministrations to her body.

†

Lara walked back into the kitchen with the bottle of wine in her hand and looked around. She wondered where Sophia had gone. The two cell phones lay side by side on the counter with their black screens ominously shining. She had a sudden image that they were passing silent judgement on her.

"Sophia?" Lara called into the empty room. Her voice echoed in the cavernous space. It was a premonition to the sudden loneliness she felt. Her face scrunched up in bewilderment, but deep inside she knew.

She picked up her cell phone, pressed the button as the eerie glow of the text message mocked her. She'd fucked up for the last time and the verdict was swift. Justice would sentence her to a lifetime of meaningless sex—devoid of love, compassion, tenderness, or acceptance. She'd made her lonely bed and now she had to lie in it.

Her earlier realization that Sophia was the love of her life hadn't been enough to offset her sick addiction. Power, control, sex had all overpowered the sliver of love and humanity buried inside.

For the first time in her life, Lara sobbed as the pain of her loss registered in her mind. She remained bent with her head in her hands as the river of grief flowed freely.

Chapter Twenty-six

Six months later.

The rain fell lightly as Sophia watched the boats sway in the harbor. A storm was kicking up, but she didn't care, because in a few hours she was to marry the love of her life. This time she was sure her choice was rock solid.

The only regret she had when she left New York that day was leaving behind her beloved cat, Fawn. In a last minute gesture of compassion, she'd decided she wouldn't take Fawn away as well, because that would leave Lara with nothing. The only consolation was that Espresso glommed onto Sophia right away.

When Lara attempted to call, Rachel made it clear that if she failed to sign the divorce papers in a reasonable amount of time, she would make her threat of turning Lara in to the authorities a promise. Sophia heard Rachel declare that it wasn't her first choice, but if Lara gave her no other option, she wouldn't hesitate to take that step.

Lara had finally given up and she'd heard somewhere that she was dating Chelsea Martin. The two were a perfect pair. She was surprised that the news hadn't upset her more.

She felt Rachel's arm wrap around her and her body got that same tingling feeling she always got when she felt Rachel's touch. Since that very first night when she'd showed up on Rachel's doorstep and declared her love, she knew the difference when making love with your soulmate. Rachel took her to a whole new dimension of intimacy.

"Remind me why we decided to get married in dreary December?" Rachel asked.

"Joy couldn't get away until then, Dad needed a bit more time to recover, we needed to make sure my divorce was final, and *you* didn't want to wait any longer."

"Oh yeah, it's coming back to me now. You keep distracting me with your sexy ways. I never know if I'm coming or going anymore." Rachel turned her around and kissed her bride to be.

"Joy and Marie are going to have a joint hissy fit, you know. Tradition says we aren't supposed to see one another until the ceremony on the day of our wedding."

"Since when did we ever pay attention to tradition or convention? My God, you do know you're marrying your ex-wife's, secret wife? It doesn't get any more non-traditional than that. I suppose I should thank Lara."

"What the hell for?" Sophia asked.

"Well, I never would have met the love of my life is she wasn't such a two-timing lesbian bigamist."

"True. Let's stir things up tonight and toast her," Sophia joked.

"You are positively evil." Rachel laughed.

"Yes, but I'm your evil," Sophia quipped.

"Yes, you are and I plan to keep it that way. Let's go poke the bears and find Marie and Joy."

Sophia and Rachel walked arm in arm back into the Empress Hotel, laughing loudly.

About the Author

Annette Mori

Annette is a health care executive living in the beautiful Pacific Northwest with her new wife (got to love Washington State) and their five furry kids. Well, actually, it might be more than five, but they do not count the ones they only feed. Annette is fifty-six years old and believes it is not too late to try something new. As an avid reader, she is pleased there are thousands of good books to choose from, and hopes that one day hers will be one of the many for readers to consider. She reads at least three to four books a week, so please, keep them coming. She has a habit to feed, after all.

No matter if you loved it or hated it, I would love your comments. Feel free to e-mail me at annettemori0859@gmail.com. I will always be a WIP (work in progress—just learned that) so feedback is a gift.

Other Books from Affinity eBook Press

Keeping Faith by TJ Vertigo
Join the antics of Reece, Faith, Cori, Vi, and even The
Animal, one final time in *Keeping Faith*. Faith has finally
made the big screen, but how will Reece handle her success?
Will the love that they share be enough to save their
relationship and soothe The Animal?

Bound by Ali Spooner
A rogue master vampire threatens the existence of the New
Orleans vampire clan. Lord Jordan enlists Devin Benoit,
sister of the Baton Rouge Alpha, and her witch lover, Tia, to
assist with cleansing the city from potential disaster.

The Circle Dance by Jen Silver
Jamie Steele has moved to another town, trying to forget the
heartbreak of losing her lover of six years. Sasha Fairfield
finds her thoughts taken up with her ex-lover and thinks she

wants Jamie back. Follow this captivating romance as love dances through the lives of these women to its surprising conclusion.

Search for the White Moon by Natalie London
Kathryn Austin, a government agent, is given opera singer, Adriana Desi, as her new assignment. Their lives and futures are in danger as the White Moon terrorists hunt them. Immerse yourself in this fast-paced romantic thriller by debut author Natalie London.

Take Me As I Am by JM Dragon & Erin O'Reilly
When Jo Lackerly and Thea Danvers meet, an unexpected friendship develops, proving a catalyst for both women to change their lives irrevocably. Follow them on a journey of discovery that will have your heart smiling, blood boiling, and senses entangled in a wonderful romance.

Carved in Stone by Jen Silver
Join the characters from *Starting Over* and *Arc Over Time* in this final book from the Starling Hill trilogy. Ellie Winters thinks she might be going mad when the ancient queen wants a proper burial for herself and her consort. *Carved in Stone* has romance, adventure, a treasure hunt, and a happy endings for all, living and dead.

Anywhere, Everywhere by Renee MacKenzie

Gwen Martin's life in the Ten Thousand Islands area changes irrevocably when Piper Jackson comes into her life. Without trust, can the budding relationship between Gwen and Piper survive? Or will the answers to the questions continue to haunt them?

Venus Rising by Ali Spooner
Levi Johnson arrives at Venus Rising, an exclusive lesbian-only tropical resort in the Virgin Islands and finds more than she expected—a sizzling hot love triangle. Torn between her attraction to two women, she struggles to choose the right woman to share her life.

The Devil's Tree by Ali Spooner
Torn between her love for the pack and her need to find what's missing in her life, Devin Benoit travels to New Orleans. Will the previous happenings at the Devil's Tree help or hinder Devin in the fight of her life, and the life of Tia, the woman who now owns her heart?

The Beggars' Coppice by Erica Lawson
Edda Case is a woman in crisis who discovers that things are not as they seem. Is it truly a message for her from beyond the grave or is something more sinister taking place? Can Edda solve the mystery of *The Beggars' Coppice*?

Locked Inside by Annette Mori

How much does the power of love matter to someone who must overcome obstacles far greater than most people face in a lifetime.

Line of Sight by Ali Spooner
Sasha and her lover Kara are back. Continue the thrilling adventures of this couple from the Sasha Thibodaux series.

Requiem for Vukovar by Angela Koenig
Requiem for Vukovar continues the Refraction series and the exploits of Jeri O'Donnell and her partner, Kelly Corcoran. In an epic siege largely ignored by the wider world, Kelly, who was prepared to give up comforts and certainties when she became part of Jeri's nomadic life, encounters more than physical danger. Her ability to maintain her core integrity is assaulted by the inevitable ugliness of war. For Jeri, the true battle is confronting her attraction to violence as she struggles against losing herself in the exhilaration of combat.

Against All Odds by JM Dragon
From award-winning and bestselling author JM Dragon, with significant updates by Erin O'Reilly, comes an original tale of romance where everything seems to be stacked against two women whose destinies bring them together. Life however takes a twisted path, setting both Steph and Louise in directions they never thought possible. Will love win out against all odds or will love be forever lost?

The Settlement by Ali Spooner
The outpouring of love and friendship toward Cadin helps her on her path to healing and learning to trust her heart to love once again. Join bestselling author Ali Spooner on this sensational journey that ends with a heartwarming romance.

Once Upon a Time by Alane Hotchkin
Raven only wanted to escape the blows that life had dealt her. She longed to be on the open sea and free. When she came upon a beautiful young girl sitting alone in the middle of a meadow, little did she know that her destiny would be changed forever. Will they become the pawns of the ancient vision or will both paths lead to the same port of destiny? Find out in this exciting high seas adventure that will capture your imagination.

Asset Management by Annette Mori
Follow the twists and turns to the explosive conclusion. Not everything is black and white. There are many shades of gray, and sometimes it's difficult to decipher who is good and who is evil. No one is all virtue or all malevolence, but sometimes love helps us rise above.

Do Dreams Come True? by JM Dragon
How do two people who really shouldn't get on end up in a relationship? Find out in this deliciously ordinary romance.

Return to Me by Erin O'Reilly

Will Salvation bring just that to Ellie, allowing her to find peace and happiness again, or will it have her questioning all that she believes in? A wonderful romance cloaked within an intriguing mystery.

Arc Over Time by Jen Silver
Book 2 of the Starling Hill Trilogy. This wonderful romantic continuation with the characters from *Starting Over* ties up loose ends. But the question is—does everyone have a happy ending? A must read.

The Presence by Charlene Neal
Can Rebecca and Kayleigh overcome ghosts from the past and their own insecurities, or will a presence from the past tear them apart?

A Walk Away by Lacey Schmidt
Sometimes chance brings you to the right person to help you resolve some of your baggage, and you learn to like yourself a little more. Kat and Rand are smart enough to recognize this chance in each other, but they also find that there is a catch to every opportunity—walking toward something is always walking away from something else.

Possessing Morgan by Erica Lawson
The investigation has barely begun when Andrea becomes the target of a nearly fatal hit-and-run. But was it really aimed at her? Can she and Morgan find the common ground

they need to solve the case and stop the attacks, or are the gaps just too wide to bridge?

Twenty-three Miles by Renee MacKenzie
This is a story about community, and how it comes together in dangerous and devastating times. When you don't know who to trust, you better have friends who will rally around you. Will Talia and Shay find the answers they need to the mystery of the murders on the parkway, or will justice be elusive? Will they survive their quest for the truth?

Reece's Star by TJ Vertigo
Under Faith's guiding, loving hand, will Reece successfully traverse the rocky road of emotion and embrace the positive changes in her life? Or will she panic and be unable to control that Animal part of herself? Will she take that next step to declare herself fully capable of love and devotion? This third installment in the popular series that began with *Private Dancer* continues the passionate and often hilarious romance of Reece and Faith as they both grow in love and in trust.

The Chronicles of Ratha: Book 2 A Lion Among the Lambs by Erica Lawson
Can Jordana believe in herself like her Noorthi sisters do? Only then can she fulfill her destiny as The Chosen One. Follow the colorful cast of characters in this action-packed

adventure sequel as they traverse the galaxy. Of course, nothing ever goes smoothly when Jordana is involved.

Starting Over by Jen Silver
Book 1 of the Starling Hill Trilogy. There's a mystery afoot—whose royal resting place is disturbed at Starling Hill? All is revealed in this classic romance of simmering passions, anguished loss, and the wonder of love.

If I Were a Boy by Erin O'Reilly
Will Katie and Helen be able to make a life together work or succumb to doubts and the pressures of family? This story will fill you with the thrill of passion and the tenderness of love.

Terminal Event by Ali Spooner
Will the killer be caught or continue to evade authorities? Can Tally and Blair's budding romance survive the possibility? Read this intense murder mystery romance and find out.

Love Forever, Live Forever by Annette Mori
Fate intervenes and puts Nicky directly back into the path of her first love, Sara, and the corresponding events send her into a tailspin. Now she must decide—who will be the person she ends up living with and loving forever?

The One by JM Dragon

2015 GCLS Winner for Romance, Intrigue, and Adventure. The One is a romance with everything, love, intrigue, misunderstandings with a happy conclusion—the only question—who gets the girl?

Confined Spaces by Renee MacKenzie
Corporate politics, complicated romance, and long distances conspire to keep Andie and Kara all boxed in. Can love triumph despite the Confined Spaces?

Reflected Passion by Erica Lawson
Through a mirror, Françoise embraces life anew, while for Dale it is a powerful awakening, forcing her to discover not only her sensual nature, but the inner strength she possesses.

Flight by Renee Mackenzie
Some lives will be lost and others changed forever when the sisters' lives intersect. Will they be consumed by the wreckage, or will they be able to pick themselves up and take flight?

Cowgirl Up by Ali Spooner
Ride along with the MC2, for boot scootin', butt kickin', dirt eatin', rodeo adventures, with a love story thrown into the mix.

E-Books, Print, Free e-books

Visit our website for more publications available online.

www.affinityebooks.com

Published by Affinity E-Book Press NZ LTD
Canterbury, New Zealand

Registered Company 2517228